THE UNITED FEDERATION MARINE CORPS' LYSANDER TWINS

BOOK 3
NOAH'S STORY: MARINE TANKER

Colonel Jonathan P. Brazee
USMCR (Ret)

Semper Fi Press

Author Website: http://jonathanbrazee.com
Email List Sign-up: http://eepurl.com/bnFSHH

Acknowledgements:
I want to thank all those who took the time to pre-read this book, catching my mistakes in both content and typing.   Thanks to best_editor1 for her editing. And once again, a special shout out goes to my cover artist, the award-winning Jessica Tung Chi Lee. You   can   see   more   of   her   work   at: http://www.jessicatcl.com/news.html.

Original cover art by Jessica TC Lee

Cover graphics by Steven Novak

GAZIANTEP

"We're going into the city, Staff Sergeant?" Noah asked. "I thought . . ."

". . . that we don't go into cities. You're right, Lysander. We don't. Except we are," Staff Sergeant Jarvistus Cremineli said, his voice evident with disgust.

Sergeant Noah Lysander, fresh out of armor school at Camp Ceasare, was the driver for the *Anvil*, the Number 3 tank of Charlie Company's First Platoon. The company had been attached to Task Force 54/03, the Federation response to the Ataturk incursion into Cennet.

Noah was somewhat familiar with Gaziantep. His father, while a lieutenant colonel, had taken his battalion onto the planet, but in support of Ataturk against Cennet aggression. The planet had been a thorn in the side of the Federation for years, and it seemed some things never changed. At least this time, the Marines were there to support Cennet, a Federation government against the non-member Ataturk government.

Noah's big M1A4 Davis purred under his seat, a 40-ton behemoth waiting to be let loose. The fusion engine could push 2500 horsepower to the road wheels, and that made her a veritable sports car. At 185 cm, Noah was almost too tall to fit in the driver's hole, but by scrunching, he could see out the blocks and drive the beast, even if his head hit the hatch whenever he took a bump too quickly.

He wasn't concerned about his driving, however. He'd been at the top of his class during his Class Four quals, and he knew he could put the *Anvil* through her paces. What he was concerned about was the order the platoon had been given: go into Glen's Landing on a recon to see who was there.

One of a tank's most important advantages was its maneuverability. The M1 was fast and powerful, and it could engage a target at 6,000 meters and destroy it. For MOUT[1] operations, tankers liked to stand off a klick and pound the enemy in support of the infantry. Getting into the cities themselves limited their ability to maneuver and made their tanks big targets. An insurgent or militiaman, with little training, could drop an incendiary device off a roof that would burn right through a Davis' armor.

Reconing a town was not armor's job; it was the infantry's. But Kilo Company had been held up in the hills on the north side of the Pierpont Valley, and Glen's Landing was astride the intersection of the Demir Highway and Route 14, the main roadway in the valley itself. Colonel Bhekizizwe, the ground element commander, wanted that intersection secure before he committed Lima and Echo Companies into the assault on New Antalya, the only major Cennet city that the Ataturk forces had been able to capture. The commander's intent was to eject the Ataturk forces from New Antalya and force them back across the border, then deploy along that border to let the Federation teams negotiate from a position of strength. Leaving the Demir Highway unsecured would be begging for someone to cross the border at the river crossing south of Glen's Landing, and then hit the Marines from their rear.

The platoon's four tanks were in hull defilade about two klicks from the town with mostly open bottom land in between. A small creek ran down the valley and into the town. While it might be large enough to slow straight-leg infantry, it would be nothing to a PICS platoon nor the tanks. The sandy creek bottom was more than firm enough to hold up the tanks' heavy weight without bogging down.

As the driver, Noah didn't have the optics available to the TC, the tank commander, nor to the gunner. Still, he zoomed in the insert in his center block to the max 6X power and scanned the town. He could see nothing, no movement. His insert had night-vision capability, but no heat sensors, so if some Ataturk armor was waiting for them, engines running, he couldn't pick up the heat

---

[1] MOUT: Military Operations in Urban Terrain

signatures. Both Staff Sergeant Cremineli and Sergeant Cayenne "Chili" Fulford, though, had that capability, and as neither one of them was saying anything, Noah took that as a positive.

He toggled the route planner, and the big combat AI's up on the *FS Jerry-John Crossland* mapped out the quickest and what they considered the safest route to the town, then overlaid it right onto both his center block and digital display screen. Noah could use the overlay in a pinch during periods of zero visibility, just following the projection on his screen, but he preferred to use the Alpha Mode, with him seeing the real terrain through the blocks and with the tracks in HUD-mode[2] merely guiding him. As good as the display was, he trusted seeing the real world through the blocks more.

"Charlie-One, prepare to advance in a wedge," Lieutenant Amanda Moore passed over the net, with what sounded like a hint of nervousness in her voice.

Like Noah, this was the lieutenant's first combat mission as a tanker. Most of the platoon had never fired their main guns in anger. Only the platoon sergeant and two others had been on real missions, at least in tanks. Noah wasn't positive, but he figured everyone had seen some sort of action during his or her first tour with the grunts. Noah hadn't seen much combat with 3/14, not like his sister, but he'd gotten a taste of it, at least.

Noah flipped off his overlay. He had no control over his route now, so it would just be a distraction. When the platoon was in a wedge, his job, as the driver for Tank 3, was to lock himself onto Tank 4's right rear as its wing tank. Charlie-One-Four, which was the platoon sergeant's tank, would guide on Charlie-One-One, the platoon commander's tank, and Charlie-One-Two, the wing tank for the lieutenant, would be to the left rear of her. The lieutenant would be leading the way, and the other tanks would guide off of her, or in Noah's case, off the platoon sergeant, to the objective. Noah's job was to keep his distance and guide on Tank 4, but he also had to watch what was right in front of him. It wouldn't do anyone much good to drive into a ditch and flip or hit something and lose a track.

---

[2] HUD: Heads Up Display

"I want to get to the release point quickly," the lieutenant said, something to which Noah, not wanting to spend time in the open, heartily agreed. "As soon as we reach it, Red Section will enter here, and Blue, I want you to enter here."

Noah looked down at his display where the lieutenant had highlighted in red where his section of two tanks would enter and in blue, where the other section would enter the town. Blue Section's entry point was two blocks to the south of where the lieutenant was going to enter the town, which let the platoon cover more ground, but left the two sections unable to support each other quickly if need be.

"Initial speed, 45, but ping on me and be ready to dash on my command."

Noah could match the designated speed by entering it on the autorev or controlling it manually. The autorev worked well on highways, but over open terrain, most drivers, Noah included, preferred to keep control themselves.

He revved the motor, watching the tac-line as he waited for the order to move out. The fusion generator could put out 200,000 watts, or 7,000,000 kilojoules/hour, and it was pretty foolproof. That was more than enough to power the tank's systems, but the motor could be touchy at times, lagging the power surge. As he checked it, the rev was smooth, though, with nary a blip on the readouts.

"Don't blow the motor," Staff Sergeant Cremineli yelled down at him from the commander's hatch.

Noah had been the staff sergeant's driver for only a month now, but one thing that had become evident was that his tank commander didn't trust the beasts. Sure, a Davis could break down, but they were well-made, and the motors didn't "blow." At school, the instructors had told them that the initial Teledyne motors had some issues, but those had been worked out and fixed years ago.

This motor only had seven hours on it, practically brand new. After landing at Konrysville, the tanks had been loaded onto HE haulers, large flatbeds designed to transport Marine armor over long distances, saving wear and tear on tanks and Aardvark personnel carriers. The *Anvil* had only started this road march at zero-dark-thirty this morning, 17 klicks back up the valley.

He didn't bother to argue, though, and cut back on the power feed. His filters were at 94%, so he flipped the flow, forcing air out in a powerful blast.

"What the hell, Lysander? You trying to let everyone know we're here?" the TC shouted back through the hatch again, this time kicking Noah in the shoulder. "Cut that shit out!"

Like they can't see us now, if they're even there?

Technically, the reverse blast of air could be picked up by some types of scanners, but they'd just come down the valley in the open. If eyes were looking for them, they'd have already been spotted. And now, their guns were trained on the town, so it wasn't as if they were invisible even to a set of Mark 1, Mod 1 eyeballs.

Once again, however, Noah complied, smiling, though, when his filters read 98%. Clogged filters would shut down a tank to keep from destroying the motor. The Davis could still fire when that happened, but an immobile tank became a dead tank right quick.

"On me, move out," the lieutenant passed over the platoon net.

Forty meters to his left, Lessa Franklin, Charlie-One-One's driver, goosed the *Kiss of Death* over the small rise and forward to the town. Looking out his side block, he watched as the *Kiss of Death* pushed her nose into the air, exposing her underbelly for a moment before crashing down and heading out. As soon as the platoon commander's tank reached 20 meters out, Charlie-One-Four pushed forward, moving into position.

"Get ready, Lysander," the staff sergeant told him. "And don't expose our belly!"

Which was impossible, Noah knew. Unless he turned and drove down the wash to get around the rise—which would put him way out of position—the mere fact that he was clearing the rise would expose the *Anvil's* undercarriage for a second or two.

Noah ignored the TC. He waited until the gunny and *Ba-Boom* were 20 meters out, then hit the dual accelerators. The *Anvil* surged forward, nose high until enough of the tank crossed the top of the rise and fell forward with a lurch.

"Damn it, Lysander! I said don't expose us!" the staff sergeant shouted as his feet lost purchase for a few moments as the tank bounced.

If you were buttoned up, or even open-protected, you wouldn't be having that problem with your footing.

Noah's TC was rapidly getting on his nerves. The man was too cautious, worrying about everything. Yet here he was standing half out of the hatch, exposed, when he should be in his seat with either the hatch closed or open 10 centimeters, the "open-protected position," which still provided fairly decent protection while providing better visibility than being completely buttoned-up.

He pushed that train of thought out of his mind and focused on his one job, to keep in position. Chili Fulford, the gunner, and the staff sergeant on the .50 cal, would be watching for the enemy and would engage if need be. Noah had to trust them for that.

The acceleration of a Davis was impressive, and Noah quickly brought the *Anvil* up to 45 KPH as the platoon dashed across the lowlands. The ground was relatively smooth, but the big tanks still bounced around, their suspension unable to completely dampen the bumps and jolts. Twice, Noah's helmeted head slammed into the closed hatch. He'd have liked to have the hatch open, but the lieutenant had ordered the drivers to close up.

"I'm down, fuck it!" Gunny Hattori shouted over the net as the *Ba-Boom* suddenly swerved to the side and stopped in a cloud of dust. "Piece of shit Brysons!"

The Bryson Adjusting Track was new to the fleet, able to adjust on the fly from 500mm to 950mm in width with elevation points on the treads from 1mm to 70mm in depth. This was great in theory as it made the tanks far more maneuverable over a wide range of ground surfaces, but the life-span of the new tracks was far less than that of the older tracks they'd replaced. Still, after covering only 18 klicks, the tracks should have held up, especially over this terrain.

Should have . . .

Noah started to slow down, not sure what to do.

"One-Four, stay in place and provide overwatch. One-Three, guide on me," the lieutenant ordered.

Noah goosed the *Anvil* forward, passing the stationary *Ba-Boom* and rushing to take her place as the remaining three tanks rushed to close the gap to the town.

"One-Three, your entry point is now this one. I'll be taking yours," the lieutenant passed.

Noah glanced at his display to where the platoon commander had highlighted the positions. The *Anvil* and the *Kiss of Death* were switching entry points into the town. It didn't make much sense to him. The lieutenant needed to be where she could best control any coming fight, but she was going in alone, without a wingman, which made the *Kiss of Death* far more vulnerable. She probably thought she needed to take the more dangerous position, but in reality, that might put the entire platoon in a more tenuous position.

"Release," she passed as they reached 200 meters from the edge of the town.

They hadn't rehearsed crossing paths, but Noah figured that the hard-charging Lessa would be aggressive. He was right—she bolted right in front of him as she headed for the right entry point. Noah let her cross his path, then he turned left to his entry, pushing ahead of Charlie-One-Two, the *Ball Shot*.

He couldn't enter at 45 KPH, so he slowed down, causing the staff sergeant, still in the open hatch, to fall forward and have to grab at the rim to keep himself in. Noah thought he was stupid to stay exposed like that—all the *Anvil's* reactive and ablative armor did him no good if an enemy soldier decided to take a pot shot at him. Tankers didn't have "bones," the armor inserts infantrymen used, in their tank suits, and the durable cloth alone wouldn't stop a round. One round to the chest, and he'd have to be resurrected and go through regen, if that was even possible.

"Keep your eyes peeled," the staff sergeant said as they passed the first building and entered the town.

Noah checked the four APCD's that were on each corner of the tank. These little boxes, the "Hashers," were the close-in defense against enemy infantry. With a range of only 15 meters, they were nevertheless effective against ground troops, with both compacted-tip flechettes and sonic bursts that would kill or decapacitate anyone within their kill zone. As the tank's driver, the

APCD's were Noah's responsibility. He was also the secondary gunner of both the coax M104, the automatic 4mm hypervelocity mag rifle, and the M519 .50 cal. The gunner had both the tank's main gun as well as the coax, and the TC was the primary on the .50, but if required, either weapon could become the driver's responsibility.

With only three crewmen to a tank, each Marine had to be flexible and handle each other's function. Noah could even aim and fire the *Anvil's* 75mm hypervelocity rail gun from his driver's hole, if he had to. It had seemed confusing at armor school, but with the tank's AI assisting, it became routine.

Noah wasn't sure the railgun was the best choice for them as he drove down the deserted street. The railgun, with its sabot round, was the premier armor killer in the Marines, although he knew the Wasp pilots might take issue with that. It would destroy any known armor to 6,000 meters out at least. With that kind of range, it was not designed with MOUT operations in mind.

The Ataturk forces were equipped with the Teresas, the upgraded version of the older Tonyas. Made on Gentry, the Teresas used fuel-cell-powered motors, an upgrade over the older Tonya's bio-diesel engines. The Teresas could lay quiet, and with a simple turn of a switch, be at full power. The fuel cell technology limited their endurance when compared to the older Tonyas and the Marines' Davises, but they cost far less than the fusion generator-powered Marine tanks. Like the Tonyas, the Teresas were armed with the Gentry 90mm smoothbore canon. Neither had the reach of the Marine's 75mm railgun, but within an urban area, that extreme range would never come into play. And at close range, both the 90mm HEP-T and HEAT rounds would do a number on a Davis.

Noah found himself wishing the *Anvil* had the Marines' version of the 90mm cannon. The barrel was much shorter than that of the railgun, and the rate of fire was quicker. With the MGS system, a Davis could be outfitted with the railgun, the cannon, or a 20 mega-joule meson gun. The platoon had been outfitted with Weapons Mix B, which was two 75's, one 90, and one meson gun. The *Ba-Boom*, now down and outside the town, had the energy mod, the lieutenant had the 90mm mod, and the *Ball Shot* and *Anvil* had the anti-tank mod.

Noah kept to the middle of the street as he slowly drove the *Anvil* forward. It left him in the open, but it made it more difficult for anyone on top of one of the buildings to easily engage them while simultaneously making it easier for the TC to engage an enemy soldier with the .50 cal.

If there even were soldiers there. The place was a ghost town. There was no sign of anyone, military or civilian. The scanners onboard the *Jerry-John* had shown nothing in the town, but still, it seemed almost too quiet to Noah as he approached the first intersection. But if the Ataturks hadn't deemed the crossroads strategic enough to hold, then that was fine with Noah.

Noah was creeping the *Anvil* along at 10 KPH. At this speed, the big tank was surprisingly silent. There wasn't any of the creaking and groaning of the first 200 years of tanks, and with the fusion generator, the propulsion was silent. The city might be deserted, but the *Anvil* and the *Ball Shot* were 40-ton ghosts making their way through the town. Two blocks away, his display showed Noah that the *Kiss of Death* was paralleling them 300 meters to the south, but equally as silent.

"Stop!" Chili shouted as they crossed the second intersection. "I think I've got something."

Noah immediately applied the brakes, the *Anvil* scraping on the road as it slid to a halt, the first real sound it had made. He checked the Hasher once again, and the green activation lights were a steady reassurance.

"Tank!" the sergeant shouted as the wall of a building 40 meters ahead seem to dissolve as a 90 mm gun started swinging around to them, the gun disrupting the projection field that had hidden it.

"Engage," the lieutenant ordered.

There was a sharp crack as the electromagnetic field accelerated the 12 kg sabot round to almost 5,000 KPH. Almost instantaneously, the Teresa exploded in a blinding flash of light, the turret, with the gun still attached, visible until it flew out of sight.

The familiar smell of ionized air swept into the crew compartment through the TC's open hatch.

"Holy shit!" the sergeant said, his voice filled with awe.

All three of them had fired the railgun back at Camp Ceasare, and Chili had fired the *Anvil's* main guns during pre-deployment quals, but firing at an enemy tank and destroying it took things to another level. Noah was in awe of the amazing power of the railgun. Just five minutes before, he'd wished they had the 90mm smoothbore on the tank, but his concern had evidently been misplaced.

His display rang for attention, and Noah tore his eyes away from the flaming hulk that had been a 60-ton tank only moments before.

"We've got more tanks," the lieutenant passed as two energy blooms blossomed onto his display and started to scatter.

The Ataturk tanks had been lying quiet, and from where the destroyed tank's gun had been pointing, they had evidently been oriented towards New Antalya. Noah shuddered to think what would have happened had they moved with the rest of the task force to the intersection at Route 5 and the Demir Highway, then come down south to hold this objective. As the lead Davis in this two-tank section, they would have eaten a 90mm shell at point-blank range. The *Anvil* would be the smoking hulk instead of the Teresa.

"Two and Three, take the left tank," Lieutenant Moore ordered.

"Two, you take the left," Staff Sergeant Cremineli ordered, pulling up an overhead map and swiping his finger on his display, drawing a red arrow onto the road he wanted Staff Sergeant Kyle Mauser-Lopez, the *Ball Shot's* TC, to take. The tank was still 50 meters behind them, and with a quick pivot, headed down the road.

"Lysander, go, go! What are you waiting for?"

"Which way?"

"Down the road," he shouted, bending over back into the compartment, using his hand to point.

That's all Noah needed, and the *Anvil* responded to his commands, almost leaping ahead, a lion chasing a wildebeest. Except a wildebeest didn't fight back. The Teresa had teeth.

"Noah, I want a right front quarter aspect, if you can," Chili passed. "Don't let them get behind us."

Noah turned left, smashed a road sign, and accelerated the *Anvil* down the road. A small voice of caution surfaced, reminding himself that if he'd been the Ataturk armor, he'd have mined their rear. There were hundreds of military mines available that could disable, if not destroy a Davis. But his TC said go, so he tried to push that concern away.

The *Anvil* had far more power and massed much less than the Ataturk Teresa, and he quickly closed the gap and edged ahead while running parallel only a block over. The excitement of the chase rose within him. Just two more blocks, and he thought he could take the next cross street and cut the Teresa off—until the Ataturk crew turned their tank to the right and away from them.

"Shit! Get on his ass!" Staff Sergeant Cremineli shouted.

Noah spun the *Anvil* around on its axis in a neutral steer, tracks going in opposite directions, then dashed forward, hoping to reach the street the Teresa was on in time to give Chili a shot up the tank's ass-end. Just as he reached the road, however, almost sliding the *Anvil* around the corner, the Teresa turned left, taking it out of Chili's line-of-fire.

Just as Noah could see the Teresa on his display, he knew the Ataturk crew could see the Marine tanks. They were trying to counteract his attempts to get into position to fire while maneuvering their tank to fire on the *Anvil* and *Ball Shot*.

"I'm switching to AI routing," the TC passed.

Immediately, the AI highlighted the routes it calculated for both Marine tanks as they tried to corner the Teresa. Noah would rather be choosing his own route, but he followed where the AI directed him—which changed each time as soon as the Teresa changed its direction.

"It's trying to hook up with the other one," Staff Sergeant Mauser-Lopez passed.

Noah realized that the *Ball Shot's* TC was right. The Teresa was darting around like a bird in a cage, but it was slowly making its way towards the south side of the town where the lieutenant and the other Teresa were maneuvering against each other.

They'd never learned anything like this at armor school. The battles there had been in wide open spaces, covering long distances. Maneuver had been on a larger scale, not individual tanks darting up and down small roads and alleys in a city.

Six or seven years ago, there had been the historical Hollybolly flick, *David Bowie Takes on Wall Street*. Set in the 20th Century, Old Reckoning, the hero Bowie had challenged one of the Wall Street princes to an ancient game called Pacman. The game had made a very brief reappearance as part of the marketing for the flick, and as a big-time gamer, Noah had played the modern release a few times. Used to modern games, Noah had been bored with the slow and one-dimensional play, but what was happening now reminded him of that game. In this case, the three Marine tanks in the fight were doing the chasing, but his display looked like that of the ancient game, with figures chasing each other through the maze of roads and alleys.

"Lieutenant, he's going to be on your ass!" the gunny passed from where he was monitoring the action.

Noah took his eyes off the road for a moment to look at the *Kiss of Death's* avatar, and the gunny was right. Her target had doubled back, and in a moment, it would emerge behind her with a free shot up her ass end. Sergeant Juniper was rotating the main gun, but there was no way she could get it around in time to engage.

Noah held his breath, staring at the screen, as the Teresa emerged and pivoted to take the shot just as the *Kiss of Death* darted down a side alley. The display registered the shot, but the Marine tank kept moving, untouched.

Pay attention to your own fight, Noah scolded himself as he let out the breath he'd been holding.

The flash and explosion took him by surprise, the clang against the top of the *Anvil* reverberating throughout the crew compartment. Immediately, another Teresa had appeared on his display, but he could see it with his naked eyes, just a couple of meters away off his left side where it had been hiding in ambush inside a shop of some sort. The muzzle of the 90mm gun looked huge, so close he thought he could reach out and touch it.

A Teresa was larger than a Davis in both weight and height. The Ataturk tank's 90mm was depressed as far as it could go, and the *Anvil* was beneath the line-of-fire. The Teresa's round had skipped off of the turret instead penetrating. If the eager gunner had just waited ten seconds, the *Anvil* would have been far enough away for the Teresa's main gun to be depressed enough to score a direct hit.

More on instinct than anything else, Noah swerved the *Anvil* into the Teresa, slamming into it with a jolt that knocked Staff Sergeant Cremineli completely out of the tank. He fed the power, keeping contact, and started pushing the Teresa back into the building, walls being smashed as the two tanks struggled against each other.

The Teresa's 90mm gun extended over Noah's hatch. If he opened the hatch, he could reach out and touch the barrel. As Chili brought his longer 75mm railgun around, it ran up against the Ataturk gun, locking together with it.

Noah's initial burst of power pushed the Teresa back, but as its own tracks began to gain purchase, it started to force the *Anvil* back, more walls collapsing as the two tanks banged into them. The Davis had a much more powerful motor, but the Teresa was 60 tons to the Davis' 40. The *Anvil's* tracks started to slip on the hard floor of the building, so Noah adjusted the tread elevation, raising them— and immediately started getting pushed back even quicker. He reversed the elevation, making them almost flat, and that was better, but the Teresa was slowly gaining an advantage. The *Anvil* might have more power, but the Teresa's low-tech polyuthe treads were giving more traction on the building's slick flooring.

"I can't fire!" Chili shouted out, his gun stuck fast, aiming over the front of the Teresa. "Get us out of here so I can take a shot!"

But Noah couldn't just back up, even had the two tanks not been locked together. With the angle of the two guns, as soon as he disengaged, the Teresa would be in position to fire first. He looked out his front port block to try and visualize exactly how the guns were situated, and he caught sight of the Ataturk tank commander, looking down at him through the blocks in his commander's hatch. To his surprise, the commander smiled and nodded at him.

Noah didn't nod back. The Ataturk tank commander was not part of the fight. This was now between both drivers and both gunners.

"*Ball Shot*, cut off that Teresa!" the gunny passed over the platoon net.

Noah risked a glance at his screen. The Teresa he'd been chasing had turned around and was heading back. The *Anvil* was slowly being pushed back out into the street as the two tanks struggled like bull moose during the rut, their antlers locked together. As soon as that first Teresa reached their street, it would have an easy shot up the *Anvil's* ass end. Noah figured they had 30 seconds until then, and he didn't think the *Ball Shot* could get there in time.

Noah could feel it as the *Anvil's* tracks began to gain better purchase. The two tanks were probably beginning to tear up the road and the building's shallow courtyard, which would give his higher-tech tracks more of an advantage and maybe give him the chance to do something with his tank's greater power output. But he had to steer clear of the Teresa's gun, which was still positioned right over the *Anvil*.

"Do something, Noah!" the sergeant shouted.

He just couldn't quite visualize how the two tanks were locked together.

Screw it, he thought with resignation as he popped his hatch.

It opened half-way before hitting the Teresa's gun, but he twisted far enough around to see how the *Anvil's* 75mm had traversed up and in front of the enemy gun, lodging between the turret and the front of the tank. If both tanks stopped and slowly backed away, they could come clear of each other—not that either one of was going to stop and suggest that. Noah was pretty sure he could back up on his own, but that would leave the Teresa aiming down at the *Anvil* and Chili still aiming forward off target.

And then it hit him.

"Traverse back!" he shouted over his headset.

"I can't! The fucking turret!"

"Just grubbing do it! Now!"

A split second later, amid the roar of the battle, he heard the whine of the turret servos as they strained to bring the 75mm around. At that instant, Noah reversed his port tracks and slammed the starboard into forward. For a moment, Noah feared that his tracks would just spin, doing nothing, but enough of the road had broken up that the tank started to rotate, ass end first, counterclockwise. The driver of the Ataturk tank didn't realize what was happening, and probably thinking he had an opening, pushed forward, which was exactly what Noah had hoped he would do. He caught a glimpse of the tank commander, eyes wide as he started shouting inside his tank. He could see what Noah had intended, but it was too late. With the Teresa pushing forward and the *Anvil* rotating, the two tanks slid apart, the Teresa's main gun pointing more than 90 degrees away from the *Anvil*, the *Anvil's* much longer 75mm railgun pointing almost on the Ataturk tank.

"Fire, fire!" Noah shouted as both guns started to traverse, but the *Anvil's* 75mm didn't have as far to swing.

Noah reached back just as Chili brought his gun to bear. He didn't quite get the hatch closed when the sergeant fired and the Teresa erupted into a blinding flash of fire, the force of the explosion slamming Noah's hatch down with enough power to smash his left hand and push the *Anvil* several meters back.

Noah didn't wait. The first Teresa was just reaching the intersection, and Chili Fulford was out of position to engage it.

"Tank, eight o'clock!"

He slewed the *Anvil* around, using his tracks to rotate, seeing the enemy tank as it emerged from the side street, its 90mm swinging over to engage them. His display showed him both his tank's main aspect as well as that of the main gun. He forced himself to look down from his port to the screen, using his tracks to orient the main gun. He couldn't go too far, or he'd take the gun off the target, but he couldn't wait for Chili to traverse, either. It would take too long, and the Teresa would get off the shot first. The two Marines had to work together.

He stopped just short of what he thought the alignment should be, letting the gunner aim in the gun. Only then, did he look up and out the blocks at the Teresa, 70 meters away, and its big 90mm seemingly pointing right at them.

Fire, Fire!

And Sergeant Fulford, UFMC, did.

The hypervelocity round, traveling 5000 meters per second, crossed the 70 meters and slammed into the heavy frontal armor of the Teresa, penetrating the crew compartment with enough kinetic energy to blow the turret off and send it 100 meters into the air to crash down on the roof of some building in the distance. Pieces of the tank shot in all directions, several chunks hitting the *Anvil* with resounding clangs.

Noah leaned back in his tight hole, his head hitting the hatch mount as he slowed his breathing. His heart was pounding at a million beats a minute, and he wasn't sure he could breathe.

"Mother fuck," Chili said, his voice quiet with awe.

"What now?" Noah asked him, looking down at his screen.

Three enemy tanks were burning hulks, and the avatars for two more could now be seen. As he watched, the *Ball Shot* fired through a building, it looked like, the sabot round passing completely through to hit the tank on the other side.

"Target down," Staff Sergeant Mauser-Lopez passed.

"Two and Three, help me with this asshole," the lieutenant passed, still playing cat-and-mouse with what was now the sole remaining Teresa.

Noah started to reach for his controls, and he screamed out in pain. His hand was on fire. He held it up, and it looked pretty bad.

"You OK, Noah?"

"Uh, yeah. I'm OK."

There was a clatter on the outside of the tank, and Noah reached for his Ruger as a body dropped in through the commander's hatch. Noah fumbled to bring his handgun up when Staff Sergeant Cremineli's familiar voice asked for an update as if nothing had happened. When the TC had fallen out of the tank, Noah had figured he'd been crushed in the struggle or blown up when the Teresa had exploded, but here he was, looking none the worse for wear.

"We're on our way to back up the *Kiss of Death*," Chili told him.

"Then let's go, Lysander."

Noah reached out with both hands on his yokes, but his left hand wasn't working. He'd somehow managed to use it to get the *Anvil* around for the third kill, the one coming around the corner, but now, it was useless. The *Anvil* lurched forward, smashing into the side of a building, sending a shower of debris down on the TC.

"What the hell, Lysander? You drunk or something? Drive it right!"

"I . . . I don't think I can. I'm down one hand."

The TC bent over in the hatch and looked at Noah, who held up his now throbbing hand.

The staff sergeant shrugged, then said, "Switch with me" as he started to slide, feet first, into Noah's hole.

There wasn't any room for Noah to slide past him in the constrained crew compartment, so he had to open the hatch with his right hand, then crawl out, feeling very vulnerable as he scrambled to the commander's cupola, dripping bright red blood onto the dusty skin of the *Anvil*. He almost fell through the hatch, then pulled it closed after him.

The staff sergeant was now the driver, with the hatch open, of course, and his head sticking out, he put the *Anvil* into motion, ready to join the last fight. They didn't make it. Before they'd driven 200 meters, the *Kiss of Death* and the *Ball Shot* had cornered the remaining tank, forcing it to surrender.

One short Marine tank platoon had defeated a five-tank Ataturk platoon, destroying three Teresas, disabling one, and forcing the surrender of the fifth. For a bunch of previously untested tankers, that wasn't too shabby.

ITZUKO-2

Chapter 1
Ten months earlier . . .

"Here, let me look at you," Miriam said, turning Noah around and touching his collar, straightening what was already straight. "OK, give me a kiss, and don't be late."

Noah obediently leaned in and gave her a quick peck on the cheek.

"Are you going to be OK here today?" he asked.

"I'm a big girl. I think I can handle being on my own for the day. Now go," she said, turning him back around and giving him a slap on the ass.

"OK, I'll be back as soon as I can."

Noah slipped out the door, walked down the hall, and descended the decrepit stairwell. Miriam was putting on a good face, but he worried about her. Camp Ceasare was an unaccompanied tour for students, even if he would have been a sergeant, so there was no base housing. He'd been assigned a shared room in the barracks, but with Miriam with him, he didn't plan on spending too much time there—even if the conditions were much better in his assigned quarters. As a corporal, without rating a housing allowance, the only apartment they'd found that they could afford was a run-down shithole that catered to transients, drug-heads, and other Marines in his situation. He didn't feel good about leaving Miriam alone there.

It would have been better if she'd been able to find a job, any job. It would help with the rent, but more importantly, give her something to do. He had a nagging fear that after a month or so, she'd give up on the situation and run again, and that meant giving up on him. He was confident that she loved him, but her past record of sticking with something when things got rough was not encouraging.

But there was nothing he could do about that now. Today was the first day of the Marine Corps Armor Operator's Course. He was going to be starting his journey to become a Marine tanker. The course trained Marines to maintain and fight the two Marine tanks, the Davis and Mamba, and the Aardvark armored personnel carrier, but for Noah, only the Davis would do. Despite his concern about leaving Miriam alone for the day, he was excited as he boarded the maglev to the front gate of the camp, an excitement that only mounted as he got off the train and looked up at the huge Garcia mounted on a pedestal at the gate. The largest land vehicle ever used by the Federation military and FCDC at 120 tons, it almost took his breath away. At 40 tons, any modern Davis could defeat an old Garcia, but even so, the sight of it still filled him with awe.

He only had to wait a few minutes before the shuttle arrived, taking him and the other 20 or so waiting Marines and civilians into the main base, a good 20 klicks in from the gate. Camp Ceasare was a huge, expansive base leased from Itzuko Daihatsu, the corporate owner of the "Itch," as the Marines called the planet. A sparsely-populated commercial planet, the company had been happy to lease the 1,350,000 hectares of what had been unused land to the Federation. Most of the built-up area of the base was located at the 40,000-acre far eastern tip of the base. The rest consisted of firing ranges and maneuver areas. While the base population was small, the land area made Camp Ceasare the largest military base in the Federation and the second largest in human space.

Noah sat quietly in his seat, looking at the other passengers, but not saying anything. He wondered if any of the others were in his class. Camp Ceasare was home to the United Federation Marine Corps Training Command, and there was more going on than just the armor school. Marine pilots received their level two training at the camp, and almost every type of mechanics, technicians, artillery Marines, and engineers also received their training onboard. The vast spaces also provided First, Second, and Third Marine Divisions with their combined arms ranges.

Noah might have been happy to just sit there in silence, but not everyone was so reticent.

"You going to armor school?" another corporal asked him, her voice kept low.

"Yes," he said. "First day."

"Well, yeah. First day for the course for everyone," she said, rolling her eyes.

Duh, Noah. Of course, it is. The next class won't convene for another six months.

He didn't know how to respond, but she reached out a hand and said, "Patricia Chopra. They call me 'Killer.'"

Noah took the hand, but he couldn't help but question her nickname, simply asking, "Killer?"

"That's me. And you are?"

"Noah."

Some Marines put a lot of importance on their nicknames. They'd even come into a unit making up a name that they felt fit them better, or at least how they wanted others to see them. That rarely worked as it was pretty easy to check on the undernet, and when caught, the new nicknames were rarely something anyone wanted. If this small Marine, who couldn't have massed more than 40 kg, said her name was Killer, then so be it. He was sure others would check up on that.

Killer or not, she seemed to be somewhat of a chatterbox. Noah had heard her life story before the shuttle pulled up in front of the armor school. Even if 50% of what she'd said was was pure BS, then maybe the nickname was deserved. Noah had broken out laughing several times at her stories, and two other Marines had joined them to listen as well. After arriving, the four of them walked up the steps of the school, following the signs to Classroom A in the main building.

They swiped themselves in at the door, then entered the large classroom, where at least 70 Marines were already in their seats. Coming from an infantry battalion, as were probably all of them, it was different to see that about half of the class were female. He'd expected it—with the size limitations to serve in armor, a higher percentage of enlisted women Marines gravitated towards armor, just as a higher percentage of female officers gravitated toward air.

He looked at Killer as they entered, half-expecting her to join some of the women, but she seemed happy with her new-found friends, and the four took their places in the back.

There was a stage in the front of the room—a plaque with the words *Si vis pacem, para bellum* prominently displayed across the wall behind it. To the side was a simple sign with the capital letters YATYAS. Noah had seen that back at the armor ramp at Wayfarer Station, but he still wasn't sure of its meaning. Sergeant Phong never explained what it meant.

Ten minutes after the four Marines had taken their seats, a Marine captain and a master guns entered the classroom, the master guns calling the class to attention. The captain walked up to the lectern, put them at ease, and looked out over the class before speaking.

"Welcome, Class 42-06. I am Captain Jurveous, your OIC. For the next 34 weeks, you will be learning how to fight in the Davis, the Aardvark, and the Mamba. By the time you graduate, you will know every connection, every plate, every track on the three vehicles. You will be able to fight in them, and you'll be able to repair them in field conditions. You will live in them, sleep in them, eat it them, shit in them. You will learn to love them and hate them.

"This is a professional class, and each of you has already proven yourself as a Marine. We will not be babysitting you. It is up to you to do what is necessary to pass the course. If you want to go out in town and down a beer, no one's going to stop you. However, my military and civilian instructors' word is the law. I don't care what your rank is, when you are in your vehicles, you will do what they say.

"This should be a rewarding course, and you will emerge from it as a tread-head, the noblest job in the Corps. And with that, I'll turn it over to Master Gunnery Sergeant Andreiko. Master Guns?"

The master gunnery sergeant called the class to attention, and the captain climbed off the stage and strode up the center aisle.

Just before he reached the hatch, he turned and shouted, "YATYAS!" before exiting.

"What the hell does that mean?" Noah asked.

"You don't know?" Brock Eastern asked.

Noah and the other two Marines looked at him expectantly, but he shook his head.

"We can't say it, but you'll find out later," he said.

At least the other two didn't know either. Noah was tempted to pull out his PA and look it up, but there was obviously something significant about it, and that seemed almost like cheating.

"Class 42-06, today is T1. After my orientation, you will remain in this classroom for Dr. Polytermis' class. But first, we've got to get some admin out of the way, so pull up the class app and listen up . . ."

Noah turned on his PA and pulled up the app. Thirty-four weeks might seem long right now, but he had a feeling that so much would be crammed in that time would be of an essence. If he was going to pass the course, he'd have to pay attention, starting right now.

Chapter 2

"I'm Terrance Duval," the young man told the four of them. "I'll be your primary instructor for your M1 prac apps. For all intents and purposes, I'll be the one who teaches you through this rotation.

"So you know my background, I served two tours as Marine tanker, all on the Davis, and one with the FCDC before coming here as a civilian employee."

Two tours with the Marines, three if you count his grunt tour, and one with the FCDC? How old is this guy? Noah wondered.

He looked younger than any of them. Either he had really good genes or the good plastic surgeons had gone to work on him. Noah had hoped for a Marine instructor, but with only two of them and one FCDC instructor teaching the prac apps, he was stuck with a civilian. With the total force numbers limit, more and more civilians were taking over the support and training missions in the Corps.

"This right here is your training tank, B103."

"No name?" Killer asked. "Just B103?"

"No name. Only combat tanks are named. This is just a training device. I'm sure you'll give her a name, though, by the time you're done with her, at least something you call her under your breath when she's covered with mud that has to be scraped off or she throws a track. She's been here for a long, long time, and she's feeling her age."

Noah had helped Sergeant Phong clean the Mambas on Dixie once, and that had been bad enough, but that was just sand. Mud had to be much worse.

"First, some rules. There will be no horseplay on the ramps, as in none. Forty tons of tank will crush you flat in an instant. We've got eight trainers here for the class, and as you can see, the school ramp is a little cramped. So, head's up at all times. You're all coming from the grunts, and there, if you collide with a fellow Marine, no harm no foul. If you crash your tanks, that can result in lots of damage. If you let one run into you when you're dismounted, however, we won't have enough to scrape off the ground to send home to your parents."

Brock grimaced at that. He was a crèche baby from Adelaide III, and he'd never known his parents. He could get a little sensitive about it at times. Noah bumped him with his hip. This civilian had control if they graduated or not, so it wouldn't do any good to antagonize him over some half-assed comment.

"If you receive three safety down-checks, you're out of the course and back to the grunts," Mr. Duval said, his voice dripping with scorn as if that would be the worst thing that could happen to a Marine.

Noah really wanted to become a tanker, but he took offense to Duval's tone. He'd enjoyed his time as a grunt, especially being a PICS Marine, and while he looked forward to being a tread-head, they were a support unit, after all, supporting the infantry.

"You're lucky that you've got Rotation 1 first. Once you've mastered the M1, the other two vehicles will be cake."

Two weeks into the course, the class had been broken into three training groups. They would still PT together, still attend common classes together, but the specific vehicle training would be done in one six-week rotation, then two five-week. The theory was that as all three vehicles had essentially the same controls, so after mastering driving one, it wouldn't take as long to become familiar with the other two platforms. Noah, and his three friends had been assigned to the M1s first.

He risked a quick look at the other three Marines. It hadn't been coincidence that they were together. Unlike boot camp or even getting assigned to the fleet, the staff didn't seem to care who joined up with whom. They were simply told to form training groups of four each. Killer, Skeets, Brock, and Noah had immediately come together and locked in their group while most of the rest of the class were just beginning to ask each other if they wanted to hook up. They were the second group to get their names in, and they'd been assigned to Rotation 1, which was the M1 Davis training module, much to their delight. Half of the class would end up going to tanks, with the bulk of them going to M1 units, while the rest would go Aardvarks. Noah knew the Aardvarks were vitally important to the infantry, and the smaller Mamba assault tanks could be lifted to places where the M1 was impractical, but he joined armor to fight in the biggest, baddest piece of gear in the Marine Corps inventory. Being trained on the Davis first was in no way a guarantee that he'd eventually get tanks, but he was still pretty pumped.

"So, now that we've got that out of the way, let's climb up there and get acquainted with the lady," Mr. Duval said, jumping up on the nose of the tank.

Noah jumped up, eager to take a look. Duval might not think much of B103, but if she was showing her age, Noah couldn't tell. She sure looked beautiful to him.

Chapter 3

"Corporal Lysander, you're up. Get in your tank," the gunny said.

Noah leapt out of the stands, his legs springs as he rushed to where B103 waited for him. It didn't have the MGS module on nor the .50 cal attached, so it was somewhat toothless, but she looked sexy as all get-out to him. He'd spent over 40 hours on the simulator, but this would be his first time driving an actual tank.

First time driving a Davis, he corrected himself.

He'd driven the Mamba back on Dixie when Sergeant Phong had given him the opportunity, but the Mamba assault tank, as excited as he'd been back then, was not a Davis, and with 40 hours of sim time behind him, he knew he'd be allowed, no, expected, to put 103 through her paces.

"Show us how Marine does it!" Killer shouted out from where she was sitting with Brock and Pie, his three closest friends at the school.

Noah knew they were all aching to get their chances, but with the second highest sim scores, Noah was the second student in the class to get his chance. Killer's comment referenced the fact that Sergeant Opania Bester, FCDC, had come out of the sims with the highest score, and for a "fuckdick" (not that Noah used the term himself, especially within earshot of the other eight FCDC troopers in the class) to be at the top of a Marine Corps class was simply unacceptable.

"Corporal Lysander, let's see what you can do today. Just remember, this is for real, not like the sim," Mr. Duval said from the TC's cupola as Noah ran up. "Listen up to what I have to say. You'll be in control, but if I say 'Stop,' you stop, understand?"

He wasn't going to be totally in control, Noah knew. Duval might be the one to tell Noah what to do for the next twenty minutes, but he also had mirror controls in the commander's seat, and his controls were primary. He could stop or steer the tank out of trouble if he needed to, and from the holos they'd been shown during the class that morning, the instructors evidently had to inject themselves into the training quite often. The Davis had 2,500 horses under her skirt, all raring to break free, and more than a few new students had unleashed them and then panicked, not knowing what to do.

Not me, Noah vowed as Mr. Duval went through the rest of his brief. *Just get it over with. I read everything you're saying already.*

"So, if you don't have any questions, why don't you get into the driver's hole?"

Noah didn't have to be asked twice. He vaulted over 103's prow and in through the open hatch. Many of the shorter Marines could jump in, turning as they entered, and land sitting on the seat. Noah had tried that, time and time again, and all he ended up doing was to almost knock himself silly. As tall as he was, he had to land standing on the seat, turn, and sort of slide down, his feet moving into position.

It might have taken him a split second longer than it would most of the class, but he was sitting in the driver's hole, ready to go. His gaming background probably helped him in getting a leg up in the simulators, but this was the real thing. If he wanted to get Davises for his first assignment, he had to kick butt starting now. He sat in the driver's hole, hatch open, waiting for his next order.

"Comms check," Mr. Duval said over the net, his voice relayed out of the speakers in Noah's helmet.

"Roger."

"You may start the motor."

A Davis' fusion generator is always on, but dampened. The moment Noah reached down and flipped the switch to turn on the motor, the generator surged, sending power to meet the demand. There was no noise, no roar of engines, but there was a slight vibration as the tank's systems came alive. To Noah, it seemed as if the 103 was a race horse, snorting at the starting gate, ready to bolt as soon as she was released.

"How are your readings?"

Noah had forgotten to check them, so hyped was he to get moving. He gave them a rapid eye-over, then told the instructor that all were within the green.

"I've got a 5 KPH limit on, so use the manual and get us to 13B."

"Roger that," Noah said as he pushed the two thumb paddles forward.

With a jerk, the 103 jumped into motion, only to steady out at the glacial 5 KPH. He understood it, though. There were eight training tanks and eight training ranges. There would be tanks travelling back and forth between those eight ranges, and the instructors didn't want newbie drivers crossing paths at speed. At 5 KPH, they could stop the tanks if it looked like a collision was imminent.

Noah tried to ignore his impatience as he trundled 103 behind the ranges to get to 13B. He turned into his range, brought the 103 to the raised starting platform, and stopped her.

"Still green," he told Mr. Duval, remembering to check his readouts.

The Davis was a sophisticated tank, and the tank AIs would inform the crew of problems and would even shut her down to prevent further damage is something went wrong. But in the school, the AIs were toned down, only to kick in for a dire emergency. For the most part, it was up to the students to monitor their vehicles.

"I just removed the limit," the instructor said. "I want you to give me a clockwise neutral steer."

Noah complied, then slowly advanced power to the left track in forward, the right track in reverse. The 103 jerked into motion, but then pivoted in a clockwise circle. He was pretty sure he'd nailed it as he completed the entire rotation.

"Counterclockwise, neutral steer, do it."

He reversed what he'd just done, and the tank started pivoting in the opposite direction. He drifted slightly forward this time, but he still managed to stay on the platform. The Davis had voice control, and Noah could have simply told the B103 to complete the neutral steer, but the voice control had been deactivated for the training session. He was supposed to be learning how to drive the tank, not simply to issue verbal commands to the tank's AI.

"Very well," Duval said. "Now, take us down the track."

Noah felt a surge of excitement sweep through him. The "track" was a five-kilometer trail up the range and then back. They'd cover more difficult terrain later in the course, but at least he'd be doing real driving. He'd driven just about every real armor going back to WWI and more than a few fictional tanks in his gaming, and some of those games had seemed pretty realistic, but this was the real deal.

He edged the 103 off the platform and steered her to the starting flag. The trail was marked with orange flags on three-meter poles, but it was hard to miss the trail itself, carved by thousands of tanks tearing up the ground. Noah drove to the head of the trail, and without pause, started down it. The rutted soil left a chute, like those used for bobsleds, that he needed to follow. It had recently rained, and the ground was a little muddy, but the compensators kicked in, keeping slippage to a minimum as Noah took the first two turns, his confidence building.

Driving a tank takes into account many different factors, from yaw, to the slewing force required to overcome turning resistance, and all of those are different depending on the surface characteristics. It is not simply a matter of a one-size fits all application of the outer track, the driving force, and the inner track, the braking force. Speed is a major factor as well, and a driver has to look ahead at the ground and determine the correct inputs for the tank to follow the desired course. That is why despite all the advances in auto-driving technology, unless a tank was following a paved road, a trained human was still the best driver. Noah had just taken the first two turns without Mr. Duval interfering, and he was beginning to feel he had this driving thing figured out.

He powered up a small slope, adjusting his speed to minimize slippage, cresting the rise and tipping over to head back down. At the bottom, he could see brown standing water, collected from the recent rains. He blasted out a scan, and the return confirmed his initial impression he'd made from looking at the ground on either side of the trail that the water hole was shallow and with a somewhat level bottom. Noah goosed the 103 forward picking up speed. The depth of the water might be only a meter or so, but he wasn't sure as to the condition of the ground under it, so the text book solution was to pick up speed.

With a feeling of joy, he hit the water hard—and was immediately drenched in a muddy torrent that flowed over the nose and flooded the driver's hole. He was blinded, and he brought the tank to a stop on the slope on the other side of the hole.

"You might have wanted to close your hatch before hitting the water," Mr. Duval told him.

Noah tried to wipe the muddy water from his eyes, doing a pretty poor job of it. Finally, he could see enough to get going, and he applied power to the treads again, slipping as the tank tried to gain purchase on the slope to make it back up to somewhat even terrain.

"Stop," Mr. Duval said. "Check your medkit, take out a pad, and wipe your face."

An embarrassed Noah fumbled around until he felt the kit and pulled it open. He pulled out a large pad pack, opened it, and extracted a pad which he used to wipe his face the best he could. It took three pads, but finally, his face was clear, and he could see again.

"OK, now get up this slope."

Noah kept the power to the treads low, and the 103 made it up the slope to the top.

"Part of driving is a full comprehension of the terrain, Corporal. You don't want to plunge into a river only to find out it's five meters deep."

Noah turned to tell Duval that he'd checked the depth when he saw a completely clean instructor, a tiny smirk on his face, looking at him from a mud-covered hatch. And it all clicked. Duval had known what would happen and had buttoned up. It was all part of a set-up and a lesson in driving.

Duly chastised, he didn't say a word and continued his route. He'd gotten a little cocky, and it had bitten him in the butt. Still, he was driving a Davis, and within a few moments, he was back to being thrilled with the idea. It wasn't as if anything drastic had happened. He'd just been doused with muddy water, and that was just a Marine shower, right?

On the return leg, the trail crossed the same low-lying area. Noah pulled his hatch closed, then hit the water, sending up another wave. Lesson learned.

He reached the end of the trail, then returned to the raised starting platform, shutting down the tank. Turning his body in the diver's hole, he looked expectantly at Duval, who was entering some data on his PA.

"OK, Mr. Lysander," the instructor said. "Not bad. I'm giving you a 93. You need to be more cognizant of your surrounding terrain, and you need to get a better feel of the necessary slewing forces for a given soil condition. We'll work more on that later. No down-checks."

Noah let a breath out that he hadn't realized he was holding. He was positive that the muddy water incident was a set-up, and to hear that he hadn't been given a down-check seemed to support that.

"Take us back to the stands. And Corporal Lysander, you are not to discuss your performance until after everyone else has driven."

Noah took the B103 along the back of the range, bringing her to a stop where Skeets was waiting. He pulled himself out of the driver's hole and clambered down to the ground.

"Hey, what happened to you?" Skeets asked, hands out to indicate Noah's mud-covered body.

"It was grubbing awesome," Noah said, realizing that it had been just that. He'd driven a Davis and acquitted himself well. "Have fun."

As he walked back up to the bleachers, he caught sight of Sergeant Bester, her body covered in almost as much mud as his was. She gave him a smile and a thumbs up, which he returned.

He plopped down beside Brock and Killer, his heart still pounding with excitement.

"Hey, watch it," Killer said, scooting to the side as Noah's muddy shoulder touched her. "What'd you do, go mud-diving?"

"No, I just became a tank driver," he said. "Not like you weak-ass Marines."

"Oh, great, it's gone to his head," Brock said with a laugh.

Each of the first eight drivers came back with some degree of muddy clothes, as did most of the second, to include Pie. Marines aren't totally idiots, though, even wanna-be tread-heads, and the remaining students started figuring it out. More and more were returning with only their backs and butts dirty from sitting in muddy tanks.

"Watch the first water hole," Noah said to Brock after Killer left for her drive.

He wasn't supposed to say anything, he knew, but he was pretty sure others were telling their crewmates.

Finally, everyone was done. The gunny conducted the after action. Two drivers had received down-checks. Noah looked around, trying to see who might have received them. Overall, the gunny told them their aggregate score was 86%.

They formed up for the march back. The instructors drove the tanks—there were three tank crossings on the four-klick ride from the range to the ramp, and the students were not yet qualified yet to drive off a range. The students marched, going over their experiences, full of energy. Noah's stomach was rumbling as they came around the last bend into the ramp. He wanted to shower, change clothes, and get to the chow hall. When he saw the tanks lined up, instructors standing in front of them, a sinking feeling hit him.

"Class, you got them dirty, now you'll clean them," the gunny announced as they fell into formation in front of him.

There was a collective, if mostly silent, moan. The tanks were caked with mud, and if the B103 was any indication, all of the other tanks had mud inside them as well.

Mr. Duval seemed to take glee in showing his crew the metal tools they'd use to peel off the slabs of heavy mud that had caked the road wheels and treads. They'd have to use them to take off the bulk of the mud before they could move on to the high-pressure wash racks. Noah wasn't sure how long it would take them, but it wouldn't be quick.

He may not have received a down-check today, but evidently, there was always some sort of price to pay for having such a kick-ass time.

Chapter 4

An exhausted Noah pushed open the door to his apartment.

"Finally!" Miriam said, as he stumbled in, which then turned to, "Oh, no! To the shower," when he moved to their beat-up couch.

Noah had hosed himself down at the ramp, which had gotten rid of most of what was on him, but that had hardly made him clean. He let himself be steered away from the couch and into the tiny bathroom because the thought of a hot shower was enticing.

When Mr. Duval had told them they might come up with names for their tanks, nasty names, he hadn't understood. Now, he did. They'd just spent six hours scraping, pulling, and extracting tons of heavy, sticky mud off the B103, and more than a few names had been suggested. Pie, in particular, had a wealth of suggestions, none that Noah could repeat in public.

He considered himself in good shape—he was a Marine, after all. But the work on the B103 had been exhausting. His body ached, and he'd considered just crashing at his quarters on base instead of coming home.

Miriam stripped him of his overalls, holding them up between her thumb and forefinger as if they were infected with some sort of contagious disease before dropping them on the floor and kicking them aside. She turned on the water, and Noah gratefully stepped in, the hot water jets pounding at his body.

"I thought we could go down to the Anchor tonight. Liquid Potash is playing there, no cover, and it's still happy hour, and I thought, well, you know, maybe one beer apiece, that wouldn't be so bad, right? Manuel and Dot are going, along with some other couples, and this can be, you know, we can socialize, get out and meet people."

Manuel and Dot were in the same position as Miriam and him. Dot was a sergeant, but a student at the Aviation School, and she and Manuel were renting the next-door apartment. Noah had met them both, but despite both couples promising to get together sometime, it hadn't happened yet.

And Noah didn't really want it to happen tonight. All he wanted to do was to hit the rack.

He'd been so pumped earlier in the day after driving his Davis, only to crash down when faced with the reality of being a tanker. He knew that all of that was intended by the instructors. Being a tanker was not just driving around and firing weapons. There was maintenance that had to be done, more of that than Noah had expected. He should have realized it. Almost every time he'd gone to see Sergeant Phong, she been on the ramp working on her tank.

He didn't regret making the transfer to tanks, and he realized that it wasn't always going to be fun and games. But today, he was just dog-tired.

He was just about to tell Miriam that he didn't want to go out, when she slipped out of her clothes and into the shower. She lathered up his back, going on and on about Liquid Potash and how they could make it big if they just caught a break. Noah knew he should stop her, to tell her he just wanted to stay at home, but her hands felt good on his back as she rubbed in the soap.

She turned him around and washed his front, his eyes closing as she ran her hands over his chest. Still, he didn't say anything. It just felt good to have her taking care of him. She took down the shower head, rinsed him off, and turned off the water.

"OK, baby, you're all clean," she said, leaning up against him. "Now get ready. I've got your clothes laid out."

She stepped out of the shower, grabbed a towel, and started drying herself, half-singing a song he recognized as from the recording she had of Liquid Potash. She really, wanted to go, he knew. She'd been stuck in the apartment every day since their arrival. They barely had enough money to survive, so they hadn't had too many nights out on the town—or any time, for that matter.

Noah loved her. He was going to marry her, if he had his way. He just didn't have the energy to go out tonight.

"Come on, lazy boy. Get your cute ass moving."

With a sigh, he got out of the shower, taking the towel she offered him. He dried himself off, then sat on the edge of the bed where she'd laid out her clothes.

OK, OK, I can do this, he thought as he let himself fall onto his back. *Just let me rest for a moment.*

He awoke to a darkened room, under the covers. The clock on the wall was at 2314, the red LED blinking accusingly at him. He pushed off the covers and sat up.

What the heck happened?

The clothes Miriam had set out were gone. Noah pulled on a pair of underwear and a T, then padded out of the room. Miriam, in her fleeces, was sitting on the couch, watching a show on the holo.

"I'm sorry, Miriam," he said, walking up behind her and putting his hand on her shoulder.

She tensed up at his touch.

"I was just so beat today. But you could have woken me up."

"No, it's OK," she said, not turning around to look at him. "It wasn't that important. You were tired, so I just let you sleep. We can do it another time."

The words were fine, but the tone of her voice wasn't. She was upset, but trying her best to hide the fact.

Noah felt horrible. He felt horrible because he'd let her down, but even more so because he was relieved, even now, that he hadn't been dragged to the bar. Despite knowing how she'd felt, how much she'd wanted to go, he was happy that he had gotten his own way in the end.

"I love you," he said, the standard get-out-of-jail phrase he used when he didn't know what else to say.

Noah's father had been the ultimate Marine, and there was no doubt that he loved his family, even to the point where he was willing to sacrifice his life for them, but the truth of the matter was that he hadn't always been the best father, the best husband. Life as a Marine sometimes—well, often—got in the way. Noah had sworn to himself that he would never end up like that. Family came first.

Not going on a simple night out was not universe-shattering. It wouldn't register to most people. But to Noah, it was an ill portent, a truth he didn't want to acknowledge.

Maybe I'm not so different from Father after all, he told himself as he walked back into the bedroom to go to sleep, leaving Miriam alone on the couch.

Chapter 5

This was the day they'd all been waiting for. Driving the tanks had been fun—the daily maintenance maybe less so—but it had lost a little of its luster. They spent the last week attacking increasingly difficult terrains, and most of the class had been able to handle them with only two students dropped. They still had the mountain package to tackle after the three rotations were completed, but Noah and his three crewmates were confident that they could drive a tank wherever their commanders needed it.

But so far, they'd just been bus drivers, taking their 40 tons of armor from here to there. A tank's treads were its mobility but not its raison d'être. A tank's purpose was to put big bangs on the bad guys, and today, they were finally going to put that to the test.

Seven of the eight tanks were lined up at the firing line. B107 had frozen on the ride over, its AI shutting it down to prevent further damage from whatever the problem had been. A mobile tech team had been dispatched, but the 107's three students had to fire, so they'd caught rides on the other seven tanks and would fire with them unless the tech team could get 107 up and running in time.

The instructors were back with the gunny, going over the training, but the four of them were looking at the eight M-309 Mobile Weapons Systems Loader and nine MGS modules lined up looking so dangerous. They'd spent a good portion of yesterday back on the ramp practicing installing and removing each of the three different modules, and by the end of the day, they had it down to slightly less than half an hour to make the switch.

At last, Duval and the other instructors broke away and headed out to their crews. The four Marines stood up straighter, waiting for their final instructions.

"We've got the Mad Mike first," he told them. "I'd appreciate it if you weren't the last ones ready to fire."

It was to be expected that the installation would turn out to be a competition. Most things in the Corps were, whether who would come in first on a run to which ant would find the sugarpop some Marine had thrown onto the ground. Quite often, bets were made, and Noah was pretty sure the instructors had credits riding on this as well.

Mr. Duval went through the rest of the brief while Noah stood impatiently, trying to look attentive. If they hadn't heard the same brief five times already, it might have made a difference. But the Corps never believed in a Marine's ability to comprehend after hearing something once when they could instead hammer it in over and over again.

After he was finished, Duval joined the other instructors moving to the bleachers while the four of them walked over to stand behind one of the 309's waiting for the word to go. Then they had to stand there while the range safety officer, a man who looked old enough to have fought in the old World Wars back on Earth, gave them the same brief, almost word for word. At long last, he was done, and he gave them the OK.

Immediately, the four Marines sprang to work. Skeets and Killer started maneuvering the 309 forward while Brock and Noah stood ready at the lock-downs. The 309 could be programmed for a hands-off connection, but for this entire training evolution, it was to be in the manual mode.

The M-309 was a very simple looking device resembling a full rack in the gym. It was strong, steady . . . and slow. As it started to straddle the MGS-MC, Noah reached forward for the first snake, grabbing the head and leading it right to the coupler. His pulling on it wouldn't make a difference, but he couldn't help but make the effort. Finally, he felt the small tug as the connector ends detected each other and pulled together. With a click, they fused, and the telltale flashed green.

"Two connected," he shouted out a moment before Brock announced that number One had connected as well.

The two snakemen jumped back to help guide in numbers Three and Four, almost jumping back as the final two connections were made. They bolted forward to the B103 while Killer and Skeets walked the 309 up, Skeets on the controls, Killer monitoring the MGS.

There hadn't been a reason for the two Marine to sprint ahead. They waited impatiently on top of the tank while the 309 trundled forward. The MGS was fairly lightweight as armor weapons went, but it was not exactly without much mass. While the 309 had no problem lifting one, if the MGS started to sway, that could keep feeding on itself until the MWSL became unstable and even tip over. It was Killer's job to make sure that didn't happen, lowering the MGS to the ground, if necessary, but it was better to just keep any oscillating from even starting.

"Look at that! A race of the snails," Brock said.

Noah had to laugh out loud. It did look pretty funny. All eight crews were slowly walking forward, a slow-motion race to get their MGS's to their tanks. Everyone looked so serious, too.

It took a couple of minutes for the first of the teams to reach their tank, and by the time Killer raised the MGS to clear the top and Skeets eased the 309 forward, they were in second-to-last place.

"Come on, come on," Noah said, watching the alignment from inside the tank.

There wasn't much he could do from inside to make sure the MGS came down in position—in fact, he was not allowed to reach out to help. A slight shift, and his arms could get crushed between the MGS and the tank body.

But between Killer and Pie, the MGS came down smoothly, all alignment lights green. Noah flipped the connector switches, checked the circuits for continuity, waiting for Brock's "All secure" from outside of the tank where he was locking the MGS in place.

He received that 15 seconds later, and he immediately powered up the weapons module, watching the readouts. The Mad Mike, the nickname for the 2.5 KJ meson cannon, took a lot of energy to power up, whereas the MGS-AT railgun and the MGS-HE 90mm canon would be ready to go almost immediately. The B103's crew was already behind most of the other crews, and handicapped with the Mad Mike, Noah wasn't sure they could catch up. One after the other, the red lights turned green as the whine of the charging cannon grated on his ears.

Finally, the last light turned green, and he shouted "Gun up!" before scooting out of the crew compartment.

To his relief, it looked like there were two more crews still setting up. He gave Pie, who was backing up the 309, a thumbs up.

Noah had to wait for the chief weapons instructor, retired Sergeant Major Sylvester Tarpon, to reach them. He down-checked 122, which surprised the heck out of Noah.

How can you get down-checked? Either you're green or red.

That made him nervous, though, as the sergeant major climbed up on the 103. He wondered if he'd forgotten anything. The sergeant major never completely entered the tank. Hanging upside-down with his head in the gunner's turret, he barely took five seconds to emerge with an up-check, much to Noah's relief. It took another ten minutes until all seven tanks were given the up-check and were deemed ready to fire.

But Noah and his crewmates had to wait. The firing line was constrained, and while all Davises were supposedly hardened to each other, it was theoretically possible for the side lobes or leakage from a Mad Mike to set off sympathetic explosions in the 90mm rounds fired by the MGS-HE. Safety regulations required that the MGS-MC's maintain 40 meters distance between them and other tanks while firing on ranges, so the B103 and B129 remained back at the ready-line while the other five tanks loaded their rounds and moved into their firing positions.

Noah and the other three sat on top of the 103, watching, as the first tank was cleared to fire. The crack of the 75mm sabot round as it blew past the sound barrier almost hurt his ears, so sharp was it. Almost instantly, it seemed, there was a flash as the round punched through the sides of a hulk so damaged that Noah couldn't tell what it had once been.

"Get some!" Brock said, fist-bumping Killer.

Noah was impressed. While the 90mm rounds to be fired today were the blue practice rounds, there was no such thing as a "practice" 75mm railgun round. It was an inert hunk of death shot at hypervelocity speeds. They didn't have a warhead, relying on simple mass and inertia to destroy a target.

The gunner fired two more rounds before the next tank in the line was ready. This would be the MGS-HE, firing the 90mm round. Unlike the sharp crack of the railgun, the 90mm shook the firing stations with the concussion of the chemical propellant. Noah could feel it, as if someone was thumping his chest. Downrange, the impact was a little anti-climatic, but that was because the rounds were inert and not nearly as fast as the 75mm rounds. Whereas the railgun was a superb anti-armor weapon, and while it did have an HE round that could be used, the 90mm was a much better choice against fighting positions and soft targets. And just as the railgun had an HE round, the 90mm had a sabot for anti-armor.

It took over an hour for each of the students in all five tanks to get his or her three rounds, but eventually, the tanks were backed off the firing line, and the two MC tanks took their positions. With the kinetics, the range officers had been standing next to the tanks. Not so with the two MC tanks, and for the same reason that the offset was required. So much power was about to be released that any leakage could mess up a person's day something fierce. For that reason, a range officer was inside each tank, making an already-cramped situation even more so.

Given Noah's higher driving scores, he was the first one in the gunner's seat. He hadn't done as well as Killer and Skeets in gunnery drills in the simulator, but he wasn't about to give up his first-to-fire status.

Noah imagined he could feel the angry powers of the electrons and positrons, jockeying for release as pi neutral mesons. He was sitting right next to an immense pool of energy, ready to send it downrange.

The meson cannon could stop an infantry attack in its tracks. It could destroy or put out of action almost any unshielded equipment, sweeping the terrain with the force of an angry Norse god. Yet, it had limitations. A meson beam had problems with simple rock and earth, so dug-in infantry were difficult targets, and armor such as the Brotherhood's Romakh was hardened enough to deflect any land-based meson or plasma weapon. None of that was on Noah's mind as he waited for the signal to fire. All he could think about was 2.5 KJ about to blow past his head.

"You may fire when ready," the range officer said into his mic.

Noah was sighted in on a hulk 1034 meters downrange. His display had the cannon at 100%, ready to fire. His mind "itched," if he could say that with the amount of energy that seemed to hover around him. Slowly depressing the double thumb paddles, he released the fires of hell.

He would swear later that he could see the bones in his hands on the paddles, even if he knew this was impossible. What he knew was possible was the tightly focused meson beam that reached out and enveloped his target—he just hadn't realized how intense the beam would be.

"Grubbing hell!" was about the best he could manage as the afterimage still burned in his eyes as the charger whined as it strained to get the cannon ready for the next shot.

He'd only fired from a sitting tank on a controlled range, a range officer at his side, but still, Noah thought he understood at a gut level now what it meant to be a Marine tanker.

Chapter 6

"I want another apple," Killer said, already two sheets into the wind.

"Me, too!" Miriam chorused, and just about as far gone as Killer was.

She punched the order into the console, and leaned back against the small Marine, her arm companionably around her shoulder.

"My man's a sergeant now, so we can afford this!"

Noah glanced at the readout, grimaced, but forced a smile back on his face. The bill had already climbed to devour at least two months' worth of his increase in pay. Wetting downs were a tradition and part of Marine life. He'd enjoyed himself often enough at the expense of other newly promoted Marines, so he couldn't very well complain.

With a loud whoosh, which Noah was sure was mostly for show, two red apple-shaped containers came down the overhead track to land in their table's center cradle. Killer and Miriam grabbed their ice-cold ciders, clinked apples, then sucked on the extended "stems."

The apples were the latest craze, but to Noah, the cider contained in them was bland and over-manufactured. He lifted his own glass and took a sip.

Much better, he thought.

If he was going to drink cider, at least he was going drink a naturally-brewed cider from a local supplier. Miriam, God bless her, didn't have much in the way of a refined palate, and she was more impressed with the slick packaging rather than the drink inside.

Most of the party had drifted away. This would be the last weekend before the final Armor War, an eight-day practical application exercise that was the last graded event of the school. For those who passed—and most everyone who was left should pass—they would be receiving their first set of orders within a day of Endex. Even at this stage of the game, no one had a firm idea of where he or she would be going. Noah had remained near the top of the class, buoyed by his Class Four Quals in driving all three platforms (where he ended up third in the class), but his Class Three gunnery and Class Two maintenance scores had been more to the middle. The Honor Grad was probably going to be Opania Bester, who was sitting across the table from him right now, and while it hurt his ooh-rah to have an FCDC trooper receive it, he had to admit she deserved the honor. And she'd turned out to be a "cope," what some of the younger generation was now calling people or things that his slightly older generation and even older had called "copacetic."

Noah wanted to cut Miriam off. He wanted her clear-headed, but she was enjoying getting out of the apartment and being able to socialize.

Two more of the Marines got up to leave, congratulating him on his new rank. "Sergeant Lysander" did sound good to him, he had to admit. As a sergeant, the Marine Corps deemed him mature enough to get married. It seemed stupid, in many ways, that yesterday, he wasn't capable of being a Marine and a married man, but today, suddenly he was, but Noah had long ago simply accepted the many incongruities of being a Marine.

"Well, sister of another mother, it's time I pull chocks," Killer said, pulling Miriam in for a kiss on the cheek.

"No, Patty! One more, OK?" Miriam protested.

Killer looked over Miriam's shoulder at Noah, who quickly shook his head.

Killer nodded at him, then said, "No, really. We've only got tomorrow to get our vehicles ready, and the Dead Eye's got problems."

The four crewmates were starting the Armor War in the Aardvarks, and unlike with Davises and Mambas, each training Aardvark had a name. "Dead Eye" was more often called "Dead Ass," by the crew for her continually breaking down.

"We'll get together after the war, OK? Noah may be a bad-ass sergeant now, but I've got him handled. He'll do what I say," she said as Noah rolled his eyes.

"Sergeant Bester, are you on your way back?" she asked the FCDC trooper.

"Sure. I guess I'm ready."

She started to take out her PA as if to pay, and Noah had to reach out to stop her.

"My bill. Tradition."

She didn't bother to put up a fake protest, but nodded and said, "I'm glad we don't have the same tradition in Feds. That would have bankrupted me when I made sergeant. Congratulations, though."

"What about him?" Miriam said, draining her apple and looking at Brock, who was slumped down, head back, and snoring.

"It's an autocab for him. Here, help me get him out of here."

Brock mumbled a few times, and only half-way moved his feet while they mostly dragged him to the entrance, then poured him into the cab, programming and paying for the trip back to the main gate.

"YATYAS!" Killer yelled out the window as the cab pulled away.

"YATYAS," Noah yelled back.

It hadn't been until after their Phase 2 rotations that Noah had learned what it meant. "Now, it had become almost a habit, much like "Ooh-rah." Depending on whether shouted by a tanker or tracker, it meant "If You Ain't a Tanker (or Tracker), You Ain't Shit!"

Miriam intertwined her arms in his as they watched the cab until it turned the corner and was out of sight.

Miriam pulled Noah down and whispered into his ear, "I've never fucked a sergeant before."

Noah pulled back in surprise. Miriam was a little earthier than he was, but she was rarely so coarse with her language. The word "fuck" may be the most commonly spoken word in the Marines, but this was different.

And it kind of turned him on, even more so when her hand strayed to his crotch.

Not now! he told himself.

He pulled her across the street and into the park, and for a moment, she seemed to think he wanted to have at it outside in some dark corner, and she started pulling him along, only to be surprised when he stopped and sat them both down on a park bench.

"What, you don't want to fuck me?" she asked.

"No," he started until he saw the expression on her face change. "I mean yes, of course, I do. I love f . . . fucking you," he managed to get out. "But first, there's something I want to say."

She sat back, arms across her chest, the expression on her face not too inviting.

Oh, shit. Now I've got her mad at me. This isn't going like I planned.

He'd had three drinks that night, and while not drunk, he knew it could be clouding his mind. A rational Noah would just go home and make love to her. A slightly tipsy Noah, though, wanted to get things straight. The last 30 some-odd weeks had been rough on them. He'd felt them drift apart a little, and he wasn't 100% sure about where they were with each other. Even though Miriam had been around Marines on Wayfarer Station, being in a relationship with one, living with one, had to be an eye-opening experience. For a Marine, duty interfered with family life, no matter how hard the Marine tried not to let it get in the way. Noah knew that Miriam had been unhappy, and he'd feared he was losing her. He had to find out just where they were before he received his next orders.

He should have done this before going to his wetting down, but to be honest, he'd chickened out. He'd thought a drink might calm him, but that turned into three for him and four or five for her.

Doesn't matter. Just go for it.

"So, what are you going to say that's so damned important?" she asked.

"Look, honey," he said, reaching out to take her hand.

At least she's not pulling it back.

"I know, things have been rough for you during the school, and I've not always been there for you."

She stared at him with an emotionless expression on her face, which made Noah more nervous.

"And, I don't know where my next set of orders will be to yet. I can't tell you if two days after I get there, I won't be off deployed, leaving you there alone to get our home put together."

Still nothing from her.

"But I want you to know, that I still feel the same way about you. I love you, and I want to be with you, and now that I'm a sergeant, well, the Marine Corps—"

"Are you proposing to me?" she asked, her brows furrowed together in confusion.

"What? Well, yes. I mean I'm trying to," he said, pulling the ring box out of his pocket.

She tilted her head back in laughter—not the sweet giggle of someone excited, but the belly busting laughter of someone who'd just heard something hilarious. Noah had expected a happy hug or a sorrowful rejection, but not this.

"And is that the ring?" she asked, trying to stifle her laughter.

"Yes," he admitted softly, opening up the box to reveal the ring that now looked way too small, way too insignificant to him.

She took the box from him, turning the ring to catch the glare from the streetlights.

"And, why are you asking me this?"

What? he wondered, at loss for words.

He gaped at her like a fish out of water before he was able to strangle out, "Because I love you."

"And I love you, too, Noah," she said, putting her hands around his necks and pulling him forward until they were forehead to forehead. "But why are you asking me this? We decided all of this on Wayfarer Station."

"Not exactly, no, we didn't."

"Yes, my muddle-headed sergeant. You said you wanted to marry me. I said I would, and I said you were mine. Hell, why do you think I followed you to this shithole of a planet?"

Noah tried to think back to their conversation. He had said something to the effect that he would like to marry her, as in sometime, but he hadn't thought it was actually decided. And with her moping around the apartment, he wasn't sure things were still on track.

"I don't think I actually—"

"Get on your knees? No, you didn't. You didn't have to."

"But—"

Oh, goodness gracious, Sergeant Lysander. If you're that traditional, then be a Marine and go for it," she said, swinging him around and off the bench.

This wasn't at all as he imagined it, and for a moment, he wanted to pull back and sort things out. But looking at her smiling face, he was smart enough to know what to do.

He pulled the box back out of her hand, knelt, presented the ring, and asked, "Miriam Seek Grace, will you marry me."

"Yes, I will, Sergeant Noah Lysander." She pulled him in for a kiss, then whispered into his ear, her tongue flicking his lobe, "Now that that is out of the way, I still haven't fucked a sergeant. Are you going to help me get that box checked?"

"Oh, yes, I am, ma'am! Yes, I am!"

GAZIANTEP

Chapter 7

Noah's eyes kept darting to his display, trying to keep track of each avatar on it. He felt like the proverbial bull in a china shop, except instead of fine dining ware, there were Marines out there. Tankers might joke about making "gruntcakes," but the reality was stressing him out.

"You're drifting left," the TC shouted at him. "Keep your head in the game."

They'd had very minimal maneuver training with ground troops on the Itch, and mostly with other students playing the infantry role. Even during the Armor War, most of the engagements has been simple armor force on force, with an active duty mechanized task force playing the OPFOR. The standard deployment method for armor was just this, though, protected by the infantry while supplying them with the support needed to take out heavier enemy targets.

Somewhere up ahead of them were between ten and fifteen Teresas, a platoon of older Tonyas, and a rash of anti-armor weapons. The images ahead, deployed along the southern approach to New Antalya, kept shifting as the Ataturk jamming and spoofing programs were broken by the Federation Navy's surveillance AI's, only to have more spoofing appear. Somewhere in the back-and-forth was a real picture of their disposition, but that was at the back of his mind at the moment. He was happy to have the grunts with them, but they made driving the *Anvil* more difficult and much more stressful.

As a PICS Marine, Noah had maneuvered in combined arms exercises with the smaller Mambas, and if one of the assault tanks had collided with him while he was mounted in his combat suit, his combat suit might have been damaged, but he, the Marine would have survived. These straight-leg grunts seemed to be running around like crazy with little regard to where he was. The Law of Gross Tonnage was such that even if it was Noah who made the mistake, the Marine infantryman would still be the squashed gruntcake.

The platoon had remained in place at Glen's Landing until relieved by a company of Cennet militia and the gunny had switched-out the damaged track on the *Ba-Boom*. Back up to full strength, they'd made a quick, nerve-wracking run up the Demir Highway to its intersection with Highway 4 coming in from the west, holding it until the link-up with the rest of the task force. Now, in the broad valley leading up to New Antalya, the platoon was the right-hand forward element of the mechanized infantry wedge approaching the city. The grunts had been mostly on foot for the last 15 klicks, leaving their Aardvarks as the threat became greater.

Noah muted the infantry avatars for a moment. One of the task force's two Aardvark platoons was advancing in the middle, right between First and Third Platoon. They were no match for the Teresas up ahead, but their 25mm chain guns could wreak havoc among any Ataturk ground troops as well and knock enemy drones out of the sky with ease. The Ataturks employed the WWK-40 drone, which could lift and fire a single Lancet anti-armor missile, so Noah appreciated their armored personnel carriers' presence.

He'd had fun back at Armor School driving the Aardvark, but he'd never felt really protected in one. While fairly well shielded from most energy weapons, a simple rifle grenade had the ability to take one out if it hit the right spot. Noah was glad they were there with them, but he was gladder than he wasn't driving them.

Almost on cue, one of the Aardvarks, some 800 meters to his left, opened up with the chain gun, buzzing like an angry insect. On his display, a red avatar for a drone appeared, only to disappear as the drone itself was knocked down 1400 meters to their front. Noah tried to see if it was the WWk-40, but the Federation AIs weren't passing that to the command net.

Noah switched his display back, and all the ground-pounders' avatars reappeared on the screen. A squad was arrayed 25 meters in front of the *Anvil*, which was too close for his comfort level. If he had to maneuver, they weren't giving him much room. Even some of his active armor, if deployed at their full range, could pose a threat to them. His AI would take that into consideration, and it wouldn't deploy measures to counteract incoming while the grunts were within the ECR[3] of any detonations.

An explosion sent dirt flying 100 meters to the front. They'd been being peppered with small mortar rounds fired from inside the city where the enemy rightly assumed that the *Jerry-John* wouldn't engage them. New Antalya was a Cennet city, and the government didn't want it destroyed, and a few harassing rounds weren't enough to trigger a massive response. Of course, what was "harassing" to an entire unit was not so harassing when you were the Marine being hit.

"I think I have a target," Chili passed.

Several of the task force's tanks had fired already, but only one target ended up being an actual vehicle. The rest had been ghosts, figments of the Ataturk spoofing programs. With technology so readily available, even a small power such as the Ataturk military could afford equipment and AIs that could spoof even the best that the Federation had to offer.

"I'm sending it up," Sergeant Cremineli passed.

Less than 15 seconds later, Chili was given the OK. The infantry was told to hit the deck, the servos whined, and a few seconds later, the crack of the round reached Noah. He eagerly watched the impact, but it was only a small geyser of dirt instead of an explosion. They'd been spoofed.

Noah frowned, shaking out his left hand. His hand had been smashed, breaking several bones when the hatch had closed on it, but after going through his nano-scrub and being fitted with support servo-glove, he'd been given the OK to remain on full duty. Back at Camp Archuleta, he'd have been put into a week's worth of regen, but even if the current mission was not the most threatening to a

---

[3] ECR: Effective Casualty Radius

Marine task force, there just wasn't anyone else to assign to the *Anvil*, and it was better for him to drive than for the tank to go out with only a two-man crew.

There was an immediate blare of an activation alarm, and Noah's heart jumped. He swerved to the direction indicated, presenting the stronger front of the tank to the enemy when Staff Sergeant Mauser-Lopez, in the *Ball-Shot*, passed, "Threat destroyed," as the alarm stopped its raucous blaring.

"Thanks, Sergeant Crawford," he continued. "That was a little too close for comfort."

"The grunts cut the guy down," he passed, this time on the platoon circuit. "He just popped up out of nowhere with a Mantis on his shoulder. Never saw him until too late. There was no way we could've taken him out in time, but the grunts cut the fucker in half."

A Mantis was a man-packed anti-armor missile with a pretty big punch. Presenting the front of a Davis to the missile probably would save the tank, but a hit on the sides or the rear could disable a Davis or even destroy one. The *Ball-Shot* was pretty lucky that the grunts around him had reacted as quickly as they had.

"You heard Staff Sergeant Mauser-Lopez. The threat is out there, so keep your eyes open," the lieutenant passed. "But make sure your IA's are at max discrimination. We've got our infantry friends all around us."

The Intercepting Armor was one of the base components of the Davis' Armor Protection System. Consisting of automated detection systems that identified incoming threats and shot out small shape rounds from one of eight gimbals, it was not very effective against an enemy tank or artillery round, but it could knock out an anti-armor missile or deflect an anti-armor grenade. Out in the open, the target acquisition discrimination was set low, and the IA's would probably fire at a passing bird. With the grunts in such close proximity, the discrimination was set high, but that meant some real threats might be ignored.

Noah had just swung back around to continue the advance when one of the Aardvarks went up in a huge explosion. Noah couldn't see it through his blocks, but he could see the column of black smoke reach up to the sky. Noah's display did not indicate living, wounded, or dead Marines, but with a sinking feeling, he was pretty sure that the three crew members were dead. The blast had been so massive that it had to have been a mine. Noah automatically dropped his glance to the bottom of this display where the forward probes weren't registering anything. The waves being blasted into the ground as they advanced indicated nothing, but the *Anvil's* probes were the same as that on the Aardvarks, and they evidently hadn't done much good. A Davis had far more protection than an Aardvark, but from the size of the blast, Noah didn't think that mattered much. The fact that the grunts had just walked the ground didn't matter, either. Anti-armor mines ignored dismounted infantry.

As if the detonation of the mine was a signal, four separate blooms of plasma reached out from previously concealed positions two klicks and still farther away. The power levels and range rendered the streams ineffective against tanks, and for a moment, Noah wondered why they had exposed themselves, but he was thinking armor, not combined arms. The energy weapons were not targeting the armor but the infantry. Strip away the grunts, and the tanks would be far more vulnerable to man-packed weapons such as the Mantis.

Noah kept a steady advance as Chili, along with probably every other tank in the lead two platoons, fired. From above, the avenging angel of the *Jerry-John* reached out to smote the plasma cannons. Within seconds of their firing, all four of the robo-cannons were silenced, but not before several Marines had been hit.

Noah drove the *Anvil* into a wash, momentarily blocking its view of the battlefield.

"Watch your nose," Staff Sergeant Cremineli said as he pivoted slightly to take the edge of the wash head on.

Just shut up, already! he thought as he gunned the power.

Just as the *Anvil* powered up, there was a loud clang right in front of Noah, and his hatch split open with a six-centimeter gash. The breach alarm sounded.

"I told you to watch your nose!" the TC shouted.

Noah's Number 3 block was a spider web of occluded palladiglass, and he could stick his finger out of the gash in the hatch itself.

Holy crap! he thought as he touched the gash.

"You OK?" Sergeant Cremineli asked, bending forward from his seat to look at him.

"I'm fine, but we've got a breech."

They'd been buttoned up on orders from the lieutenant, which gave them the most protection. Now with a breech, they were more vulnerable, particularly from powerful-enough energy weapons. The static field around the *Anvil* would not be as effective in shunting aside an energy blast, and some energy could enter the tank at the gash—just a few centimeters from Noah's head—not good for the *Anvil*, and particularly not good for Noah.

He gulped, took a deep breath, and checked the readouts. The IA's had deployed, but not the PRA, the Plasma Reactive Armor, which covered 94% of the *Anvil's* skin. Noah's vision blocks and the hatch were not encased in PRA, and whatever hit them had creased his hatch. The *Anvil* was still battle-ready, even if a bit more vulnerable, but it had been an extremely close call.

"Target, armor, direct front, 3,000 meters," Chili said.

"Engage," the TC responded.

The whine of the railgun's capacitors sounded different with the gash in his turret, as did the crack of the round as it left the muzzle. Noah realized that that could just be his hyped-up imagination, but as he'd never heard firing with his driver's hatch open, he couldn't be sure.

Chili fired twice more over the next minute as Noah tried to give him the best shot while keeping the grunts around him out of harm's way. A railgun round could easily burst an eardrum of someone nearby the muzzle, and while the grunts were all in full battle rattle, to include their helmets, it was still a good practice to keep them far away from the muzzle and the trajectory of the rounds.

Noah was concentrating on just driving the tank, not really watching the battle unfold as rounds, missiles, and the *Jerry-John's* energy beams crisscrossed the landscape. The *Anvil* took one more hit, but the PRA defeated whatever had targeted them. And suddenly, almost as if turning off a switch, the furious firefight was over. The Ataturk forces had withdrawn on carefully planned routes, out of any of the advancing Federation force's lines of fire. The *Jerry-John* kept pounding away, and a few of the Federation's surviving battle drones took a few shots, but the direct-fire weapons fell silent.

Noah flipped up the overall battle screen. Fourteen Ataturk weapons systems had been destroyed: twelve unmanned gun systems and two Teresas. On the Federation side, one Davis and two Aardvarks had been put out of action, six grunts had been hit, probably by fire aimed at the Federation Armor, and two Davises were down for mechanical reasons. The surviving Ataturk armor was in full retreat, bolting for the city. Technically, Noah knew the short battle was a victory for the Marines, but he thought the cost was too high. Fighting Gen 7 armor, he'd have thought the victory would be more lopsided.

With the enemy running, Noah's instincts screamed to jump into the chase to stop them before they reached New Antalya, only a klick or two away from them. But he knew the command would be more deliberate. The retreat of the Ataturk armor could just be a ruse to pull the Marines into a trap, and even if it wasn't, there could be plenty of surprises in front of them, from mines to hidden hunter-killer teams. Despite the 2,500 horses in the *Anvil*, Noah would be constrained to the walking pace of the infantry.

Twice, artillery fired out at the advancing Marines from inside the city, and both times, the *Jerry-John* took it out regardless of collateral damage to the surrounding buildings. The Cennet rep up on the ship was probably apoplectic, but there was no way the colonel was going to risk Marines for a few buildings.

A blast sounded 100 meters to Noah's left.

"Hit a mine. No significant damage, and we're still up," the lieutenant passed.

"Watch out for mines," Sergeant Cremineli passed to him immediately after that.

No shit, Sergeant. I guess Lessa wasn't doing that?

Noah was becoming less and less enamored with his TC. He might have been right when Noah had gotten his hatch almost blown off, but the guy's constant warnings and stating the obvious were beginning to grate on him.

Two more tanks and an Aardvark hit mines before they reached the wrinkle in the landscape that formed a shallow ridge stretching out across the valley floor 1,500 meters from the outskirts of the city. One of the tanks lost a track, but neither of the other two vehicles were put out of action.

Noah edged the *Anvil* up to the top of the small ridge.

"More," Chili said as he looked down the barrel from the inside.

He had the gun depressed, and between the two of them, they wanted to get as much of the *Anvil* as they could behind the ridge while still allowing the sergeant to fire the 75mm gun. To make sure the gun was clear, the sergeant had opened the breach and was looking down the barrel. If he could see dirt, then any round fired would hit it.

"More . . . more . . . halt!"

There was a clamor behind Noah, and he turned to see Staff Sergeant Cremineli push himself into the gunner's seat. Chili was crouching beside him, a frustrated expression on his face. From his vantage, Noah couldn't see what the TC was doing, but he was sure the staff sergeant was checking the bore to make sure the gunner had done it right and that the sergeant wasn't happy about that lack of trust. Staff Sergeant Cremineli had only been promoted the month before Noah had arrived, so only two months ago, he and Chili had both been the same rank, and that had to grate on Chili as well.

Noah didn't get any orders to move the tank, so he knew Chili had positioned the *Anvil* correctly. From his lower position in the tank, all he could see was the dirt in front of him, so he switched to his display so he could watch the infantry and Aardvarks as they advanced to the city itself. For the moment, there wasn't much he could do except monitor the display. Any fighting by the *Anvil* at this position would be by Chili—unless the staff sergeant took over control of the main gun. Noah wouldn't put it past him. He was the main gunner for the .50 cal, which could reach into the city, but Noah thought he might want to take over as the *Anvil's* gunner.

A shadow crossed over Noah, and he looked up to see the staff sergeant standing just outside his driver's hatch. The TC knelt, then stuck a finger inside the gash in the turret. Noah had to suppress a strong inclination to smack the two fingers that were waving in his face.

The staff sergeant motioned for him to open the hatch.

"There's no way we're going to fix that ourselves. I'll put in a call for a reaction team," he said before walking back on top of the tank to his hatch.

Which was not a surprise to Noah. They'd been trained on how to work on the tanks, and there was a lot they could do with ingenuity and elbow grease, but repairing a break in the armor didn't fall under that category. This was a Class 4 repair, and while the reaction team might be able to slap on a temporary patch, Class 4 repairs had to be done at a full facility. The *Anvil* wouldn't get completely repaired until they were back at Archuleta.

Noah turned back to his display. He didn't have the more sophisticated surveillance capabilities that the gunner and TC had, and he couldn't even scan the city with his naked eyes to spot anything, so this was the best he could do. The advancing mechanized infantry quickly closed the distance to the city. Half of the grunts disembarked as they reached the outer edge while the rest remained in their APCs. Noah had never been straight-legged infantry. He had been a PICS Marine, and he would have fought in the city in the armored combat suits. That made sense to him. It made sense for straight-legged infantry to get out of the Aardvarks as soon as they reached the built-up area. It didn't make sense to him for the infantry to stay buttoned up inside an Aardvark within the city itself. He'd felt vulnerable at Glen's Landing in the *Anvil*, and an Aardvark was far more vulnerable. It might have most of the same APS as a Davis, but the basic bodies of the two vehicles were completely different.

Fighting was sporadic, though, as the infantry advanced. Noah tried to follow along, but he was losing concentration, and eventually, the long days were catching up to him. He started nodding, catching himself a few times as his head jerked too far down, but weariness overcame him, and he fell fast asleep, only to be woken when the *Anvil's* 75mm fired.

Noah jerked back awake, hands reaching for his yokes, ready to attack or retreat.

"I can't tell if I got him," Chili was saying. "His firing position is gone, but he might have pulled back before I engaged."

Noah looked at his display, then keyed in the weapons feed, jumping back 30 seconds. He could see the gunner zoom into a steeple, barely visible between the other intervening buildings. Chili manually tweaked the aiming point, then fired.

The 75mm round was quick, very quick, but still, gravity and other forces acted upon it. The range to the steeple was 5214 meters, and the space between the other buildings was extremely narrow. Just the slightest wind could push the round right into one of those buildings. But as Noah watched, the trace of the round was clearly visible as it threaded itself between the two buildings and struck the steeple with a decent-sized explosion.

"If the sniper retreated, at least you denied him that firing position," Staff Sergeant Cremineli said.

And Noah realized what had happened. Normally, religious buildings and artifacts were to be left alone, but if a sniper was using one as a firing point on the Marines, the religious purpose of the structure was meaningless. With the positioning of the buildings, it was probable that the *Anvil* was the only tank with a possible shot, so they'd received the mission. Chili had fired an HE round to take out the sniper. A 90mm HE would have carried a bigger punch, but at over 5,000 meters, that was at the very edge of the bigger gun's range.

Noah rubbed the sleep out of his eyes. The TC hadn't noticed that he'd fallen asleep. It hadn't mattered in this specific case, but that was no excuse. If he'd been called upon to move the *Anvil*, he wouldn't have been able to react immediately. He shook his head, then slapped his face, admonishing himself to stay awake.

Twenty minutes later, the Ataturk commander contacted the colonel. He was ready to surrender. The *Anvil* remained in position—once a surrender was offered and accepted, breaking it was considered a war crime, but it had happened before, so the two forward tank platoons remained in place with Second Platoon displacing into the city. The rather sparse Ataturk forces were throwing down their arms and surrendering, and the Cennet militia moved through the Federation lines to start processing the prisoners.

The Marines searched the city, and by nightfall, Colonel Bhekizizwe declared the city secure.

The war wasn't over, but the Marines had given Cennet the upper hand again for the negotiations. With no orders to pursue the Ataturk forces over the border, the Marines settled in for what could be a lengthy occupation of the city.

Chapter 8

"Hey, you got any of that peach crumble left?" Chili asked.

"Peach crumble, he says," Noah muttered as he rolled over and pulled the packet of stasis dessert from his pack.

The only reason he even had it was that they had to police up their trash and he couldn't just dump it on the ground. The peach crumble was a gloppy mess of sugar and cinnamon fabricated by industrial units somewhere. As far as Noah was concerned, it was a waste of a perfectly good field stasis pack. Supposedly given out as treats for the Marines, Noah wouldn't eat them, as Chili well knew.

He tossed the packet to Chili who snagged in out of the air, eagerly tearing open the top and using his fingers, the same grubby fingers that hadn't seen a shower in three weeks and which had been working on the *Anvil*, to reach in and pull out the orange goop. He put his peach-laden fingers in his mouth, pulling them out slowly and savoring the crumble left behind.

That's one way to clean your hand, I guess, Noah thought as he closed his eyes, trying to drift off into a nap.

"Don't know why you won't eat the P-Crumb. It's good shit," Chili said. "All the more for me, I guess,"

Noah didn't reply. Chili had an iron stomach, which was probably appropriate for someone whose parents named him Cayenne.

Sleep was evading him, so he opened one eye and checked the time. He had another 23 minutes before he relieved the staff sergeant. No time for a nap. He sat up and scooched over until his back was against the *Anvil*.

Noah was pretty proud of the old girl and what they'd accomplished in both Glen's Landing and outside New Antalya, but he was getting a little sick of using her as billeting. She was a monster in battle, but she was seriously lacking as a condo. When he'd moved to armor, he thought he'd have it better than the grunts. Little did he know.

The grunts were all back at New Antalya, billeting in appropriated buildings, with only two platoons at a time moving forward to the border area. All of the armor, Davises and Aardvarks, had been deployed 200 meters from the border and placed in a line, guns pointed into Ataturk. No one expected another incursion. The Federation armor, along with a hodgepodge of Cennet armor, was merely window dressing to help spur along negotiations. Every day, the Cennet bio-diesel armor fired up, belching out black smoke, just to remind the Ataturk watchers that they were there.

At first, the respite had been welcomed. A reaction team had slapped on a temporary patch on the gash in the *Anvil's* driver's hatch, which made the integrity of the tank whole again, even if not as strong. That had been a huge relief to the three crewmembers, and they started taking care of the more routine maintenance on the tank. Noah, with the servo-glove on his left hand, had been relegated to assisting the other two rather than working the tools himself.

Almost as good as getting that patch had been the ability to get some sleep. They'd all been running on empty, taking vivostims to keep going and almost getting to brain wash territory. All the stimulants in the world could not take care of brain fatigue—the only way to combat that after the stimulants wore off was to undergo a wash, which relaxed the brain cells and allowed for the artificial cerebral spinal fluid to flush the brain awake. It was an effective and supposedly safe way to renew brain function, but no one liked the process. "Hated" might not be too strong of a word. Without the chance to sleep, they'd been about a day away from getting the orders, so it was a relief to let their brains rejuvenate through natural sleep.

But what had been a relief was now utter boredom. There wasn't much else they could do to the *Anvil* out in the field, so they just sat, taking four-hour shifts in the gun turret and spending the other eight either scrunched up inside the tank if it was raining or sitting outside directly behind her if the weather was nice. They got hot chow once a day and ate field rats for their other two meals.

It had been quiet, too quiet, since they arrived, so the explosion 200 meters to their rear shocked the two Marines into action. Chili dropped the peach crumble pack into the mud and vaulted up onto the rear of the *Anvil* only a split second behind Noah.

"Just EOD blowing up a mine," Staff Sergeant Cremineli said as the two scrambled for their positions.

"What?"

"A controlled detonation. Nothing to get excited about."

"Well, you could have told us," Chili said, his chest heaving as he slowed his breathing.

"If you had your helmets on, you would have heard," the TC said, turning back to look over the border.

"Right," Chili muttered, quiet, but loud enough for the staff sergeant to hear. "As if we sit around all day with them on."

He turned around and walked to the rear of the tank, then vaulted off.

"Fucking great! My P-Crumb's ruined," Noah could hear him say.

No great loss.

Noah stood for a moment, taking in the line of armor. He had to admit that they looked pretty fearsome, arrayed as they were. The Cennet armor added to that. Nothing the Cennets had could stand up to a Davis, and they'd be hard-pressed in a fight with a Teresa, but the big Cennet tanks looked the part. Their ancient FBR-3's were over 100 tons of metal, each sporting a huge 135mm main gun. Over a century old, unwieldy, not very maneuverable, and with limited range, they still looked fearsome. And with that big gun, if they could hit a target, that target would sure know it.

Noah almost wished something would happen, just to fight the boredom. It was a stupid thought, and he knew it, but almost anything would be better than simply sitting there.

"I'll take over, Staff Sergeant," he said, walking up to the gunner's turret.

"You sure?"

"I'm ready. I might as well take over."

"OK, your choice. There's been the normal movement, nothing different. Three Ataturks have been up in the tower, glassing us, and there's been some vehicular movement. You can check everything in the log," the TC said, pulling himself out of the turret. "And shave yourself," he added when he got closer to Noah. "Regs are still in effect."

Noah tried not to roll his eyes as he sidled past the staff sergeant and lowered himself into the turret. Who was going to see them out here in the boonies? The lieutenant had come by an hour before to check on them, and she hadn't said anything.

Sliding into the seat, he pulled up the log in the display. As the staff sergeant had said, there wasn't anything noteworthy, but each sighting was notated. Noah deployed the sights, first zeroing in on the watch tower that looked over the border crossing. Three Ataturk soldiers were readily visible with one glassing the Federation lines. Nothing else stood out.

The scan took him all of four minutes.

Two-hundred-thirty-six minutes to go, he thought. *No, belay that. I relieved him early. Two-hundred-forty-five minutes.*

With a sigh, he reached into his cargo pocket and brought out his shaving wand. Shaving would take him all of a minute.

He'd never realized that combat could be so boring.

QUINTERO CRAG

Chapter 9

The bus pulled into Camp Archuleta, home of the 11th Marines. Noah had barely spent time at the camp after reporting in, but still, it felt good to be back. The mission on Gaziantep had dragged on for almost nine weeks after the battle at New Antalya, with Noah and his crewmates living in the stationary *Anvil*. The *Jerry-John* had been a welcomed relief with showers and a real rack, even if they had to hot-bunk them, but the Navy ship was not as good as getting back home.

The *Anvil* would be trucked back to the battalion at Camp Tainio, the division headquarters, tomorrow for Cat Four maintenance to repair the gash in the driver's hatch, so the three Marines would be without a tank for at least two weeks. Which was fine with Noah. They had a 96[4] coming up, and he planned on spending every minute of that with Miriam.

He scanned the faces of the spouses, children, girlfriends, and boyfriends who'd lined the parking lot, most with balloons, banners, and signs welcoming their Marine home. He didn't spot Miriam, but there were a lot of civilians milling about, so that wasn't surprising.

"OK, as soon as we stop, get off the bus and into formation," Gunny Torrington shouted out. "No one's getting dismissed until the captain gets the OK."

"But I'm horny!" someone shouted from the front of the bus to the laughs of everyone else. "My man's waiting for me!"

---

[4] 96: A four-day pass, not charged as leave.

"You'll just have to wait, Corporal Sanders, like all of us," the gunny said, but in a light tone. There were hoots and hollers and more ribald comments, which the gunny let go on for a few moments before shouting out, "OK, that's enough with the language. We've got families out there."

The bus pulled to a halt and sank onto its skirts. Noah was in the back with Lessa Franklin and Chili, and it took some time for all 60 Marines and sailors to debark.

"Over to the right," Staff Sergeant Reiser kept saying, pointing the way. "In back of Weapons Company."

There were shouts from the crowd as they spotted loved ones, and several Marines "accidently" strayed close enough to catch a quick kiss and hug as they made their way to the formation.

Noah walked slowly, trying to spot Miriam, but to no avail. He was one of the last Marines in the company to fall in. Shouts of "We love you daddy!" and "Welcome home" reverberated from the families as the buses lifted up and drove off. A little girl, probably three or four years old, suddenly broke from the crowd, darting past her mother's grasp, and ran to Fox Company to latch onto the leg of one of the company lieutenants, much to the delight of the crowd. The lieutenant stood there stoically for a moment before bending over and picking her up. He gave the Fox Company commander an embarrassed look, then took the little girl forward and handed her back to his wife while the crowd broke into applause.

Noah joined the rest of the Marines in laughter. Marines didn't break ranks to laugh as a rule, but this was a homecoming, and those rules were different.

Five minutes after they formed up, the commanding general and the regimental commander made their way to the front of the formation. Colonel Bhekizizwe called the task force to attention, and the general put them at ease.

"Welcome home, Task Force 54/03!" the general said to the "ooh-rahs" of the Marines and sailors. "I'm very proud of all of you, not that I expected anything less. You were given a tough task, and you accomplished it in the best tradition of the Corps. Now I'm not going to keep you standing here long. I think I'd get mobbed by the families gathered here who want to welcome their Marines and sailors home," he said, turning with a theatrical sweep of the arm to indicate the crowd.

The general might have said he wouldn't keep them in formation very long, and maybe 20 minutes wasn't long for him, but for the Marines in formation, and for those family members who were there waiting, it might as well have been an eternity. The general went on about tradition, then recounted the push toward New Antalya. As was usual, most of his comments were centered around the grunts, barely mentioning any of the other units, which stuck in Noah's craw just a bit. But he just wanted the CG to shut up and let them go. He wanted to find Miriam.

A baby starting squalling, his or her little lungs putting out an enormous amount of sound. The general turned around to spot the child, hesitated, then seemed to give up. Turning the task force back to the colonel, he stepped back to the applause of the crowd.

Within moments, the order to dismiss was passed down. The officers were dismissed, and the first sergeant reminded each platoon about its weapons turn-in time, and at last, the company was dismissed. Already, a good third of the Marines were rushing to meet their families, and families were rushing forward.

The tank company was made up of more senior Marines, and so a better percentage of them had families there. The junior Marines in the line companies were mostly single, and they initially stood around, slapping each other's backs and loudly making plans to meet out at the various bars outside the main gate.

Sucks to be you, Noah thought as he pushed his way through the gaggle of single Marines. *I've got someone waiting for me!*

But try as he might, he couldn't see her. He pulled out his PA and tried to call her, but all he received was a message.

"Hey, Sergeant! Where's your fiancé?" Lessa asked as she saw him walking aimlessly about.

"I can't find her."

"So, call her."

"I did," he said, holding up his PA. "No answer."

"Ah, she's around here somewhere. We've got weapons turn-in in 20, though."

"I'll be there."

Noah was sure Miriam was around somewhere. She'd told him she'd get off work early, that she missed him, that she'd be wearing something sexy. But he was getting a little depressed. He'd returned from deployments before, but never with someone special waiting for him. When his father had come back from deployments, it had been a pretty big thing with the family. They'd made signs, decorated the house, and their mom, who never paid attention to fashion, hair, and the like, had gone through the process to look her best. They'd gone all out for their dad, and now, Noah was expecting Miriam to have done the same for him. But she was nowhere to be seen.

As if to add salt to the wound, Cliff Bloomer, the *Ball Shot's* driver, stopped to introduce his fiancé to him. Roseapple was a good 10 cm taller than Cliff, and judging by the way she was clinging to him, along with an amazing outfit that left nothing to the imagination, as soon as his weapons were in the armory, they couldn't wait to be alone with each other.

Roseapple was an impressive-looking woman, but Noah wanted to be with *his* woman. But he couldn't find her.

He kept trying to call her until it was time for the platoon to turn in their weapons. That took about twenty minutes, and then they were technically free until noon tomorrow. They had some admin to take care of before being released on their 96.

The single Marines were rushing back to the barracks to change, and the married ones were quickly leaving for hovers or the shuttle to the main gate. Noah wasn't sure what to do. Miriam still wasn't answering.

He sat on one of the tables set up in front of the company office, butt on the tabletop, feet on the bench, to wait for her. Marines started to pour out of the barracks, flowing like lemmings out in town to celebrate a safe return and to toast the few Marines who'd fallen. Several shouted to him to join them, but he just waved and sat.

Almost an hour-and-a-half after they'd returned, and with the area almost deserted, a sultry voice from behind him asked, "Hey, Marine. You looking for a good time?"

Noah turned around and almost fell off the table as he scrambled to hug Miriam, who was standing there in her waitress uniform. Horrible thoughts of what might have happened to her had been flooding his mind, and relief flooded over him to see that she was OK.

And then a bit of anger replaced that relief.

He pulled back out of the hug and said, "I've been waiting for you. Where were you?"

"I'm so sorry, babe. I told Fanny that I needed to get off early, but we got slammed, and I had to take my tables. I didn't even have time to go home and change."

Their financial situation was a little better than it had been on the Itch, but not by much, and until they were officially married, they wouldn't be drawing Family Support Allowance. So, to help with the budget, and to keep from going stark-crazy mad, Miriam had taken a job at a restaurant.

"But I tried to call you!"

"I'm sorry, baby. We can't use our PA's at work, and I forgot to turn it back on when I left. I was in such a hurry to get here. Forgive me?"

"I was worried. Really worried."

She snuggled closer to him, pulling him back into a tight hold, and whispered into his ear, "I think I have a few ways to make it up to you. While you've been gone, I've been coming up with some very, shall we say, 'interesting' things to do together?"

Her hands fell to grab his butt and pull him in closer, and she bit his earlobe.

Noah wanted to protest. He was still upset. This was his time to experience what his father always did, what military men and women have experienced for thousands of years. He wanted that homecoming, and he felt cheated out of it.

But he also realized that Miriam had taken the job for both of them, and it hadn't been her fault that she was late. Her hands on his butt excited him, and passion began to push disappointment away. Making more out of her being late wouldn't do anyone any good.

He made a conscious decision to forget it. He loved her, and that was what mattered.

"So, you've come up with ways to make it up to me?" he asked. "Then what are we waiting for? Let's go home!"

Chapter 10

Noah watched out of his blocks, expecting to see something, anything, even a shadow, but there was nothing. His display was off as the *Anvil* was powered down, so he was blind from that as well. Noah wasn't sure how anyone could pick them up, even had the internal systems been powered, but their orders had been specific.

Noah was usually relaxed inside the *Anvil*, but for the first time, he was claustrophobic. He was not feeling comfortable.

The *Anvil*, along with the *Ball Shot* and the *Kiss of Death*, were at the bottom of the Gold Strand, the top of their turrets eight meters below the surface of the murky water. They'd been sitting there like huge snapping turtles waiting for prey to wander too close for over seven hours, slipping into the muddy river a klick upstream under the partial cover of darkness and carefully navigating the river bottom to their present position. Blind in the darkness and the water, and relying only on the *Anvil's* proximity alarm to keep from colliding with the *Kiss of Death*, the underwater march had been among the most stressful things Noah had ever undertaken in a tank, and that included combat on Gaziantep.

Now, as they sat on the bottom, Noah's mind wandered, bringing up images of water pouring in. He kept glancing at the lip of his hatch, running his finger alongside the rim to make sure it was dry. His eyes told him that, but he needed to feel for confirmation. The Cat 4 techs had assured him that the entire new hatch they'd installed was as good, if not better, than the one that had been damaged, but that was hard for him to accept.

Noah knew the technical abilities of the Davis as well as anyone. They could stay completely submerged for up to 20 hours, longer if they used auxiliary O2 tanks. He'd even been completely submerged before, doing river crossings on the Itch. But this was different. He wasn't actively driving with his mind focusing on what he was doing, but simply sitting, and he imagined he could feel the weight of the water pushing down on them. He had an irrational fear that once he powered up, the *Anvil* wouldn't respond, and they'd be stuck down there forever.

Chili evidently didn't have the same problem. His snores reverberated throughout the crew compartment. The staff sergeant didn't seem to mind if his gunner was asleep, so Noah didn't say anything. If he could, he'd catch a few z's, too. They'd been up for three days and were running on stims, and he knew he could use even an hour of sleep, but he also knew there was no way he could sleep with the river pressing down on him.

His simple proximity alarm indicated that the *Ball Shot* was ten meters to his left, and the *Kiss of Death* was 15 to the right. He'd feel better if he could see them, but the water was way too murky for that.

Grubbing hell, I didn't join the submarine Navy, he told himself for the hundredth time.

Noah didn't know what was going on up there on the land. They were lying quiet, all systems turned off. When it was time to move, they'd get the word via a very old-tech low-frequency message blast. Noah just hoped that the order would come sooner rather than later.

The sunlight had earlier turned the water a yellowish-brown, and as it started turning darker, he knew the sun was getting closer on the horizon. They'd been in the river for 16 hours now, approaching their limit. One way or the other, they'd be emerging, and Noah hoped it would be in daylight. He didn't want to spend any more time sitting underwater in the darkness.

He'd just reached for the piss-tube when the order came. Dropping the tube, Noah flipped the switch, sending power surging to the motor. Displays turned on, but he couldn't make much of what data was streaming in.

"Go, go," the lieutenant passed on the now active comms.

"Wake up, Fulford," the TC said, then to Noah, "Let's take her out. Give me a 280-degree heading as soon as you can."

Noah glanced at the display as both friendly and enemy vehicles appeared, but he couldn't study it. He had to watch where he was going, even with almost zero visibility. Despite all the *Anvil's* capabilities, he didn't have a kind of sonar that could map out the river bottom ahead of him. Coming down the river, they'd crept along, but now, with surprise paramount, they had to get out of the water immediately.

He gunned the big tank forward, feeling the lurch as his treads, with the elevations fully extended, dug into the muddy bottom. They should be 40 meters from the shore, which on land could take mere seconds, but this wasn't land.

His stomach flew into his throat as the *Anvil* dropped down into a hole, but to his relief, immediately climbed back out. He could tell they were rising, and the brown water turned more to yellow as they rose closer to the surface. Noah hated the fact that he was driving blind, but the closer to the river bank, the better he felt. And then, the short barrel of the *Anvil's* 90mm broke the surface right above Noah's head.

"Release the Kraken," he muttered as he goosed the accelerators, and like the legendary creature breaching the ocean, the *Anvil* emerged into the afternoon sun.

"Tank, two o-clock!" Staff Sergeant Cremineli shouted out.

Noah concentrated on the best spot to climb the low bank, but he could see the muzzle of their main gun traverse. There was a blast, and then a "Target destroyed" from Chili.

The *Ball Shot* emerged from the water, and Corporal Vestle, her driver, swerved to her right, bringing her tank too close to the *Anvil* for comfort, but Noah reacted by pushing the *Anvil* forward and up on the bank. The elevated treads grabbed into the bank and almost threw the tank up and onto the semi-forested land beyond the bank. They hit with a thud, and Noah reduced the elevation to better manage on dry land.

"Weapons free!" Lieutenant Huang, the Second Platoon commander passed.

If the Second Platoon commander was giving the orders, then that meant both the skipper and the XO had been taken out.

"Wedge, on the *Anvil*!" Lieutenant Moore passed.

Noah's display was flashing with avatars and streams of data. He had to concentrate on driving, but at first glance, things were not good. There were too few blue avatars and too many red. Within 3,000 meters, there were only two more friendly tanks, both from

Second. There was no sign of the *Ba-Boom*, which was supposed to have been the bait to draw the enemy in close. Within that same 3,000 meters, there were nine enemy tanks.

It looked like the surprise had been total. The nine tanks seemed to be focused on Lieutenant Huang in the *Saber* and Staff Sergeant Juarez-Akito in the *Winston United*. Within moments, two of the red avatars switched to black as Chili and Cliff fired up their rears. Noah's elation faded immediately when both the *Saber* and the *Winston United* were knocked out.

Noah extended his range out to ten clicks as he charged the enemy force, but no blue avatars appeared. It looked like it was the three of them against seven of the opposing forces.

Not good odds.

Prissy, on the *Kiss of Death*, took out another of the enemy tanks before they seemed to realize what was happening and started to swing around to meet the threat.

As the center tank in the wedge, Noah pushed forward, not worrying about the other two. It might be better to break up and conduct a hide-and-seek attack, taking out the enemy one-by-one and not letting them concentrate their forces, but until the lieutenant changed her order, it looked like it was going to be a full frontal assault, and if he could close quickly, he could minimize the number of tanks that could fire on the *Anvil* at any given time.

"Grubbing hell, you mothers!" Noah shouted as he closed the distance.

He juked to the right just as Chili fired, throwing off the shot.

"Damn it, Noah! Keep me steady!"

That made them an easier target, but Noah simply shrugged. If that was how it was going to go, so be it. There wasn't much hope that Charlie Company was going to come out on top, but they could take out as many of the opposing tanks as they could.

Chili got in one more kill before the *Kiss of Death* was knocked out. That left Staff Sergeant Cremineli as the acting company commander.

"Break off!" the TC immediately shouted. "Get some cover in the forest."

Noah was in berserker mode, and with the way things were playing out, he just wanted to continue the charge. He wasn't surprised, though, that Cremineli wanted to bug out. And maybe that was a sound tactical decision, but it rubbed Noah wrong. He didn't argue, though, and swung the tank to the right—only to be hit as soon as he presented the *Anvil's* left side.

"Fuck!" Chili shouted as the *Anvil* shut down. "I could've got me another one, Staff Sergeant!"

"That was the right decision, Sergeant!" the TC protested.

"In your dreams," Chili said, pushing the envelope with the rank-conscious tank commander.

"The *Ball Shot's* still in it," Noah said. "They'll kick some Alpha ass."

And as if in response, the *Ball Shot* was hit and knocked out.

"And that's that," Noah said, disappointed.

This was the second time that they'd gone up against Alpha company over the last three weeks, and it was the second time they'd had their asses handed to them. All 15 Charlie tanks were killed, while only 10 of the Alphas had bit the dust. The fact that they'd managed to come out on top over Bravo meant little when they were oh-for-two against Alpha. Noah had even heard that unless Bravo managed a win against Alpha, the battalion commander was going to pit the company against a combined force of Bravo and Charlie Companies. Noah would be professionally mortified if that came to pass.

It looked like the small river force had been a good decision, and they'd managed to knock out four of the opposing force tanks, but in the end, it hadn't mattered. They'd still lost.

Power came back on to the drive train and turret.

"All hands, return to the ramp for debrief," was passed over the net.

"Well, at least we got two of them," Staff Sergeant Cremineli said as Noah opened his hatch and headed for the main track that would lead back to the range ramp.

"Maybe, but we still got our asses shot off, and to top it off, we've got some heavy maintenance to do after sitting in the fucking river for a day," Chili said in a sour tone of voice.

Shit, he's right, Noah realized. *It's going to be a long night.*

One of the Alpha company tanks reached the trail from the opposite side at the same time as the *Anvil*. Noah didn't know if that was one of the surviving Alpha Company tanks or not, but he motioned for the other driver to precede him.

It may have only been a training exercise, but to the victor belonged the spoils.

Chapter 11

Noah looked at the table one more time, then made a minute adjustment to the fork's placement. Miriam wouldn't notice, but he was stressing out, and that nervous energy had him going anal on the meal.

He'd made veal piccata, one of Miriam's favorites that he could whip up on short notice. The veal was fab veal, not real, but by going heavy on the lemon, not even he could tell much of a difference, much less his fiancé. The veal had been browned and was in the warming tray, and the sauce was done. All he had to do was throw in the spaghetti in the water and put the veal in the pan once she arrived, and within ten minutes, they'd be eating.

He took a quick look inside their small oven where the Canadian Cobbler was bubbling away. Miriam still wasn't 100 percent sure on just where or what Canada was, but she loved the dessert made from ghostberries and raspberries, the red and white berries that matched the colors of the Canadian flag and gave the dessert its name.

He kept watching the clock on the wall in the living room, waiting for Miriam to show. Unable to keep still, he checked the veal five or six times, lifting up the top cutlet, and poking the next one with his finger before letting the top one back down. He fretted that they would become too soggy, and wished he'd waited to sauté them.

When Miriam finally opened the door, still dressed in her lime green and pink waitressing uniform, he jumped up to greet her, giving her a kiss on the cheek. She smelled like old frying oil, something that continually bothered him since she started working at Harstons, but that he never voiced to her.

"What's this?" Miriam asked, dropping her bag on the floor.

"I wanted to make something special for you," he said.

Her brows furrowed together for a moment, then asked, "What's the occasion," her suspicion obvious.

"You've been working so hard, lately, and I thought you'd like some piccata."

Hearing what he said he'd made, she perked up.

"I had a bombburger at the restaurant. It was sent back to the kitchen for being overcooked, so I just helped myself. But I can still eat."

"Good. Why don't you just sit down and relax. Dinner will be ready in ten."

She ran her fingers through her hair and said, "I should shower up, but that'll take half-an-hour to get Harstons off of me."

"Don't worry about it. Just sit for a few minutes."

"OK, if you say so," she said, flopping heavily in their overstuffed couch. "I need to get off my feet."

Noah dropped the pasta in the water and turned up the heat in the pan. He had piccata programed into their fabricator, and with a simple code input and a push of a button, he could have dinner in 30 seconds, but he enjoyed cooking, and he thought it was more personal when he home-cooked food, even when like this evening, some of the ingredients were fab-food.

He dropped the veal back in the pan, cut a lemon in half, and squeezed the juice into the dish.

"Smells pretty cope, honey," Miriam said from the couch, not bothering to turn toward him.

"I know how my lady likes it," Noah said.

"I'm such a lucky girl marrying such a good house-husband," she said.

Noah snorted. He could cook, but as for the rest of the daily chores that kept their apartment running, he was somewhat helpless. He could screw up putting his uniform in a Wrinkle-free, which was supposedly foolproof.

If he hadn't enlisted, he'd probably have gone into the culinary arts, either as a chef or as an engineer. And nothing like Harstons, where every dish was fabricated. The restaurants didn't even need a wait staff—they could have the dishes automatically delivered to the tables, but the owners thought the waiters and waitresses would make them more popular with the Marines on base as well as the longshoremen from the port.

Enlisting had delayed his passion for cooking, but he realized that cooking at home for Miriam was a far cry from running a real restaurant. The hours were rough, maybe worse than being a Marine, and taking any passion and making it a chore was a good way to cool the ardor.

He finished off the piccata, drained the pasta, and set up the plates.

"It's ready, honey."

Miriam got off the couch with a sigh, then came over to sit down, her eyes lighting up when she saw her meal.

Better than a bombburger, right?

"I've got a Canadian Cobbler in the oven, too."

"Yeah, I can smell it. You outdid yourself. Did the lieutenant let you out early today?"

"No, normal time, but these are quick dishes."

She dug in, slurping loudly as she ate. Neither of them said anything. When they first started living together, they talked non-stop. But now, even though they weren't married yet, eating, watching the holo, or reading in bed seemed to take precedence.

The word "married" in his thoughts brought him back to why he was nervous. He toyed with his meal, barely eating, while Miriam shoveled in her veal as if she hadn't eaten in weeks. Finally, with a satisfied smile, she mopped up the last of the sauce with the last of her spaghetti, put it in her mouth, and swallowed.

She leaned back and said, "Cope to the max, Noah, cope to the max. Now how about the Canadian Cobbler."

"Uh . . . another ten minutes, I think."

"Oh. OK. I can wait. And thank you. I appreciate the effort."

He hesitated, then decided just to get it over with.

"We got new orders today. A month-long mission to Opal Lexus 3. Training."

She looked up at him, and asked, "Training? No combat?"

"Just training."

"A month, though? Well, that's the life of a Marine, I guess. And a Marine wife's. Uh, when is it? I will be a wife then, right?"

"That's the thing—"

"Why do I have the feeling I'm not going to like this? The dinner, and now the look on your face?"

"We're deploying October 3."

"The third? Of October? So, you're going to be leaving me before the wedding? So, I'm going to have to get everything arranged with your family?"

"Uh, baby. We're scheduled to come back on the 19th."

"The 19th? Oh, that's not so bad. That's less than a month."

"Of November. November 19th."

Her mouth dropped open, and she looked at him for a moment before saying, "And we're getting married on the eighth? How's that going to work?"

"It isn't. We have to re-schedule."

"You've got your leave request in. It's already been approved."

"And the first sergeant told me today that the approval's been rescinded."

Miriam stared at him, with an expression he couldn't decipher. He wasn't sure he wanted to.

Finally, in a brook-no-nonsense tone, she said, "Noah Lysander, I agreed to marry you, and I was fine with just going down to the city center and getting it done. You were the one who wanted the family wedding, not me."

"We can forget about the wedding. We can go to the city center tonight, if you want—"

She held up a hand to stop him.

"I've already been working on this with your family, mostly your grandmother. If we cancel, they'll think it was because of me, and that will put me at odds with them. With your father and mother gone, and with your sister evidently not the marrying type, this wedding of yours . . ."

"Wedding of yours." That's not good.

". . . is a big deal. You've been paying no attention to any of this. And if we just cancel the wedding now, after they've gotten so embedded in it, well, I'm the bitch who doesn't want a family. I'm the bitch who turned you away. And that's not going to happen.

We'll just re-schedule it and make the Marine Corps the bad guy. What with your father, that's already a given."

She hadn't raised her voice, but the steel in it couldn't be missed. She was adamant about it.

"Uh . . . uh, OK. We can reschedule, if you want."

"If *I* want? This is all on me? Not a good way to put it, Noah. Not good at all. What I want is not to be put into this situation," she said before standing up. "And what I want right now is to take a shower."

She strode off to the bedroom, not saying another word. Noah sat there, wondering how he'd blown it so bad. He wasn't sure what he could have said differently.

It's not my fault.

The dinger rang, and he was tempted to ignore it, but wasting food was not in his DNA. With a sigh, he stood up, went to the oven, and removed the cobbler. It smelled great as he put it on the sideboard to cool. He wanted to pout, he wanted to be mad, but he couldn't help but bend over to let the aromas wash over him.

He got out some bowls and scooped out two helpings of the steaming dessert. The white and red berries had formed a pinkish syrup that held them together. They needed something else, though. Stepping over to the fabricator, he dialed up two portions of vanilla ice cream, plopping them on top. They immediately started to melt, sending a thick white stream into the cobbler.

The simple act of making the dessert had calmed him down. He knew Miriam had every reason to be upset. She'd put a lot of work into the wedding, a wedding that she hadn't wanted in the first place. And Noah, using his duties as a Marine as an excuse, had not helped much.

He placed the desserts on the table, walked to the bedroom, and knocked softly on the door.

"Miriam? The cobbler's ready."

She didn't respond.

"Miriam?"

Silence.

With a sigh, Noah went back to the table and sat down to wait. The ice cream had half melted, the pool of vanilla now covering the rest of the cobbler. He picked up his spoon and ladled some of the melted ice cream back to the top of the remaining frozen part, but it slid back down. He scooped up another spoonful, this time picking up a few of the berries, but instead of dumping it back over the top, he shrugged his shoulders and put the spoonful into his mouth.

Two minutes later, his bowl was empty, and he picked it up to lick any remaining traces.

"Miriam? You coming?"

He waited for a moment, but she didn't answer.

With one more dramatic sigh, which was wasted as he was the only one there, he reached across the small table and picked up Miriam's dessert. He held it for a moment, listening for any sound coming from the bedroom. When he still didn't hear anything, he plunged his spoon into the cobbler.

No use wasting good food.

OPAL LEXUS 3

Chapter 12

"The Rangers suck big time," Chili said, flicking a gummy bear at Corporal Knight Lewis, the *Ba-Boom*'s new driver.

"Bullshit. They may be down inna pisshole now, but they'll be a'coming back up," the corporal said, catching the candy after it bounced off his face and popping it into his mouth. "Wit Kuyiko at center, things are gonna change, you jes watch."

Noah tried to ignore the two, sticking his nose deeper into the novel he was reading. He found the constant bickering about sports rather mind-numbing. It wasn't easy to keep rooting for teams while traveling around the galaxy. Growing up on Tarawa, he'd been a casual fan of the planetary teams, even getting up for some of the rivalries within the sector. He wasn't the die-hard fan that his sister Esther was, but still, he could get excited. But with Marines coming from every corner of the Federation and even from some non-Federation worlds, they represented a vast array of not only teams, but sports that were only played locally. Yes, he watched the Olympic games, along with most of humanity, and of course he watched the Gladiatorial combat with the Klethos, but he'd lost interest in most professional sports. Heck, he didn't even know what sport the two Marines were arguing about. There had to be a dozen professional sports that had a center as one of the positions.

But sitting in the White Cliffs Hotel, there wasn't much else to do. They were not allowed out into town, so hanging out or hitting the hotel gym were the daily *riguer du jours*. Without their tanks, there wasn't even the daily maintenance that would keep them busy. And they were getting more than bored. Just the night before, Lessa and Jadelle Portis had gotten into a knock-down, drag-out fight that had broken Lessa's nose and gotten both Marines restricted to their respective rooms. They were lucky at that. If the captain had gotten wind of it, they'd both have faced NJP.

Chili flicked another gummy bear at Knight, but it flew past his shoulder to hit Noah in the chest.

"Grubbing hell, Chili! Watch what you're doing!" Noah snapped.

"Well, fuck me royal, Noah. Sorry to ruin your entire day."

"Just . . . just . . ." Noah started before giving up and turning on his side, presenting his back to the other two Marines.

"Shit, Lewis, I guess Her Royal Highness has got her pussy in a tizzy," Chili said, flicking one more gummy bear, this time aiming for and hitting Noah's back. "Let's me and you get out of here and leave her to play with herself."

Noah didn't say anything as he listened to the two Marines get up and leave. He knew he was out of line. Chili was a pretty good roommate, and they were all bored, but his mood was sour. He looked at his PA, on which he'd opened a window for Williamson time on Prosperity. It was 1233 in the afternoon there, November 8th.

With a sigh, he turned back to his book, but while he could see the words, nothing was registering. He had no idea what he'd just read. Giving up, he turned off the book and folded it up.

He got up and walked over to the window. The view was great, he acknowledged, and the hotel was a high-end resort. But it was a gilded cage. They were essentially prisoners, free to use the grounds, but nothing else.

They'd arrived on the planet and been bused directly to Camp Amethyst where they'd been scheduled to provide training to the planetary militia's newly formed armor regiment. All had gone as planned for the first few days, with the company starting the training syllabus. On the third day, however, that training came to a screeching halt. On the fourth day, the Marines were packed up and transported to the White Cliff.

Politics had reared its ugly head, and the Marines—along with the local armor regiment—were the ones to suffer while the politicians blustered and maneuvered.

Opal Lexus 3 was a newly autonomous world, taking control over their own governing from Exlar, the big conglomerate who'd terraformed the planet over 100 years prior. The local government was friendly to the Federation, but Exlar was almost fanatically devoted to neutrality—and the company (one of the few with only a UAM charter) still wielded significant power on the planet.

The fledgling military had requested aid from the Federation which was more than happy to provide it, and Marine rifle, armor, and air units had been dispatched on training missions. That only lasted until Exlar-leaning politicians saw the reporting on the news holos, much to their surprise and displeasure, and they stepped in. The Marines were whisked away and hidden from sight while the politicians played their political games, with the Federation keeping in the background. That was a month ago. And while Marines and sailors of Charlie Company and 2/11's Echo Company had initially been impressed with the pure luxury of the White Cliff, that had quickly soured. They'd been cut off from the outside worlds, and that included calls back home.

The initial contract was to expire in a week, and no one thought the training would commence before then. They couldn't even leave early, though. The Opal Lexus government—both factions—didn't want to officially antagonize the Federation by breaking the contract, so the Marines were put up in luxury for the duration.

Noah's stomach growled, and he looked at the concierge on the table between the two beds. He'd skipped lunch with the rest of the Marines, choosing to go back to his room after the makeshift hip-pocket class Lieutenant Huang had given about living wills, only the latest in a series of classes the skipper had them attend each morning. That wasn't a big deal, though. Room service was part of the package, and with a simple call, he could get a meal sent up, and as much as he almost hated to admit it, the food was pretty darn good. He'd snuck into the kitchens a few times to talk with the staff, and he knew he was out of their league.

No, I'm not going to call for room service, he told himself forcefully.

It was rather childish, he knew. He was not a happy camper, true. He didn't like the situation, true. But it made no sense to refrain from one of the advantages of the place just because he wanted to hold onto his resentment, to keep reminding himself that the situation sucked the big one.

His PA, which he'd left on the bed, buzzed. Snapping back to reality, Noah took two steps and picked it up. The time in Williamson was 1259. He stood there motionless, holding the PA, and watched it count to the new hour.

"I do," he whispered as it hit 1300.

Without this stupid deployment, he'd be on Prosperity now, standing in the front of the cathedral, waiting to see Miriam emerge on the arm of his Uncle Caleb. He'd be getting married.

The Big Suck, the Green Weenie, could and did make demands on Marines. Noah had eaten his fair share of shit in his career, as had all Marines. But this was the first time he'd resented the Corps. He was missing his wedding, and for what? So, he could sit in some sort of resort—one that would be great, in all irony, for a honeymoon—and be a bit-part spear carrier in a larger game of thrones. He didn't need to be here, but the unit was bigger than the individual, and the Federation was bigger than the unit. He signed on the dotted line, so he understood it—but he didn't have to like it.

He pulled up his favorite pic of Miriam, one where she was laughing at something he'd said, and kissed the image.

"I love you."

He put the PA down on the table, right next to the concierge. His hand was next to the power-button—none of the voice-activated room genies here—and he froze for a moment.

"Screw it," he said, hitting the button.

"May I help you, Sergeant Lysander?" a real person immediately responded.

Neither Chili nor he had found any sort of surveillance device in the room, but the person on the other end always knew which one of them was on the concierge.

"Yes, I missed lunch, and I'd like a . . . a . . ."

What the heck do I want?

"I want a piece of Black Volcano," he decided.

"With snow or without?"

"With, please."

"Very well. Chef will cut you a piece right away."

If he was going to indulge, Noah thought he might as well go whole hog. The Black Volcano was the most indulgent dessert on the hotel's menu, a spongy layer of chocolate goodness with chocolate and raspberry "lava" pouring from the top. The "snow" was the ala mode plopped right in the "crater."

They'd missed the wedding date, and that was that. He realized that approaching the date, he'd been getting more and more depressed, but now that D-Day had passed, surprisingly, he felt a little better, and he thought he could move on. It wasn't as if the wedding was canceled, after all.

And if he was going to be stuck here, he might as well try to enjoy it. Maybe he could get the chef to give him a few pointers to take home.

A few minutes later, there was a discreet knock on the door. Noah let in the server, who wheeled in his dessert on a silver tray. When he put it on the table, the rich chocolate aroma filled the room.

"Enjoy, Sergeant," the server said before leaving.

Noah felt bad about not leaving a tip, but they'd been briefed that the Opal Lexus government was covering everything.

He probably makes more in a week than I make in a month, Noah thought as he sat down and looked at the chocolate extravaganza.

Miriam was not a chocoholic, but he thought she'd like it. But he was here and she was there, so he just picked up his spoon and dug in.

QUINTERO CRAG

Chapter 13

Noah tracked the incoming drone, barely leading it as it dove to take them under fire. With the rail gun, and with automatic targeting, the *Anvil* would have already engaged it, but the with Mad Mike, range was more limited. More pertinent, though, was that the targeting AI was turned off. This shot was on his shoulders.

"Four thousand meters," Chili said from where he was crouching beside him, scrunching up his 1.6-meter frame the best he could in the small space. "What's your trigger point?"

"Two thousand?" Noah said in a question despite knowing it was the textbook answers.

Ground attack drones were moderately shielded, enough so that a shot from the *Anvil's* Mad Mike would have little effect at maximum ranges. In order to assure lethality, the range needed to be narrowed—but letting the drone approach closer made the *Anvil* a more vulnerable target at well.

"And at the recycle rate, how much ground will it had covered after you fire?"

Shoot, I forgot to check.

"Uh . . . 402 meters," he said after checking his sight display. "So, I . . . "

"Don't tell me. Look at your range!"

The range display was rapidly dwindling, and the drone was at 2,200 meters and closing.

He adjusted the aim and fired, just at the drone passed the 2,000-meter mark. It kept coming as the *Anvil's* generator poured power into the meson cannon. Either the audible whine or the inaudible subsonics grated on Noah's inner ears as the gun powered up.

"No effect," Staff Sergeant Cremineli passed. "Fire again."

Noah worked the hydraulics, slewing the cannon to keep the drone in his sights. The drone fired before his cannon was charged, but the instant his go-light turned green, he triggered another shot.

"Dead on," the TC passed. "Target down."

Noah let out a huge breath of air as he watched the drone glide to the ground downrange.

"Not too bad," Chili said from beside him. "We'll check the readouts to see what happened with that first shot. But right now, how about letting me out of here? My legs are killing me."

"Oh, yeah, sure," Noah said as he popped the hatch on the cupula and scrambled out.

"Uh, Staff Sergeant, what about the shot the drone got off?" he asked as he stood up next to his TC, who was standing in his open hatch.

"Eighty-two for combat ready," the staff sergeant said, meaning that the Range AIs had given the *Anvil* an 82% chance of still being combat ready.

"That means a go," Noah said with relief.

"Yeah, a go," the TC said, almost sounding reluctant.

Noah had been concerned about this shot. With Chili moving to crew with the new first sergeant, Noah was next in line as the *Anvil's* gunner, but only if he qualified on each of her three main guns. Staff Sergeant Jones, over in First Platoon, still hadn't qualified, and so he was still a driver, the highest-ranking driver in the company. In most militaries, a driver would be a private or PFC—or the local equivalent—but even in the Marines, where all tankers had previously served a tour as a grunt, it was almost unheard of for a staff sergeant to be a driver.

Noah hadn't been concerned with auto-fire or AI assist, but the manual firing had been nerve-wracking. It would take extraordinary circumstances for him to have to manually aim and fire any of the three weapons configurations, especially the Mad Mike, but if the *Anvil* were hit with something that knocked out her systems, then he'd be tasked with turning her into a Marine-powered artillery piece, using glass sights and hydraulics to aim the tubes.

How a tank could be rendered powerless in as far as target acquisition and aiming but still have power for the meson cannon was something Noah couldn't imagine, but it was part of the qualification.

"Crap, gotta get the blood flowing," Chili said as he climbed out onto the *Anvil's* deck and flexed his legs, one after the other. "Not much room in there."

Noah looked downrange where the drone finally landed on the ground. Almost immediately, like a trap-door spider sensing prey, an RB, or Recovery Bot, darted out of its hangar to recover the drone. During quals with the railgun and the 90mm, inert rounds either hit the targets or simulated detonations, but with the Mad Mike, the cannon was powered down, and sensors on the drones relayed readings to the Range AI which determined if a kill had been achieved or not. The drone Noah had just "killed" would get recharged and be ready for another mission within half-an-hour.

"Well, I guess you passed, you lucky bastard. Shoot her straight, OK?" Chili said, slapping the cannon.

Noah looked at Staff Sergeant Cremineli for confirmation, but he just said, "Back into your driver's seat. You're not the gunner yet, and we've got to get back to the ramp."

Noah was the only Marine to get qualified today, so there wasn't another tank on the range at the moment. He didn't know why the hurry, but he nodded and stepped over to his hatch, opened it, and did his regular contortion to get inside. Chili might have been scrunched up beside him, but with the gun turret, there were an extra six centimeters in the gunner's seat that he in the driver's seat didn't have, and that would make it far more comfortable for him.

He smoothly backed the *Anvil* up, turned her, and started down the trail back to the ramp. He'd gotten used to the big girl, and he was comfortable driving her. Moving to be the gunner was the normal progression, but it was new territory, to a degree, one which he still had to get used to. For a moment, he wished he could just stay as the *Anvil's* driver, but a tank was its gun. A driver simply taxied the gun, and a tank commander merely directed where the gun would be. It was the gunner who operated it.

It was time to step up.

TARAWA

Chapter 14

Noah stood well behind the formation of midshipmen, avoiding the stands where the bulk of the guests were sitting. He wasn't sure why he didn't sit with the rest of the spectators, just that he didn't feel part of the ceremony. He also felt unaccountably nervous.

In front of the mids, the commandant of the Marine Corps had started the oath, his voice booming:

"I, state your name . . ."

Each midshipman repeated after the commandant, right hand raised.

> *. . .do solemnly swear, to support and defend the Articles of Council of the Federation of United Nations, against all enemies, foreign and domestic; that I will bear true faith and allegiance to the same and above all others; and that I will obey the orders of the Chairman of the Federation of the United Nations and the orders of those appointed over me, according to the Uniform Code of Military Justice. So help me God.*

"Congratulations, lieutenants," the commandant said as he lowered his right arm. "Now get out there and lead. The Federation is counting on you. With that, I know you have family here, so celebrate today, for tomorrow, duty calls. You are dismissed."

The group of newly minted Marine lieutenants burst into a loud "Ooh-rah!"

Noah tried to spot his sister, but the milling boot looies were like a school of fish, hugging and pounding each other on the back, whirling around and making it hard to spot any one individual.

At the peripheries of the group, enlisted Marines and sailors were gathering, the sharks, swordfish, and sea lions looking to dart in and target the lieutenants.

Noah caught sight of Esther once, but he quickly lost it, and he wasn't going to just wade into the group. There were unspoken rules for this sort of thing, and trying to be the first to salute the new lieutenants couldn't interfere with their own celebration.

He looked around. There had to be thirty of them gathered, all watching the newly-minted lieutenants. Noah didn't care about the bulk of the lieutenants—only Esther mattered, and he was not going to let any of the others give his sister her first salute.

His sister could be a real hard-ass, one who had very strong opinions on how things should go, and Noah intended to make that work to his advantage. Behind him was the statue of General Salizar. Their father had received his first salute in front of the statue. If he knew his twin, she'd want to receive her first salute at the same place. To paraphrase the old saying, in this case, if he couldn't go to the mountain, he'd let the mountain come to him. Taking one more look at the lieutenants as they broke to meet family, or in several cases, allowed the enlisted Marines to come close enough to salute, he turned his back and took up a station just to the statue's left. Now all he had to do was wait.

But Esther didn't show. Noah stepped back to where he could look over the parade deck, and the school of lieutenants was getting smaller as more and more of them were leaving. With fewer lieutenants there, he should be able to spot her, but she wasn't on the parade deck anymore.

Did I miss her?

He hadn't told her he'd gotten leave to attend her commissioning because he was afraid she'd have told him not to come. Things had been a little tense between them over the last couple of years for reasons that Noah still didn't understand. But he was her brother, her twin, and the only close family she had left. He had to be there for her. Blood was blood.

If she'd already left, he'd just have to call her up. It wouldn't be the same as what he'd imagined, but he was not going to slink back to Quintero Crag without letting her know he'd come.

He was just about to give up when a familiar figure left the stands and started marching purposefully towards the courtyard with the general's statue. A couple of fellow lieutenants grabbed her for hugs, but Noah knew she was heading his way.

I knew it, he told himself, a smile breaking out across his face.

She eventually broke free of her classmates, and a couple of Marines tried to intercept her, but she was walking quickly, head down. As she got close, Noah stepped forward, but a corpsman rushed up, arm ready to whip it up in a salute.

Not going to happen!

"As you were, Doc. She's mine," Noah barked out with all the authority he could muster into his voice.

The corpsman stopped, and it looked like he was going to argue with him, but with a smile, he nodded and turned back to what was left of the remaining second lieutenants.

Esther slowly turned around and caught sight of Noah, her eyes widening in surprise. He came to attention, and in his best drill field manner, slowly brought up his hand in a salute.

"Congratulations, ma'am!" he said, keeping his face as emotionless as he could despite the pride that threatened to well out.

Esther stood there, her mouth open, motionless. Noah froze, his hand still up in his salute. As if suddenly remembering where she was, she returned it.

"How . . . what . . . how did you get here?"

"By spaceship. That's the usual way, ma'am, you know."

"But you're at Camp Ceasare!"

"And no ships ply the space lanes from there to here? And I'm not at Ceasare any longer. I've already been assigned. I sent you a whispergram to tell you that."

"You did? Well, I've been . . . I mean, with NOTC and everything, I don't check my personals often. I'm sorry. But why come all the way here? I mean, that had to cost a pretty credit."

She was right. It had taken a good chunk of his salary, and unless Miriam had agreed to it, he wouldn't have spent the funds.

"You have to ask? You're my sister, Esther. We only have each other. You needed family here for this."

"How did you know I'd come to the statue for my first salute? That someone wouldn't grab me sooner?"

"As I said, Ess, you're my sister. You're my twin. I know you. Of course, you'd come to where Dad got his, and no one was going to get in your way for that. I saw you marching over, a woman on a mission. I'm surprised that corpsman even got as close to you as he did."

"Well, I guess you're right. And I guess I owe you this," she said, pulling the Kookaburra Dollar out of her pocket and handing it to him.

Noah gave it only a glance before a satisfied smile crept over his face.

"I was hoping that's what it would be, but I looked online. A 2123 Kookaburra's pretty hard to find."

"I . . . well, you know."

"Yeah, Ess, I know."

Most new lieutenants bought one of the many commemorative coins to give to the Marine or sailor who first saluted them. But their father, in respect and gratitude to Gunny Meader who had helped him through NOTC, had bought a 2123 O.R. Australian Kookaburra Dollar to present to the gunny after that first salute. Both of them had heard the story more times than they could count, and while Noah figured Esther would want to give the same coin, it was pretty rare and cost a pretty credit to buy, probably as much if not more than the cost of his ticket to Tarawa. He smiled and slipped the coin into his pocket before looking back up to catch his sister's eyes. But neither of them said anything, and the silence grew uncomfortably longer. But there was another reason Noah had made the trip, and he had to ask before she walked away.

"There's one more thing. Miriam and I are getting married, and we'd love you to be there. It's up to you, though. I know you'll be busy snapping in with your platoon."

He tried to make it sound casual, as if it was no big thing, but he could feel his body tense as he waited for her to respond.

Esther liked to think she could control her emotions, that she could hide her feelings. But they were twins. Noah might not know what had come between them, but he could still read her, and it wasn't good. He could tell she was embarrassed, maybe even feeling guilty because she didn't want to go. He'd hoped for a sign of joy, but it wasn't coming.

He was about to tell her it didn't matter when she asked, "When is it? And where?"

That took him by surprise, but he knew it was probably just so she could have a reason to say no.

"May 4. On Prophesy. So, you know, Grandmama can help."

"Help, Noah? You mean take over," she said, a smile cracking her features

"OK, she'll take over the entire thing," he said, laughing.

Esther might not be close with their extended family back on Prophesy, but she knew Grandmama would be fully in charge.

"And May 4? Aren't we copying our parents a little much here? Me with General Salizar and the Kookaburra, you on Mom and Dad's anniversary?"

"Just like where you had to enlist Ess? In the same recruiting station where Father enlisted? We're just like each other, in so many ways."

He could see that she didn't agree with him, and that hurt.

"I tell you what, Noah. I don't' know my deployment schedule yet. I've been assigned to 2/14."

"Ah, the Lagunari," Noah said, more than willing to change the subject. "Good unit."

"The what? 'La-goon-ary?'" she asked.

It's your unit. Didn't you bother to look up your battalion's patron corps? he wondered.

Esther wasn't much for the tradition and esprit de corps, but he thought she'd surely have looked it up when she'd received her orders. Every rifle battalion had one of the extant Marine Corps or Naval Infantries as its patron unit, and that patron's birthday celebration was almost as big as that for the Marine Corps birthday.

"The Lagunari Serenissima. One of old Italy's two Marine units. Two-fourteen chose the Lagunari as their name, but adopted the San Marco Brigade's motto, let me remember, something like '*Per Mare, Per Terram.*' Do you know, the Lagunari were Army, not Marine or Naval Infantry? The San Marco Brigade was Navy, but not the Lagunari. It's one of only two Army patrons in the Corps today."

She looked at him like he was crazy for knowing it, like he was some sort of history geek. He did love history, something he'd probably gotten from their father, but if for no other reason than to follow her unbridled ambition, this was something she really had to know in the tradition-loving Corps.

"OK, um, good to know," she told him. "But back to your question, I don't know my schedule, but if we're not deployed, and if I can get leave, I would be honored to attend your wedding."

And there it is. A no.

"It's OK. I under . . . oh, you'll make it?" Noah asked as his brain processed what she'd just said.

"It's not a promise, Noah. But I'll try. You know the Corps, though. Remember how many times Dad missed birthdays and anniversaries?"

"Yeah, yeah, of course, I know," Noah said, excitement taking over. "But thanks, Ess. It'll make Grandmama happy . . . no, strike that. It'll make me happy."

"You're my little brother, Noah," she said, just like old times in using her being born nine minutes before him to claim the title of older sister. "Of course, I'll be there."

A Marine spotted Esther standing by the base of the statue and started over, arm cocked to salute before he saw Noah and dejectedly turned to find a yet un-saluted lieutenant.

"It's a little late for that," Noah said as they both laughed and watched the sergeant's retreating back. "You've got to get an earlier jump on things."

"I think you're right. But, I need to get going. I've got a property pick-up in about an hour, and I'm not packed yet."

"You know, they only allow you two seabags," Noah said, referring to his sister's habit of traveling with a wardrobe of clothes

"I don't carry that much!" Esther protested. "And now that I'm an officer, I get a load-out box, too."

"Lucky for you. I'm betting it's still not enough," he said, still teasing.

"You'd better watch it, Sergeant! I could always order you to pack my stuff for me and carry it to TMI."

So, she's going to hold her rank over me? Noah thought, despite knowing she had been joking.

Joking or not, it still revealed a frame of mind. If there had been some sort of wall between them before, her being an officer just made that wall all the taller.

"Well, Ess. Lieutenant Ess," Noah said, forcing a smile on his face. "I need to get going. I'll let you get your things ready. Congratulations. Really. Mother and father would be proud."

He stepped forward, and the two awkwardly hugged. Their stiff dress blues were not the only reason for that.

"Thanks for coming, Noah. It was good to have family here. And I'm proud my first salute was from you."

"I couldn't miss this," he said, reaching into his pocket and pulling out the Kookaburra Dollar for another look.

He came to attention again and gave a snappy salute, which she returned.

"Well, OK. I guess I'll see you in May?" Noah said as he turned to walk away.

"Hey, Noah!" Esther said after he'd taken several steps. "When are you leaving to go back?"

"My shuttle's at 0530."

"Unless you've got something else to do, why don't you meet me for dinner? I'm going to eat at the Globe and Laurel with one of my classmates. His great-grandfather will be there. He was a Marine in the War of the Far Reaches, and his grandson—my friend's father—fought with Dad."

"I . . . I'd like that, Ess. But . . ." he said, as he pointed to the chevrons on his sleeve.

She'd just reminded him that she was an officer and he was a sergeant, after all.

"Screw that. We're family. And Mr. Upshick was a corporal when he served. We're all Marines, right?"

"Well, right. But—"

"But nothing. Twenty-hundred, OK?"

Noah only hesitated a moment before he shrugged and said, "Twenty-hundred it is. See you then, Ess."

He turned around and walked off, but with more spring in his step. He'd hang out on base, looking up old friends, but spending time with his sister was an added bonus, one he hadn't expected.

Maybe they were becoming a family again.

QUINTERO CRAG

Chapter 15

"So, what the hell's going on?" Chili said as he slid into the seat beside Noah.

"Your guess is as good as mine."

The company had been scheduled for range driving, something it really needed, but while they were on the ramp, it had been canceled, and all hands were in the theater waiting to find out why.

"How's the new first sergeant?" Noah asked, tilting his head where she sat in the back.

Tank crews tended to sit together, but Noah and Chili had been together for a while, and he'd just switched over to the newly re-named *Night Witch* two days prior.

First Sergeant St. Cloud had been one of the first women to enlist when Noah's father had re-opened the Corps to all genders, and while there were female tank officers who out-ranked her, there were only a handful of female tankers who'd reached the rank of first sergeant so far. With the gender mix in tanks, that would change over time, but for now, a female tanker first sergeant, or any first sergeant, for that matter, was still somewhat rare.

What was pertinent to the Marines in the company, though, and why Noah was asking, was what kind of first sergeant she would be. She had a decent combat record, but so had her predecessor. He'd been somewhat laid back in garrison, and with the captain in the same mold, things had been pretty easy in the company. Noah hadn't liked the fact that Charlie was obviously lower on the pecking order than Alpha, and he'd love to overtake the battalion CO's favorite company, but the Marines in Alpha were pushed harder.

"Hard to tell. This was supposed to be our first time as a crew today."

"Not that. We know she's got tank chops. You know, as first sergeant."

"Still hard to tell. I get the feeling she's just biding her time, watching and evaluating."

"That sound ominous," Noah said as Chili shrugged.

"What about you? How's your new driver?"

"Nervous. He's barely said a word so far. Today was our first day out as a team, too."

Noah didn't know what to make of Corporal Moby Jankowski. He'd made it through Armor School, so he was qualified, but the quiet Marine certainly wasn't making an impact with his presence. Noah was now the *Anvil's* gunner, but he was anxious to make sure that the tank had a strong Marine in the driver's seat.

"He'll be fine. It's Cremineli you need to be worried about."

Ever since Chili had gotten word that he'd be moving to a new tank, he'd been more open about his disdain for the *Anvil's* commander. He hadn't openly challenged the staff sergeant, but he'd been free to express his opinions to Noah. Noah thought Chili might be going overboard, but he had to admit that there were some truths to Chili's complaints.

Noah opened his mouth to reply when First Sergeant St. Cloud screamed out, "Attention on deck!"

Noah jumped to his feet, craning his eyes to see not only the company commander, but the battalion commander stride into the theater. Whatever was up, it was bigger than Noah had guessed.

The two officers marched to the stage where the battalion CO took out a collar mic and turned it on before facing the company.

"Ooh-rah, Charlie," the lieutenant colonel called out to the return "ooh-rah" from the still standing Marines.

"That's what I like to hear. Take your seats.

"I'm sorry to interfere with your range day. I know you're anxious to get out and get muddy. So, I'll only keep you for awhile. But something's come up, and you need to know.

"As of 0400 tomorrow morning, Captain Lorre and Charlie Company will be deploying to Novyy Ural."

What? What's going on there? Noah wondered, suddenly alert.

"Approximately 14 hours ago, a full regiment of Naval Infantry from Pytor Velikiy landed at the spaceport at Manchester Center, quickly capturing it. The Novyy militia, which consists of one division, is being mobilized, and from initial intel, will march on Manchester Center to retake it. The *FS Weevil* will arrive in system in approximately four hours to block any further landings, but a fight's brewing on the ground that benefits no one."

The colonel turned around and activated the screen. Noah was vaguely aware of the Janson System, one of the few with two populated planets, and the images and data on the screen brought it into focus.

Novyy Ural was almost Earth-like, able to sustain human life, and so, it was one of the earlier planets settled during the First Expansion. Significant mineral wealth was discovered on the third planet in the system, so despite it being a Cat 2+ planet, Novyy Ural decided to terraform it. That turned out to have been too big of an undertaking for the planet, and it had to turn to BaikalBank, back on Earth, to finish the job. The terraforming had been minimal, stopping at the point where life could be sustained, but not a comfortable life.

Novyy Ural had expected to become landlords of a valuable piece of real estate, licensing it off to the highest bidder, but the contract with Baikalbank effectively cut them out of the process, a contract that was upheld after years of litigation. Over the last 60 years, the two planets had developed a love-hate relationship, emerging from similar cultural backgrounds, but with Novyy Ural feeling they'd been cheated in their own system, and Pytor Velikiy resenting their dependence on Novyy Ural food and products for survival.

"As you can see on the screen, Manchester Center is in the agricultural heartland of Novyy Ural, this peninsula that extends into the temperate zone, while the three planetary regiments are here, here, and here," the CO said, highlighting two regiments on the same continent, with the closest being 800 klicks away, and one on the other side of the planet. "Charlie Company's mission is to sit right here," he said, pointing to a narrowing of the neck that attached the peninsula to the rest of the continent, "and keep these idiots apart while the First Ministry negotiates an end to the potential for actual hostilities to break out."

The time-worn symbol for an armor company—a rectangle with an oval in the middle and a single short line protruding from the top—appeared on the neck of the peninsula.

"As you can see, there is no Federation infantry being deployed at this time," the CO said to the murmurs from the Marines in the theater.

"At the moment, Alpha is a symbol. They are not to engage," he said, and Noah could tell he didn't like the situation.

Noah didn't know how big a regiment from either side was, nor did he know their capabilities, but he did know that 15 lone tanks was not enough to survive if things got hot.

"And that brings me to you, Charlie. As of this moment, you are on Hot Alert, to be joined with a mechanized company within 48 hours."

Noah's heart fell. "Hot Alert" was the nickname for being in a Class 2 Reaction Status, able to be aboard ships and deployed within 72 hours. Marines on Hot Alert were generally not given leave, and his wedding was in five days. Miriam had already left for Prosperity to help with the final preparations.

He barely heard the rest of the CO's brief, only catching that more would be passed as plans were completed. He stood up with the rest of the company as the CO left, his mind numb.

"Wow, some shit, huh?" Chili asked. "I can't believe they're hanging Alpha out to dry like that."

"I've got to see the first sergeant," Noah said, pushing past Chili.

"What the fuck? Can't you wait?"

"My wedding," he said.

"Oh, shit. You're right. Let's go see her."

This involved Chili as well. He was supposed to be Noah's best man, but Noah was a little more concerned about what Miriam would say.

He pushed his way through the milling Marines until he saw the first sergeant, who had her PA earphone on her ear as she spoke to someone. She saw Noah and held up a hand to stop him. Noah stood there, getting a little perturbed with her as she ignored him. This was important, and he didn't need to be blown off.

Most of the Marines had filed out of the theater before she closed the connection and motioned Noah and Chili forward.

About grubbing time.

"First Sergeant, it's about—" he started before she cut him off.

"Sergeant Lysander, your leave's been granted a special compensation, but it's been cut. You've got two days on Prosperity, then you need to high-tail it back here. Sergeant Fulford, your leave's been canceled."

Noah looked at her, his mouth gaping open. "My leave? I can still get married?"

"That's what I said. The division sergeant major just got the OK from the G1 himself."

Noah didn't know what to say. He'd been ready to argue, and the first sergeant not only knew who he was, knew that he was getting married, but had been working her bolt to get him back to Prosperity.

"Uh . . . thank you, First Sergeant St. Cloud. I appreciate it."

"Have a good wedding," she said in a no-nonsense tone. "Now, get some chow. We're going to be back on the ramp at 1230. Training's still on. "I'll see you on the ramp at 1210," she added to Chili before she turned and left.

"Wow. That's great for you," Chili said. "But, sorry I can't be there too, man."

"Oh, don't worry. It's not your fault," Noah said. "Needs of the Corps."

The truth was at this point, he didn't care anymore if Chili was there or not. He would be, and that was what mattered.

PROPHESY

Chapter 16

"How do I look?" Noah asked Skeets, who'd just arrived that morning.

When Chili's leave was canceled, Noah had been left high and dry. With Alpha Company already gone and Charlie on Hot Alert, that had drastically diminished his pool of potential best men. Skeets hadn't been his first choice. He'd asked Brock first, and when he couldn't reach Skeets, he'd even considered asking General Simone. But then Skeets had gotten back to him, and he'd readily agreed to fill in. Assigned to Second Tanks, he was even in the same sector as Prosperity.

"Looking sharp, my man, looking sharp."

Both Marines were in their dress blues. His grandmother had asked only once if he'd like to get married in a traditional Torritite Gideon Suit, but Noah had given a very firm no to that, and his grandmother had not pursued it.

Torritites were not overly conservative. They liked to have a good time, and the juice of the vine was always welcomed. But they didn't take the Lord's name in vain, and the men dressed in muted colors, so outsiders sometimes assumed that they were more conservative than they really were. Their mother had been a Torritite, but Esther and Noah had not been raised in an observant household. Noah had agreed to have the wedding on Prophesy for the extended family, but he was proud of being a Marine, and he was going to get married as a Marine.

"Noah? You be decent?" his grandmother asked, knocking at the door.

"Yes, come on in," he answered.

She poked her head in the door, and when she saw him, she broke out into a smile, her eyes watering.

"Oh, my boy, you be so handsome, standing there. I can see your mother in you," she said, slowly walking over to him and giving him a surprisingly strong hug.

Marine dress blues were sharp-looking, but they were not the most comfortable uniforms to wear, but he managed to lift his arms and cradle them around his grandmother's head, pulling her into his chest and against his three medals. She didn't seem to care that they were poking her in the face.

"Thank you, Grandmama, for all of this."

"Oh, boy, thank you. I know you didn't want to go to all the fuss and bother, and I know Miriam didn't, either, but we here, we needed it. You and Esther, you both be so far from us, that we need to keep the connection, to remember your mother and father through you.

"But here I be nattering on like an old lady. I came to get you. We be ready."

She stepped back, then tut-tutted, wiping a wet spot on his chest where her tears had stained it.

"It's OK, Grandmama, it'll dry off in a moment."

He turned to Skeets and said, "Well, are you ready?"

"I think the question is if you are ready," Skeets said with a laugh.

The three left the small changing room, then walked down the hallway to the knave. The Torritites didn't have churches, per se, and it seemed as if half of the planet's Torritite community was attending the wedding, so his grandmother had rented out the local Roman Catholic cathedral. Noah had been in the Chapel of the Corps on Tarawa, and he'd seen the Wat of Reckoning on Gloucester and St. Luke's Cathedral on Addison 2, but as he entered the nave, he was surprised at how big St. Brigitta's was—and how many people turned to look at him. He was very conscious of their eyes on him as he and Skeets walked down the main aisle.

His Aunt Rebekah, who was officiating the wedding gave him a welcoming smile as he walked down the aisle. He was nervous, and he started having tunnel vision, so he just focused on his aunt, keeping her centered in his sight. The undernet was full of holos that featured grooms fainting at their weddings, and Noah's fellow Marines would never let him live it down if he became the latest victim.

All the more reason to have just gotten it done at a government center, he thought.

He managed to reach the spot Aunt Rebekah indicated and turned to face down the aisle. Skeets gave him a nudge with his elbow, not saying anything, but letting him know he was there for him.

The music, a jolt-pop tune called "My O" that Miriam had chosen that had been "gentrified" out into a statelier, almost hymn-like rendition, filled the nave. Noah had to smile, and that calmed him down. The music sounded appropriate for a church setting, but he wondered how many people knew that the words in the original Kettle Korn version included lyrics such as "Grab you by the balls and never let go," and "Light up my G-bud." Miriam had agreed to a formal wedding, but the same rebelliousness that had caused her to leave her family and wander homeless had reared its head when she picked the music. The smiling faces who'd turned to see the bridesmaids enter the nave would probably die of shock if they knew the words of the original recording.

Noah caught sight of Esther at the tail-end of the bridesmaids. He was still amazed that she had come, certain that she'd have some sort of obligation that she couldn't—or wouldn't want to—avoid. Yet here she was, playing maid of honor to someone she barely knew. He felt a surge of affection come over him as he caught her eye and smiled.

At least the gowns weren't too horrible, as far as Noah could tell. The blue and lilac gowns were flattering, and at least in the old days before they both enlisted, it looked like something the fashion-loving Esther would wear.

The bridesmaids reached the transept, filing to the opposite side from where Noah and Skeets were standing. Torritite culture leaned to the matrimonial, and there were no groomsmen unlike in many other ceremonies. Esther gave him a wink as everyone turned to the rear to watch the bride's entrance.

The music shifted, not that Noah noticed, as Miriam, on the arm of Uncle Caleb, entered the nave. Any regrets that they hadn't simply filled out the paperwork at the government center and be done with it vanished as he saw her.

She's gorgeous! he thought. *And she's mine!*

She might be on his Uncle's arm, she might be walking with the eyes of hundreds of guests on her, but her eyes were locked onto his as step-by-step, she marched down the aisle. And Noah was mesmerized. He couldn't break his gaze. Time lost meaning, and either seconds or years later, Uncle Caleb was presenting her, a huge smile on his face. Noah held out his hand, which Miriam took.

They turned to the front in unison and took two steps forward until they were a single pace away from Aunt Rebekah, who looked over the nave and spread her hands.

"Dearly beloved, we are gathered here today under the eyes of the Lord to join Noah Absalom Lysander to Miriam Seek Grace in holy matrimony. On this wondrous occasion . . ."

Noah barely heard what Aunt Rebecca was saying. He was lost in Miriam, he was lost in the moment. He somehow managed to say "I do," when prompted, and he thought he heard his bride say "I do," but that could all have been a dream.

It wasn't until he heard Aunt Rebecca give the traditional, "I now pronounce you wife and husband," that it hit him. He was married.

When she said, "You may kiss the bride," he didn't need any urging. He turned to Miriam, pulled her in, and kissed his wife.

****

Noah held Miriam's hand under the table. They'd barely let go during the dinner, the toasts, even during the Parading of the Newlyweds. It was hard to believe that finally, the two were married. Several times, it has seemed that everything was going to crash down around them, but here they were, a married couple.

Noah had been amazed at all the pomp and circumstance that had surrounded them. His grandmother had organized everything to a gnat's ass, as Miriam reminded him. On the one hand, he thought he and Miriam should have had more input, but on the other hand, it had been a relief to have someone else put it all together—and foot the bill.

This had not been an inexpensive wedding. He didn't know how much the cathedral had cost to rent, nor the reception hall. But the decoration had been extensive, and the food alone had to cost a couple of hundred credits a head. Noah hadn't managed to eat much, but he could recognize the quality of what had been fed to the guests. There had even been jamón ibérico de bellota, the ham made from black pigs who'd only been fed acorns, as an appetizer, provided by Uncle Caleb, his grandmother had told him. It probably had come from Amana, where they specialized in creating esoteric foodstuffs using ancient traditions rather than from Earth itself, but it still had to have cost a pretty credit and most, if not all of the guests, wouldn't have recognized its significance.

"Look at Skeets," Miriam whispered in his ear. "He looks like a rutting stag."

Skeets had left the head table shortly after the main meal had finished, and now he was sitting with the bridesmaids, paying particular attention to Ruth, Noah's cousin. And from the look of it, Ruth wasn't adverse to the attention.

"They say weddings bring out the romance in everyone."

"How about you, Mr. Lysander? Are you feeling romantic?"

"Uh . . ." Noah said, looking around to see if anyone had heard. "Of course. Soon."

She shifted her hand to his thigh and gave it a squeeze. "I've only got you for two days here, and I'm waiting for you to 'pla-pla-pla-pla-plant me,'" she said, quoting one of the lyrics of "My O."

Noah pushed her hand off his thigh, but he was smiling. Even after almost two years, Miriam often surprised him. He didn't think he was a prude, but his parent's household had always been a little low key.

Aunt Rebecca and Uncle Dylan, their little boy squirming in his mother's arms with their girl holding onto her father's hand, approached the two, and his aunt said, "Thank you so much for letting me marry you. It was an honor. But Micah's getting cranky, so we better be heading off. You need to come back more often, though. We all miss you."

The four of them shook hands and kissed cheeks, and Noah promised they'd try to come back soon for a longer visit.

"Pla-pla-pla-pla-plant!" Miriam whispered again, but a little louder than last time.

Noah rolled his eyes, but that was more for effect as he couldn't help but smile.

"OK, let's make our final rounds."

Hand-in-hand, the two of them went to each table again, this time thanking them for coming. Most of the tables went quickly, but as they moved to the front of the room, some of his older relatives wanted to chat, mostly relating to stories of Noah's mother when she was a girl. Uncle Josiah, who'd served in the Marines, had a few war stories, and Uncle Paul, probably a little deeper into his cups than he should be, started relating a story that made no sense to Noah at all. He'd have stood there all night, trying to figure out what the old man was saying if Miriam hadn't dragged him away.

At the bridesmaid's table, Miriam took over, thanking each of them, women she'd only met the week before when she'd arrived. Noah and Skeets stood to the side, out of the way.

"Good wedding," Skeets said. "Thanks for inviting me."

"You seem to be doing OK for yourself," Noah said.

"Hell, Noah. Look at her," he said, nodding his head to indicate Ruth. "And I can't help it if she thinks I'm a Prime Alpha Stud."

"Grubbing hell, Skeets. Only you think that," Noah said, punching his friend in the arm.

"Just 'cause you've got the cream of the crop here, doesn't mean I can't try for the second hottest girl around."

Yeah, I do have the cream of the crop at that, Noah thought as he watched his *wife* thank each bridesmaid.

Finally, they were at the head table. A few more minutes and they could leave. Noah shook hands with his Uncle Barret and got kissed by his Aunt Lysa. Noah had no idea how he was actually related to most of his "aunts" and "uncles" within the Torritite community. Uncle Caleb was his mother's brother, so he knew that, but most of the time the title was simply honorary. But his Aunt Lysa was his father's sister and Barret her husband. Lysa, along with her children, were the last blood relatives he and Esther knew of on their father's side of the family.

"Thank you for coming," Noah told his aunt.

"It's been our pleasure, Noah," she said, taking his face in her hands. "You remind me so much of your father, you know."

To you I'm my father, to Grandmama, I'm my mother.

Uncle Barret slid the key fob into his hand when they shook, saying, "It's the red Hyundai Tonora in the reserved parking. Just have Miriam keep it until she leaves so she can get around."

His grandmother had told him his uncle was lending him the Tonora, but he hadn't been sure how to approach the man to ask about it, so that was a relief. His aunt and uncle were wealthy, and lending him the car wouldn't put them out, but it was a big boon to Noah and his sergeant's salary.

He turned to see Miriam and Esther, arms around each other, speaking quietly. Noah had the feeling that Esther didn't quite approve of his wife, and he was happy to see them chatting. He felt that if they just got to know each other, they'd learn to like each other.

Noah took the opportunity to hug his grandmother, saying, "Thanks so much. We couldn't have pulled this off without you."

"Like I told you, this was for us. I know you wanted to go the easy way, and I know you don't follow all of our customs, so I be thanking you.

"But go say goodbye to your sister and take your bride to the Westin," she said, referring to the Dry Falls Westin, where they had a room for their wedding night. She pulled him close and whispered into his ear, "Light up her G-bud."

"Grandmama!" he shouted, pulling back in shock.

First Miriam, and now Grandmama? What's going on?

Esther and Miriam looked at them in surprise, while his grandmother struggled to hold back a smile.

And suddenly, Noah had to laugh. He'd thought Miriam had slipped "My O" past his grandmother, but the old lady had been too quick on the uptake. She'd known from the beginning, most likely, the lyrics to the song, and she'd played along.

Both his sister and wife were looking at him with questions in their eyes, but he ignored them, still chuckling as he took Esther's hand.

"Thanks so much, Ess. This was really important to us."

"Like I said on Tarawa, we're family, you and I. Now with you too, Miriam," she added. "I was happy to come."

"We're getting ready to leave for the Westin. Are we going to see you tomorrow?"

"Miriam just invited me to join you two for dinner tomorrow night. Is that OK?"

"If Miriam invited you, I guess you're invited," Noah said.

"Smart boy, little brother. You keep that attitude up, and you'll be OK."

Noah rolled his eyes, then asked, "You're going back on Tuesday?"

"I think I'll hang around until the weekend, you know, catching up with the family. Aunt Lysa wants me to meet the cousins, and I think I will."

After their parents had been killed, Esther had pulled away from the family on Prophesy while Noah had spent a year there. The fact that Esther wanted to re-connect was welcomed news to him.

"That's great, Ess. I think you'll find that—."

Esther reached out a hand and put a forefinger on his lips, saying, "Once he gets going, Miriam, it's sometimes hard to get him to shut up. Just take your husband and get out of here before he starts spouting obscure historical facts about the planet."

What? Noah thought before it hit him, and he could feel his face redden. *I'm not that bad, am I?*

"We'll talk tomorrow, Ess, OK?" Miriam said as she took Noah's hand and starting leading him off. "And now, Mr. Lysander, will you get me the hell out of here so we can do some serious connubial consummation?"

"Your wish is my command, Mz. Lysander, your wish is my command!"

QUINTERO CRAG

Chapter 17

"Keep your head down," Miriam said, her hands on Noah's hips.

Noah could see the worry on her face, despite her obvious attempts to hide it.

"I will. And don't worry. The *Anvil* will keep us safe."

The tanks hadn't kept the Alpha Company Marines safe, but he didn't bother to mention that.

Alpha Company had been on Novyy Ural for four months, a blocking force between the two opposing sides. Things had seemingly quieted down, and Charlie had been relieved as the Hot Alert by Bravo, then just re-assumed it two weeks prior. Yesterday, Novyy Ural time, things had fallen apart. The details weren't too clear yet, or at least, the word hadn't been passed down to the rank and file, but a hot-headed grandstanding had resulted in a skirmish between the Pytor Velikiy naval infantry and the Novyy militia, one that Alpha Company had tried to break up. Caught in the middle, four of the company's Davises had been destroyed, with six Marines KIA.

The orders were given, and Charlie was deploying to the planet to reinforce Alpha. They'd be joined by a mechanized infantry company and a section of arty a week after arriving, but with the situation still unsure, this was being treated as a combat insertion.

Noah put his hand on Miriam's belly. Sometimes, he thought he could feel the baby inside, despite everyone telling him it was too early.

"You just take care of yourself. If you think working is too much for you, go ahead and quit. We can manage."

With them officially married, Noah was now receiving a married allowance. It wasn't much, but they could squeak by on his pay if they had to.

She put her hand over his and said, "Don't worry about me. Women have been working and having babies for hundreds of thousands of years. I'll be fine. You just make sure you're back before he's born."

"That's in five months, Miriam. We should have this wrapped up by then."

"You'd better hope you're right. I don't want to go through this alone."

Noah pulled her into a hug. Over her shoulder, he could see the Marines and sailors standing around, many with families gathered around with the single and geographic bachelor Marines and sailors gathering in loose groups.

Just a couple of meters behind Miriam, the first sergeant was sitting cross-legged on the ground, one of her four children sitting in her lap, another standing, his hands on her shoulder, while she read a book to them. Her husband, a former corporal himself, if the rumors were correct, stood silently, a tiny red-headed girl asleep in his arms. He looked resigned, but the oldest child, a skinny, frizzled-haired girl of maybe seven, looked like she wanted nothing of this, of her mother leaving.

Miriam's belly was up against him, and he wondered about his future son inside of her. They'd known his gender for over a month now, but neither of them had suggested a name yet. If Noah reenlisted again after this enlistment was up, would his son understand when he deployed? Would he resent his father leaving in the same way that the first sergeant's daughter was resenting her deployment?

One of his earliest memories was crying with Esther while his father left on a deployment. Time had a way of fuzzifying memories, and he wasn't sure if he was crying because his father was going to be gone for a long time or if it was because their birthday party celebration was going to be postponed. Whatever the reason, he remembered crying, and he remembered the look on his mother's face as the bus that was taking his father to the shuttleport pulled out.

"Hey, Miriam," Chili said, walking up behind Noah. "You doing OK?"

"Yeah, no problem. It'll be good to have some freedom for a while. Noah's been trying to wait on me hand and foot since we found out I was pregnant."

Noah didn't buy that for a moment, and he was sure Chili didn't either.

"Enjoy your freedom, 'cause I think we'll be back before you know it," Chili said.

"I hope so," Miriam said quietly.

"Check out the first sergeant," Chili said. "Four kids."

"What? You're her gunner, and you didn't know that?"

"Hell, I knew she had kids, but she's pretty tight-lipped about her personal life. This is the first time I've seen them . . . or him."

Noah didn't need him to specify who "him" was. He'd been checking out the first sergeant's husband, too. First Sergeant St. Cloud had proven to be a hard-ass, a polar opposite from the skipper. She wasn't unreasonable, and Noah respected her, but she could make life tough for her Marines. When he'd heard that she was married, and that her husband might have served as a Marine, he'd wondered what kind of man would have ended up being her husband. "Pussy whipped" was the crude term thrown about when conversation drifted that way.

He wasn't talking much, simply standing beside her, but he seemed like any other guy. Give him a high-and-tight and a uniform, and he would fit right in with the rest.

There was the whine of hover fans, and everyone looked up. A moment later, a line of three buses entered the quad. It was time.

"I'm serious. Keep your head down," Miriam said hugging him tighter. "No hero bullshit."

"Don't worry. Nothing's going to happen to me."

"Easy for you to say."

"Charlie Company, say your goodbyes and mount up. We've got a zero-one-thirty liftoff," Gunny Michealson shouted out.

"Hurry up and wait," Chili said, checking the time. "We'll be sitting on the apron for three hours, mark my word."

There was a general movement towards the buses, initially with the single Marines, then as the stick leaders scanned them off, the married Marines and sailors started to break away from their loved ones.

Miriam wasn't letting go, however, and Noah was fine with that. He could feel her tears, hot on his neck. The first sergeant was saying her goodbyes, and the smallest boy suddenly wasn't having any of it. He grabbed her leg, looking up at her with tears in his eyes. Her husband stepped in, kneeling, and after a few words, the little boy released her leg and took a step back, hand clasped together, tears still welling.

"I'll meet you on the bus," Chili said.

"Take care, Chill-man," Miriam said, her mouth muffled by Noah's shoulder.

"I will. You know me."

The first sergeant hugged each of her kids, then her husband, giving him a surprisingly passionate kiss.

Why am I surprised? he wondered. *He's her husband.*

It seemed like she tore herself away, and then the first sergeant he knew, the hard-ass, hard-charging Marine, reappeared as if turning a switch.

"OK, Sergeant Lysander, time to go," she said as she caught him looking at her.

With a sigh, Noah leaned back and with his hand on the top of her head, tilted her back and gave Miriam a deep kiss. He could taste the salty tears, and she returned his kiss with passion.

"I've got to go," he told her, dropping his hands.

She gave him one more hug, then released him.

"Come back," she said.

Noah turned and went to the second bus. His gear had been put into the mount-out boxes and was already on its way. All he had was his assault pack with what he needed for the transit. Staff Sergeant Cremineli was the stick leader, and he scanned off Noah with an "About time, Lysander."

Noah spotted Chili, who'd staked out two seats on the right side of the bus, leaving him the window seat.

"Thanks, bud."

They waited on the buses for another ten minutes while two more checks were made to make sure everyone was onboard, which was ridiculous as their wrist chips could simply be scanned again, but sometimes, the Corps worked in mysterious ways. Or as Lessa liked to remind them, if the Corps did something inane like this, it was because at another time, Marines had screwed it up. That was probably true, even if Noah couldn't imagine how a chip scan could have gotten screwed up.

Finally, the numbers must have matched, because the bus lifted off the deck and slowly started moving. Noah could see Miriam standing next to the first sergeant's husband, waving. A few of the Marines from the left side of the bus crowded over to the right to wave to their loved ones, but Noah had an unobstructed view thanks to Chili.

And then they were leaving the quad, on their way to a potential fight.

NOVYY URAL

Chapter 18

"We're up," Noah told Staff Sergeant Cremineli.

"About time. I'll report it in."

"About time," you say? It might have gone quicker if you'd helped Jankowski and me, he thought sourly.

Davis tanks were transported powered and locked down. The fusion generators were turned off, and no fewer than 284 digital and manual switches were thrown to keep the tank as rigid as possible during transit. Upon arrival, the generator had to be powered up, which took almost two hours in and of itself, and each of the lock downs had to be released. Many of them had to be released in particular order, and most of the manual releases required special tools to turn them. The bottom line was that with the two Marines clambering over and inside the *Anvil*, sometimes contorting themselves enough to make a circus performer proud, it had taken close to seven hours to make the *Anvil* combat ready.

Noah sucked on his bloodied knuckles, courtesy of balky releases in confined spaces, and resisted making a comeback. Cremineli knew he hadn't helped with the scutwork, so nothing Noah would have said would render the TC suddenly apologetic.

At least the *Anvil* was in good shape. For a piece of very robust equipment, tanks often had issues after interplanetary transport, which made no sense to any armor Marine. The Navy had huge ships that flew through space, and simply sitting in a ship's hold could affect a tank's calibrations? But the *Anvil's* readings were all far into the green, exactly as they'd been back on base. She was ready to go to war.

And she might have to. Charlie was moving out in the morning to take a position where Alpha had been hit. Nine Alpha tanks were still out there, trying to keep the two sides apart.

Noah looked over to the opposite ramp. Two of the Alpha tanks had been deadlined—they were not repair-worthy. Another two were now being fixed, or at least, the attempt was being made. One had its 90mm torn right off. Normally, a damaged cannon could simply be replaced with one of the other three systems, and Alpha had brought three of each with them. However, in this case, whatever had blown off the 90mm had torn the coupling ring out of the tank as well. When Noah had first seen it today, he'd been sure that if it was ever going to fight again, it would have to go back to the factory. But the Cat 4 crew was working hard on it, and they wouldn't be wasting time if they thought it was beyond them.

The *Roar's* gunner, Olia Destaffney, had been killed when the tank was hit, and she'd been damaged too much for resurrection. Noah hadn't really known her well, but the fact that she was a gunner hit him hard. Of Alpha's six KIA, three had been gunners.

Both the Novies and the Peters, as the Alpha Marines had taken to calling them, had thrown accusations at the other side for starting the skirmish, and they had accused the other side for hitting Alpha, but it was pretty clear that the Peters had fired the shots that had taken out the four tanks.

Not that Charlie Company could take any punitive action. No public acknowledgment was to be made, and Charlie's mission was to keep the two sides apart, just as Alpha's had been.

And look where that got them.

"Go get cleaned up, Ski," Noah told his driver. "And get some chow. We'll be on field rats for the next whatever."

Jankowski nodded, then wiped his own bloody knuckles on his tank suit, leaving two red bloody swathes on each thigh.

Noah shook his head and said, "And go get Doc to clean you up. Your nanos can't fight off every infection with you grinding the crud in."

He hopped off the *Anvil*, giving her a pat on the nose. She would be all he had between the two sides to keep him safe.

Chapter 19

"I've grubbing got you," Noah said, hitting the tag command as his AI registered the myriad of details about the vehicle that would enable it to locate and target it if given the command.

The small armored car had too many transmitters on it. He was sure this was the elusive command car for the Novie forces facing them. He felt it in his bones.

Noah had spent the last seven hours registering armor, geographic points of interest, and weapons systems. Already, he had 71 targets, all prioritized. Theoretically, he could trigger a combat sequence that would hit all available targets, in order, without him being part of the process. All he would have to do would be to initiate it. Combat rarely worked out so neatly, but even if he didn't trigger the auto sequence, his display would keep track of all of his target, alerting him when any of them were picked up by his sensors.

His targeting display still amazed him. As a driver, his display had been primitive in relation to his new one. At full data input, the flow of information was simply too much to comprehend, which made the option to go full auto a nice safety valve. But he also had the option to cut back on what was displayed, so he could keep the info blast at manageable levels.

He'd been searching for command and control targets all day, and as the armored car slipped back into defilade, he felt a moment of victory.

It would have felt better if he'd been facing the Peters, however. They were the ones who'd targeted Alpha Company. But the platoon, along with the first sergeant, were facing the Novies. Second and Third Platoons, along with the skipper and the XO and 150 meters behind him, were facing the Peters instead.

Noah could pick up the Peter targets on his display as they were registered, and if he spun his turret around, he was sure he could spot some as well. But First Platoon's job was to present a united front against the Novies.

With their infantry, either side could bypass the Marines to the flanks. Fifteen tanks just couldn't cover the frontage. Even when the Marine mechanized company arrived, they would still be hard-pressed. But as the skipper had briefed them, their presence was more symbolic than anything else. As an individual unit, they were too small for the mission. But as a representative of the Federation, they cast a much bigger shadow than their mere numbers.

As far as the Alpha casualties, Intel's point of view was that the Marines had not been specifically targeted—they'd just been caught in the crossfire.

The whizz of an artillery shell passed overhead, as if in emphasis to his thoughts. Noah waited, and the round landed somewhere back in the Peters' area. Supposedly, both sides were in a truce, but no one would know it with the harassing fire that kept passing overhead.

Noah reached into his thigh pocket and pulled out an apple. It was the last of four he'd taken from the ship, and here, 21 hours later, he'd already eaten two and given Jankowski one.

These were fab apples, without seeds or core. Noah liked real ones better, of course, but he had to admit these were better for eating inside a tank. There was no waste. He twisted his body to where he could see the staff sergeant. As usual, he was standing in his open hatch, and that meant he couldn't see Noah. Although it wasn't Marine regulations, the staff sergeant was death on food inside the *Anvil*.

Noah had felt the tiniest twinge of guilt when he'd given Jankowski one of the apples and not offering one to the TC, but he was able to push away that feeling with ease. And he didn't feel the least bit of guilt as he leaned back and bit into the red Braeburn.

The tart taste filled his senses. Noah knew he could be somewhat of an elitist with regards to food, eschewing fab food whenever he could. But fab or not, this was a good apple. Centuries of food fabrication had resulted in some superior products, and most of the population liked fab food even more than real. While organics were popular (and expensive) as vegetables and fruits, the vast majority of the human population preferred fab meats to that coming from actual livestock.

Noah had watched a show on the holo that decried the fact that 95% of all agriculture consisted of growing the 27 base products for mankind's fabricators. That allowed the teaming trillions of humans to be fed, but in the case of some sort of catastrophe, that left humanity vulnerable.

"I haven't seen any more targets designated," Staff Sergeant Cremineli shouted down at him. "You day dreaming?"

"No, I'm on it," Noah yelled back, taking a last swallow of the apple and starting to scan the Novie lines again.

As much as the staff sergeant was a worry-wort, he was right. Noah knew he didn't need to be contemplating humanity's food paradigm. He had a mission to accomplish, and the more targets he identified and register, the better it would be for them if everything went to shit.

Chapter 20

"Whaddaya tink dey're gonna do?" Corporal Jankowski asked in his heavy General Optics accent, one so thick that Noah could barely detect his driver's nervousness.

Jankowski was a good kid, but unlike most Marines coming to tanks, he'd never experienced any real operations, much less combat. He'd been born and raised in the vast megaplexes of General Optics, never getting off planet until he'd received his ticket to Camp Charles, and he'd stayed with First Marines on Tarawa for his first tour, never leaving the planet except for some live-fire training on some of the Corps' remote ranges.

You just might be getting your baptism of fire, Ski.

"What I think doesn't matter. All I know is that I've been trained, just like you, and we're more than capable of handling whatever we're ordered to do."

"Cut the gabbing," Staff Sergeant Cremineli shouted back. "I'm trying to monitor what's happening."

Unlike with Jankowski, the nervousness was evident in the TC's voice.

Noah could see Jankowski, who at 1.6 meters tall was easily able to turn around and look up at him. He waved his hand, indicating for the Marine to keep it quiet, but he added a smile.

If the staff sergeant would just wear his helmet, the other two Marines could shout at each other without interfering, but he preferred the ear bud, just as he preferred riding with an open hatch. Noah had long ago decided that the staff sergeant had a touch of claustrophobia, something that was at odds with serving in a tank, and something easily treated. But he hesitated to say anything. He wasn't a corpsman, and what he knew about mental issues is just what he'd seen on the holos.

He had a feeling that Chili might have told the first sergeant, however. It could be a coincidence that the first sergeant had positioned the *Night Witch* as the *Anvil's* wingman, but Noah was not a big believer in coincidences, particularly when the first sergeant was concerned.

Noah was pretty sure that events on the ground were progressing towards if not past the point of no return, and this was the real thing, though. Over the last three days, negotiations had begun to tilt towards Novyy Ural, which made sense as it was the Peters who had invaded the planet, not the other way around. Intel had warned them that with the tide turning against them, the Peters might try to strengthen their hand to improve their position. Now, every drone, every piece of surveillance was streaming in data that showed the Peters on the move.

Noah didn't think it was a feint.

Behind the platoon, the rest of the company, joined by what was left of Alpha, was buttoned up and deployed, guns facing the Peters. The Peter armor was formidable as a planetary armor, but Noah was fairly confident that when taken together with the extensive mining the attached four-man engineering team had accomplished, even the 19 Marine tanks should be able to blunt the advance of the Pytor Velikiy mech. What worried Noah more was the large numbers of infantry that were moving through the marshy wetlands along the sea two klicks to the north. They were somewhat safe from anything the Marines could throw at them while in the wetlands, but as they emerged onto the higher ground, the Marines could intercept them—not that they should, Noah thought. Tanks against infantry at close quarters rarely turned out well for tanks.

In two more days, the mechanized infantry company, which included a platoon of PICS Marines, would be on planet, and Noah would feel much better with them taking on the Peter infantry. But now was now, and the Marines had what they had. Noah had a sinking feeling that First Platoon would be ordered to meet the Peter infantry and stop them.

He was right. Less than three minutes later, the order was passed.

Noah shook his head—this wasn't a good idea. He ran a quick diagnostic on his rail gun, which hadn't changed one whit since the last one he'd run 30 minutes ago. His gun and targeting systems were at 100%. He did yet another inventory of his loadout.

One of the big advantages of having the railgun module on was that it could carry a lot of rounds. The 90mm, which in many ways was more versatile, was more limited in numbers carried. It may have a jacketless round, with the "shell" being part of the propellant, but a Davis could only carry 40 of the rounds vice the 150 railgun rounds in the standard anti-armor Mix 1. The *Anvil* had been loaded with Mix 3, which was 90 inert anti-armor rounds and 40 of the longer HE rounds, for a total combat load of 130.

The platoon re-oriented and drove off in a staggered column, pushing the speed to get into position. The lieutenant was ignoring the wetlands. The stands of coastal scrub were tall enough to cut visibility and dense enough to provide cover for the infantry, and for the tanks to enter the morass to try and meet them would be a costly mistake. Instead, she wanted to block off the higher ground, where trees and brush didn't make for great tank territory, but the ground itself provided for better maneuverability. Noah hoped that the imposing presence of five Marine Davises would give the Pytor Velikiy infantry pause.

"Check your Hashers, Ski," Noah said.

"Roger dat."

Noah had a feeling that the four APCD's would come into play. These were the final line of defense, so-to-speak, against infantry. Noah had the coax M104 alongside his main gun, and the staff sergeant had the .50 cal, which left monitoring the APCD's to the driver.

"You on low disc now?"

"At one."

With no friendly forces around them, the APCD's could be set at the lowest discrimination level. Anything out there that came within 40 meters would be engaged.

The forward Peter naval infantry had reached the edge of the wetlands. They had to know that the platoon was a klick away and closing, and Noah had hoped they would halt and hunker down, but they kept coming. It seemed they were serious.

But so was the platoon.

The lieutenant shifted them into a wedge, which gave them far more mutually supportive fires. Normally, this meant the *Anvil* would be the last tank on the right, but with the first sergeant and the *Night Witch* with them, she took the position just outside that of the *Anvil*.

"Watch the trees!" Staff Sergeant Cremineli shouted as Jankowski blasted through a small group of 5-meter tall trees.

Noah rolled his eyes, switched to the P2P, and then said, "If you button up, you won't be bothered by the little stuff, Staff Sergeant."

"I'll worry about that, Sergeant. I'm not going to burn when Jankowski hits a mine."

Noah almost added that the TC was becoming a liability. With his hatch open, the *Anvil* was not a secured platform. An energy shot of some sort could flow inside the tank through the hatch and cook all three of them. Part of him wanted to scramble over and pull his TC inside, but he held back.

They were closing to within 300 meters when an energy flare lit up his display. Noah immediately saw that it was a small rocket of some sort, too small to take out a tank, but he zeroed in his sensors to try and pick up who fired it. He heard the staff sergeant scramble back into the *Anvil* as the rocket hit the *Kiss of Death*.

"Hell, they got one of my Hashers," the lieutenant passed.

Noah pulled up the platoon commander's tank, and sure enough, there was a red "X" right where the right front Hasher should be.

Staff Sergeant Cremineli started firing the .50 cal, which sounded louder than it would if they were buttoned up. Noah looked at the *Anvil's* diagram, and he saw that the TC hadn't buttoned up, only gone to the open-protected mode.

Better than nothing, Noah thought. With only a ten-centimeter opening, the almost-closed hatch provided decent cover, even if it still left a route for energy fire to enter the tank. But for kinetics, it would take a pretty lucky shot to make it through the gap.

More small energy flares lit up his display. A moment later, one of the rockets hit the *Anvil* with a loud crack that rang the crew compartment.

"Lost my Hasher," Jankowski said, his voice rising.

"They're frigging targeting the Hashers!" Noah said as several more were knocked out among the platoon's tanks. "What's going on with the IA?"

And he immediately knew the answer. The Interactive Amor analyzed the incoming rockets, but it was deeming them as "not a threat." And while there wasn't any way one of the small rockets could manage to pierce a Davises armor, it was evidently enough to take out the Hashers.

Noah tried to spot a target as the five tanks closed the distance. One of the advantages of armor was that it tended to cow infantry, to break their will to fight. As a grunt, Noah had gone force-on-force against a Mamba platoon, and he'd been thoroughly impressed with them. He couldn't imagine what it would be like to face a platoon of Davises. He was sure the Peters would break.

But they didn't. The five tanks were putting out a tremendous amount of fire, but salvo after salvo of mini-rockets were fired, and more and more Hashers were knocked off line. The *Anvil* had lost both of her front Hashers, and Noah felt more vulnerable as they ploughed through the forest.

He had HE loaded for the railgun, but he didn't have a target. He could see the heat signatures of bodies on this firing display, and he sent streams of fire from the coax to engage them, but he wasn't sure he was having much effect. The fight was breaking up into individual actions.

And then the ill-fated *Ba-Boom* exploded. One moment, she was just to the *Anvil's* left front, and the next, she was a ball of flame. Noah caught a glimpse of a body scramble out to fall on the ground, but then they were past, with him on the coax and the staff sergeant on the .50 pouring fire into the brush ahead. Noah still didn't have any good targets, but his suppression fire should make them keep their heads down.

And then he did see someone, a short, stocky Peter, running right at them, a limpet in his hand.

Noah depressed the coax to its max and fired off a stream of fire, at least one round taking off the top of the Peter's head.

Jankowski kept driving forward as if to pound the soldier into the dirt when Noah shouted, "Hard left!"

"What the hell?" Staff Sergeant Cremineli shouted as the *Anvil's* driver obeyed Noah, slinging the big tank around and presenting its more vulnerable side armor to the enemy.

Noah heard the TC's hatch open, then the relatively muted shots of a Marine Ruger. Noah bent down to look out of his side port, and he could see his tank commander firing his handgun down to where the Peter was.

"Back on course!" he shouted.

"Button up!" Noah shouted back just as whatever the dead Peter had been carrying detonated. A blinding flash momentarily blinded him, but the *Anvil* barely rocked. The blast had been ten meters away, and the *Anvil's* sloping armor had deflected the shock wave. If Jankowski had kept driving forward and the mine or whatever detonated underneath them, Noah was sure things would have been different.

Staff Sergeant Cremineli flopped back into his seat, and Noah felt his anger boil over. TC or not, popping out like that to shoot what had almost certainly been a dead Peter—and ordering Jankowksi to turn to the right and putting the *Anvil* in danger—was more than he could take.

"Stay the hell buttoned up, Cremineli," he shouted, bending around to pull on the TC's arm.

He was going to give the staff sergeant an earful, and he'd expected the staff sergeant to resist, but he easily pulled him over— at least what was left of him. From the base of the neck on down, most of the staff sergeant was in good shape. But that was all there was. Staff Sergeant Cremineli's head was gone.

"I'm taking command of the *Anvil*," Noah passed on the platoon net, letting go of the staff sergeant's body.

"What?" Jankowksi asked. "We dint get hit."

"The staff sergeant's gone. Keep driving. You've got the .50 cal, too."

It was difficult to be very effective on the .50 from the driver's hole, but any rounds going out was better than nothing.

"Sergeant Lysander, what's your situation?" the lieutenant passed on the P2P.

"Operational. No damage."

"And Staff Sergeant Cremineli?"

"KIA. No chance at resurrection."

There was a pause, then, "Are you combat ready?"

"Affirmative. I've got the *Anvil*."

"Roger that. Then fight her."

Noah took another glance at what he could see of the staff sergeant's body. When Noah had released it, the body had flopped to the right, and if he didn't look too closely, it looked almost normal, as if the staff sergeant had just slumped over taking a nap. Noah felt dizzy, as if he was watching from afar.

"Screw it," Noah said, slewing his main gun around. He'd just told the lieutenant that he was the *Anvil's* commander, so it was time to command. He didn't have any confirmed targets, but he knew more infantry were emerging from the wetlands, and he wanted to show them who they were messing with. He sighted forward best he could, then fired the railgun, sending the HE round 200 meters before it hit a tree and detonated. In quick succession, he fired four more, each one clearing the way for the next to go further. Noah didn't know if he actually hit anyone, but the display was impressive, and he hoped it would disrupt the Peters.

"Did you activate the command display?" the first sergeant asked on the P2P.

Shit, no I didn't.

With Noah taking over as TC, the AI opened up the command display to him, but as he was also the gunner, the AI needed his active OK—it wouldn't do much good if it interrupted him as he was about to fire.

He accepted the display, but on a split screen. Suddenly, far more data appeared. He tried to take it all in, and that ended up with him doing nothing for fifteen seconds as Jankowski drove the *Anvil* forward.

"I've got it now, First Sergeant. Thanks."

"Keep your head in the game, Lysander. You can do it."

The *Anvil's* IA deployed, and a bright flash lit up the air 30 meters to their front. The Peters had launched something bigger at them, something the AI deemed a threat. Noah would read the analysis later to see what it was, but for now, that fact that it had been neutralized was good enough for him.

There was a good-sized explosion off to the *Anvil's* left side, right where the *Ball Shot* was, but she kept going. The *Ball Shot's* avatar remained a bright blue on the command display.

The lieutenant in the *Kiss of Death* reached their objective, a raised hill that looked on the overhead views on his display to offer reasonable fields of fire. As he pulled in, he could see it did, but only out to about 150 meters. A small swale cut diagonally across the slope, and a line of 10-meter trees jutted up from it to effectively conceal what was just over the other side. Jankowski pulled the *Anvil* up along the *Kiss of Death's* right side, 20 meters away. Immediately, the dreaded put-put-put of a Morrison was picked up, and the *Anvil's* alarm blared. The Morrison was the poor man's anti-armor rocket. Cheap to make and easy to operate, it was the mainstay of both militias as well as terrorist organizations. It wasn't fast, and it wasn't as advanced as anything major anti-armor weapon in the Marine Corp's inventory, but if it hit a Davis, the Davis would be dead. The Morrison packed a huge punch.

"Orient and then take the 104 and engage that grubbing sucker," Noah yelled at Jankowski.

His driver swung the *Anvil* slightly to the right to present a frontal aspect. A Davis' armor was strongest to the front, so if they were hit, that gave them the best chance at survival.

Noah took control of the .50 and immediately opened up, sending a stream of rounds to try and knock the missile out of the air. A nice HE blast with the railgun would serve him better, but already, the Morrison was too close for that. Streams of fire crisscrossed from the tanks to the left, adding to the curtain of darts and rounds. The Morrison was also fairly well armored, so the darts wouldn't be that effective, but anything could happen. The *Anvil's* IA deployed again, and less than 15 meters away, according to his display, the Morrison exploded. A stream of plasma erupted from the missile body—the missile might have been knocked down, but in a last, wrenching spasm, the warhead detonated. With momentum behind it, the plasma splashed against the front of the *Anvil*.

Noah was momentarily blinded by the flare, and a sudden acrid smell filled the crew compartment. Immediately, the fire control foam filled the compartment to Noah's right, from where the TC sat. Some of it splashed on him in the gunner's turret.

"Are we OK?" Jankowski asked, panic in his voice.

Noah took a look at the diagnostics. The .50 cal was out of synch-mesh, and most of the forward IA pods were out hard, but the *Anvil* was still up and running.

"We're OK!" he shouted.

The detonation of the warhead had been too far out, and instead of plasma burning into the crew compartment, it had splashed across the front, spreading the damage. The *Anvil* would need time in a shop, but she was still functional.

Noah sniffed, confused for a second, then he almost threw up. The smell that was assaulting his nose was the burnt body of Staff Sergeant Cremineli. Noah had forgotten that the commander's hatch was still open, and some of the plasma had splashed through, hitting the body. The fire control system had immediately sprung into action, but enough of the staff sergeant's body had already burnt to fill the *Anvil* with the smell.

Noah listened with half-an-ear to the command net as the lieutenant argued with the skipper for support, support that didn't seem to be forthcoming. The Peter mech was probing their lines, but not pushing hard. The skipper's concern was that if he pulled a platoon out to support First, then that would initiate a full Pytor Velikiy assault.

A red flashing triangle appeared on Noah's fire-control display. Noah immediately hosed down the target with the .50 cal without bothering to identify it. He'd have problems hitting anything at long ranges with the synch-mesh out, but at this close range, he could manage. Something was being pushed into position in the tree line, and that was enough for him. There were flashes of his rounds hitting something, and the triangle on his display disappeared.

With that target taken out, Noah tried to hear what the skipper was saying while still scanning for more targets at the same time. He wondered how the lieutenant managed it: communicating with higher headquarters, commanding the platoon, and fighting the *Kiss of Death*.

"Keep pumping out rounds, Ski," he told his driver as he realized the M104 had become silent.

"I don't have a target."

"They sure have us. Just keep firing in the tree line and keep their heads down."

What was that? Did he say retreat?

While he was telling Jankowski to fire, the skipper had told the lieutenant something that sounded like the platoon should pull back if their position became untenable. Noah hadn't caught all of it, but he couldn't believe that was what he'd heard.

Noah was not comfortable with their position. All of his training had pounded into his head that tanks do not go up against infantry like this, yet here they were. The so-called high ground they occupied as a blocking force was barely a bump in the terrain, and even on the reverse slope, they were hardly in defilade. Out in front of them, the Pytor Velikiy infantry were probing, firing when they could while minimizing their exposure. One tank had been destroyed, and both the *Anvil* and *Ball Shot* were damaged. If they didn't do anything to change the dynamic, attrition would knock out the entire platoon.

If the Peters would charge the platoon, Noah had no doubt that the four remaining tanks would wipe them out. But they weren't stupid. He was sure their commander was more than happy to keep up the pressure, wearing the platoon down. He was also sure that this was the point of main effort, and the armor facing the rest of the company was the fixing force. This is what the Peters wanted to do—that is, get the infantry into the Novyy Ural's AO. Then, and only then, if the Marines reacted to the disbursed infantry, they might advance their armor.

The fact that they launched this two days prior to the arrival of the mechanized infantry couldn't be a coincidence—not that the arrival of the rest of the Marines had been announced, but it wouldn't be too hard for Pytor Velikiy Intel to put two and two together.

Noah couldn't imagine that they really wanted to clash with the Federation. But as the skipper had said, if they could show strength and the ability to take more Novyy Ural territory, then they'd be in that much of a stronger position with the negotiations.

Another clang of a mini-rocket filled the crew compartment, but with both front Hasher's already out, it would take a one-in-a-million shot down the barrel of the M104 or the .50 cal to knock either one out.

Still, Noah couldn't let that go. He fired two of his remaining HE rounds into the tree line. He might not have hit anyone, but the trees exploding into kindling made him feel good.

He was about ready to fire another two rounds when 30 meters to his right, the *Night Witch* was hit, the explosion momentarily reflecting off of his ports.

"They're behind us!" the first sergeant passed.

Noah could see smoke rising from the rear of the tank, and he felt a rush of fear. He wanted to ask if they were OK, if Chili was OK, but he kept off the net. The *Night Witch's* avatar was still blue, which was a good sign, but unlike an infantry display, his didn't show individual Marines.

Noah rotated the .50 cal to the rear, searching for a target, but whoever had hit the *Night Witch* had already gone to ground.

"We're a mobility kill," the first sergeant passed.

"Can you fire?" the lieutenant asked.

"On manual."

The lieutenant barely hesitated before giving her orders.

"*Anvil*, on me while we break these suckers. *Ball Shot*, stick with the *Night Witch*, and both of you, give us support."

"You heard her, Ski. Stay with her."

With an unknown number of infantry behind them, infantry that had to have been infiltrated in before this action, the platoon was in a very vulnerable position. And with the *Night Witch* a mobility kill, they couldn't break out to the rear. The lieutenant had decided to take it to the Peters, to break their will. Noah didn't know if this was the best course of action, but it was better than just sitting there and waiting to be taken out one-by-one. He felt a surge of his warrior spirit as the *Anvil* answered Jankowski's call and sprang forward into battle.

The *Anvil* crushed whatever bushes and small trees were between the tree line and her as Noah peppered the wash with his .50 cal. An explosion in front of him made him flinch, but it was probably the *Night Witch*, firing her 90mm. She'd be much slower with Chili adjusting her aim by hand, but it was good to know the first sergeant had their back.

With the *Kiss of Death* to the left, the two tanks crashed through the tree line like avenging angels. They dipped down into the small depression, then shot up, going airborne. Noah thought he saw a Peter diving to get out of the way, but they were through so quickly that he wasn't sure.

"Clear to the right," Noah shouted.

Corporal Jankowski skewed the big tank into a right-hand turn, ready to run the tree line.

"Brush me off, *Anvil*!" the lieutenant passed.

Noah swung his .50 to the rear, his heart rising to his throat when he spotted a Peter clinging to the back of the Kiss of Death, hanging onto the exhaust pack handles. Lessa was pivoting the tank like a bull trying to throw its rider, but the Peter was like a leach.

Noah fired a burst, blowing the Peter off in a mist of pink as the big rounds tore him apart.

"Got him for you. You're clear," Noah passed, then, "Ski, bring her back to the lieutenant."

They needed to root out every Peter from the tree line, but with only the two tanks, they had to support each other as well. This wasn't gladiatorial combat, and he had to keep his head in the game.

"Thanks for the help," Lieutenant Moore passed. "Let's keep it tight."

Jankowski spun the *Anvil* around again and headed for the *Kiss of Death*. They still had to keep moving, pressuring the Peters and giving them no opportunity to react other than to bug out, but they'd be doing it as a team.

Explosions tore apart the tree line, the small, 20-centimeter trunks no match for the *Night Witch* and *Ball-Shot's* guns. Noah sensed that the Peters were about to break. Frankly, he was amazed that they'd held it together as well as they had. It was almost Marine-like—not what he'd have expected from a planetary naval infantry. But with just a little more pressure, they'd have to retreat or risk total annihilation.

"Back through the tree line," the lieutenant orders. "I want it leveled."

Jankowski maneuvered around a three-meter-tall boulder, and turned to orient back on the tree line when the *Anvil* suddenly lifted into the air, smashing Noah against his display. Before he could register what was happening, she smashed back down on her side, knocking Noah out of his seat and into the still foamed areas under the commander's cupola. He slammed into the far wall of the tank, with the staff sergeant's body cushioning him. Still, he was dazed and confused. The open hatch was right in front of him, and more on instinct that rational thought, he pulled himself over the staff sergeant's body and out of the *Anvil*.

He stared stupidly up at his tank, which had somehow landed on its side. It took him a long moment to realize she was slowly tipping over—towards him. He scrambled back as gravity won the battle, and the *Anvil* flipped over onto its top, the left side just missing Noah as he pushed back out of the way.

It was surrealistic. One moment, they were fighting their tank, and the next, 40 tons of Marine armor was upside down in the middle of a battle. It just wasn't registering.

Noah managed to get to his feet, rushing forward to check on Jankowski. The moment he cleared the front of the *Anvil*, he saw a Peter, half out of a spider hole, whose look of triumph immediately changed to surprise as he saw him. The soldier reached into his hole to try and pull out a rifle as Noah drew his Ruger. The Peter was quick, but Noah was quicker, and he put two darts into the man's chest, dropping him back into the hole. Noah ran to the hole and looked in, ready to fire again, but the man was dead.

He felt a moment of victory. He didn't know how the man had done it, but he was sure this was the guy who'd taken out the *Anvil*, and that pissed him off to no end. Then with a loud "Ski!" he turned and rushed back to his upside-down tank.

'Ski, Ski, you OK? You in there?"

A Davis did not have a bottom opening into the crew compartment. Marines entered and exited through the regular hatches or not at all. And with the *Anvil* upside-down, the hatches were blocked. What worried Noah was that the left tracks, which were next to the driver's hole, were mangled with whatever had flipped the tank.

"Ski!"

Noah, who was regaining his equilibrium, flopped down at the left side of the tank, scooching himself into a small gap, trying to see into the driver's blocks. He could barely see one of them—the forward blocks were buried in the dirt—and that one looked like there was blood coating it from the inside.

Rounds pinged against the side of the tank, right above his legs. Noah couldn't scoot any farther underneath, so he pulled himself out and ran to the back of the tank. He did a quick inventory. His helmet was gone, and his combat knife had disappeared. All he had was his Ruger and one extra magazine. That gave him 200—198 now, he corrected himself—of the tiny darts. He flipped the Ruger over and saw he had enough power for ten magazines, so his limiting factor was the number of darts. His handgun was for self-defense, not long-distance engagements. The darts were so small that despite their velocity, they could be moved around by the wind, and they rapidly lost energy due to air friction. Beyond 50 meters, they were pretty useless.

Sergeant Noah Lysander, UFMC, was not in a good position.

He slowly edged his head around the back edge of the *Anvil*, trying to see what was happening.

The *Kiss of Death* was approaching. Noah started to call the lieutenant before realizing that without his helmet and outside the tank, he was deaf and dumb. He took a step forward, waving his arms. At least one of the *Kiss of Death's* Hashers had been knocked out, but he didn't want the other front Hasher, if it was even working, to take him out.

The moment Noah stepped forward, another spider hole flipped open, and a head popped out, a metallic sphere of some kind in the Peter's hand. The soldier propped herself up, then brought her arm back as if on a bowling alley. Noah had no idea what the ball was, but he didn't want it anywhere near the *Kiss of Death*, so he brought his Ruger up, took his best firing range combat stance, and fired a five-dart burst. The soldier dropped back into the spider hole, and the silver ball fell to the dirt before slowly starting to roll down the slight incline, right at the tank. Noah didn't know if it would cover the five meters or so and reach her, but he didn't want the think even close. He ran forward, waving his arms wildly to get the *Kiss of Death* to turn to her left.

"Come on, Lessa, turn her!"

Behind the *Kiss of Death*, two Peter's appeared, rushing forward. He was pushing the range, but Noah fired off two more five-dart bursts, and one of the two fell, but that had alerted the other one who started to swing his rifle towards Noah, who dove to the ground.

The Peter had him dead to rights, but Noah brought up his Ruger just as the *Kiss of Death's* right rear Hamster sent out a sheaf of darts and almost cut the man in two.

Noah flinched. He'd never seen a Hamster fire from this vantage. If the *Kiss of Death* turned, he was close enough that it would do so again, not caring if he was a Marine or not.

Grubbing hell, he thought as he realized his only course of action.

With an "ooh-rah," Noah stood up and charged the *Kiss of Death*, expecting to be cut down at any second. The M104 fired, but not at him, and Noah angled slightly to the right to give his Ruger's much bigger cousin a clear line of fire. Without pausing, he jumped, getting one foot over the lip of the sloped armor at the front, which he used to push himself up and on top. Almost immediately as he cleared the muzzle, the *Kiss of Death's* 90mm fired, the blast almost making him lose his footing. He reached out to grab the edge of the MGS to steady himself, and from over the turret, his eyes locked onto another spider hole opening.

"How many grubbing holes do they have?" he wondered as he fired five more rounds at the shape that appeared, then disappeared from sight as the darts hit.

These holes had not just been dug. They spoke of preparation, preparation that had not been picked up by surveillance. Now, more than ever, Noah was sure that this was the point of main effort.

The *Kiss of Death* lurched into a depression, and Noah almost lost his footing again. He'd been standing up too tall, his legs straight. He bent them, using his legs as shock absorbers to keep standing.

With only one tank and a fair amount of ground cover, the Peters started swarming forward like wolves on a moose, trying to use numbers to simply overwhelm the *Kiss of Death*. On the other side of the tree line, the other two tanks were firing, and the *Kiss of Death* had all three weapons engaged, but still, some of the Peters were getting too close, and that's where Noah came in. He stood on the top of the tank, a last line of defense—an extremely vulnerable last line of defense. If the Peters were not so focused on the tank herself, they could have easily brushed aside the Marine standing on top of her. Still, he wasn't invisible, and he'd taken a round of some kind to the thigh. It hurt like hell, but his leg still held him upright, so he ignored it the best he could.

Most of the Peters were revealing themselves too early, falling to the Marine weaponry. Two Peters, however, had somehow kept their nerve through all the fighting, jumping up out of nowhere only 20 meters away, each holding one of those metallic spheres. Noah fired off 20 rounds before they fell, but the *Kiss of Death* kept moving forward, which would put them over the spheres. Noah didn't know what would happen if the tank ran over them, but he did know he didn't want to find out. He flopped to his belly, his leg screaming out at the abuse, and poked his head over the edge of Lessa's ports. With his left hand, he signaled for her to do a right turn.

Lessa's eyes only slightly widened as she jerked the *Kiss of Death* to the right, almost throwing Noah off the tank. Noah scrambled for purchase. If he slid off, he wasn't sure he'd be able to get back on. The *Kiss of Death* hit a bump, and that actually helped him, almost throwing him back to where he could stand.

Noah snapped off five rounds at a Peter who was at least 100 meters away, well beyond his range—or at least he tried to. After three rounds, his mag ejected. He couldn't remember going through

100 rounds. He inserted his last mag, telling himself to have some fire discipline-which he totally ignored when two more Peters rushed the tank. He fired off ten rounds, which were probably wasted as the coax fired as well, dropping both of them.

With Noah on top of the tank, he was cut off from everything else. For all he knew, the Pytor Velikiy armor could have started a full-out assault on the rest of the company. As a result of being off the net, his war had come down to him standing on the *Kiss of Death* and trying to drop anyone who came near. In a way, it was a much cleaner way to fight, something on which he could focus. And because of that, his gut was telling him that things were coming to a head.

If a Marine unit were in a defensive position and about to be overrun, the commander would order the FPF, or Final Protective Fire to be initiated. What that meant was that every Marine, whether within the defensive position or outside it with the supporting fires, would let loose a holy hell in an attempt to crush the assault. It was "Danger Close," and Marines could take casualties from friendly fire. There was a certain mindset when the FPF was ordered, a sense of now or never.

This wasn't a defense, at least from the Pytor Velikiy side. This was an assault against a lone Marine tank, but somehow, Noah sensed that same now-or-never mindset. There seemed to be a degree of desperation among the Peters. They weren't waiting until the *Kiss of Death* came close to spring their little traps. They were assaulting from farther out, but they were coming one after the other, they were coming in concert with each other. Noah kept firing, dropping some, missing others, doing what he could to keep them away from the tank.

And then he was out of darts. There was nothing more that he could do. He wondered if he should get off, but whatever happened to the *Kiss of Death*, he was along for the ride. He slid to a sitting position, almost crying out at the pain in his leg, and settled in as a spectator, watching to see what happened.

He could see at least six Peters from his vantage point, but there wasn't much he could do about it. The *Kiss of Death's* .50 cal fired upon two of them, looking like it hit one. But if Noah could see six, there had to be more on other sides of the tank. They were closing in.

And then, right in front of Noah, the glorious sight of the *Ball Shot* filled his field of vision as it crashed through a few of the remaining trees in the wash, guns ablaze. Tellie swung her tank around, 30 meters off the *Kiss of Death's* right rear, while Cliff turned the turret to the rear, covering the *Kiss of Death's* six. Together, both tanks surged forward, right into the heart of the Pytor Velikiy assault.

"Get some!" Noah shouted before simply resorting to unintelligible woops.

With the *Night Witch* providing covering fire, both tanks opened up with everything they had—and it worked. Finally, the Peters broke. They'd done amazingly well, but there was only so much a fighting force could take, and they'd reached their limit. Either on their own or by order of a commander who'd taken a hard bite of reality and initiated a retreat to save what he or she could of their fighting force—and Noah was willing to bet it was the latter— there was an immediate, if haphazard, retreat.

The *Kiss of Death* and the *Ball Shot* pursued to make sure the retreat was real before the lieutenant slowed down and stopped, willing to let the infantry withdraw.

Noah let out a sigh of relief. Somehow, they'd pulled through—and he'd pulled through. That feeling was tempered by the loss of Staff Sergeant Crimineli and maybe Jankowski as well.

The commander's hatch opened up, and a grimy-faced Lieutenant Moore popped out her head.

"You still hitching a ride there, Sergeant?" she said, a huge smile on her face.

"Yes, ma'm. I got a little dinged up here," Noah said, pointing at his leg, "and I'm a tanker. I don't walk when I can ride."

"Well, we're heading back to the first sergeant. I think the skipper will be pissed if we just leave her there. You want to maybe ride inside with us?"

Sitting still on a range, it was one thing to have four Marines inside a crew compartment. Having four Marines inside while driving one, or more to the point, possibly fighting one was not only discouraged, but against regulations.

Noah didn't even hesitate, though. He clambered over the turret to the commander's cupula, and after the lieutenant hopped out, slid inside, trying to fit his long body into the tiny space between the TC and gunner.

"Sorry about the blood," he told that lieutenant as she came back in and closed the hatch.

"That's what we have steam cleaners, for, Noah," she told him, then to Lessa, "head on back to the *Night Witch*."

Noah wanted to ask the lieutenant what had happened. Why had the *Ball Shot* come forward? Was that on her orders? Or had the first sergeant sent it? Was anyone coming from the company? Was there a full assault on the company, for that matter?

But she was back on the comms, doing what lieutenants do. She didn't need him interrupting her. He was feeling woozy, and he while he was very aware of his leg, he still refused to look at it. He tried to push himself farther away from the platoon commander and braced himself.

Riding four to a tank might not be too comfortable, but for him, it sure beat the alternative.

Chapter 21

"And how long will that take?" Noah asked Mr. Purile.

"Back at Archuleta? Two days, tops. Here? I'm guessing a week. We've got to do a lot of jury-rigging."

Noah had been afraid that the *Anvil* was down for the count, so the fact that the armor tech could get her back up and running here on Novyy Ural was amazing. But that didn't mean he wasn't still antsy to get her back into service.

Not that I can ride anyway for another couple of days, he admitted to himself.

Noah had taken a dart right through the meaty part of his left thigh. It hadn't hit anything vital, and he hadn't had to be CASEVAC'd off planet. Doc had simply cleaned out the wound and given him a nano booster. The independent duty corpsman had given him a light duty chit for six days and braced his leg to keep it immobile, but Noah wasn't going to stew on his cot with nothing but his thoughts to keep him company. With Corporal Lewis assisting, he'd hobbled over to the ramp to check on his tank.

Frankly, he was surprised that she'd looked as good as she did. She'd only been recovered the evening before, but with the left-side tracks and the MGS removed, she didn't look too damaged.

The mine had detonated directly under the front of the track with most of the slow-acting force pushing like a huge catapult, flipping the tank on its edge before it fell over. The body of the *Anvil* had suffered only a minor breach—minor in tank talk, not minor as far as Ski was concerned. The blast had turned parts of the *Anvil*'s armored skin into shrapnel, riddling the young Marine and almost tearing off his left arm. He'd been put into stasis and was already on his way back to the regional naval hospital on Shiva where it was expected that with eight to nine months in regen, he'd be as good as new.

Purile—"Pure Dick," as he was known to the Marines due to the civilian's often condescending attitude he displayed to the enlisted Marines—and his two-man team would simply weld a patch and then replace four of the road wheels and the track. "Easy-peasy," he'd told Noah.

Surprisingly, at least to Noah, was that fact that it was the damage to the gun weapons turret that had taken the most damage. The *Anvil* was a tough old girl, but she wasn't designed to be upside-down. The MGS had been driven into the docking ring when she fell over. The MGS was a lost cause and would be sent back to division at Camp Tainio to see what could be salvaged. But the docking ring had been warped, and a new MGS couldn't be installed as is. With the tight tolerances and connections, this would not be an easy fix, and Pure Dick was going to have to pull a miracle out of his ass to make the *Anvil* combat ready here on the planet.

"So, unless you have any further questions, *Sergeant*, I think I'll get back to doing my job so you can get back to doing yours."

"Yeah, sure. I'll just make myself comfortable."

Pure Dick narrowed his eyebrows and frowned, but he didn't say anything. Noah knew the tech didn't want him there, but there wasn't much he could say. A tank commander, even an acting tank commander, had every right to be there, observing. Most techs welcomed Marines getting their hands dirty, even for a Cat 3 repair, but Pure Dick wasn't most techs. He was happy to leave the crews to Cat 1 and 2 maintenance—and he'd report a crew in an instant if he thought they were shirking their duties, but for Cat 3 or Cat 4 repairs, he was far more possessive of the process.

"You going to hang, Knight?" Noah asked.

"Nothing else to do, so yeah, if that's OK," his new driver said.

Nothing else to do but think, I know.

Knight Lewis had been the *Ba-Boom's* driver, the only one to escape the tank when it was hit. Gunny Hattori, who was a short-timer whose retirement date had actually been a week ago, and Dirk del Moses, the *Ba-Boom's* gunner, had been KIA in the blast. The *Ba-Boom* was destroyed, and no Pure Dick magic was going to change that. If she were deemed salvageable, she'd be going back to the factory refurbishment center. So, Lewis was without a home, and Noah was without a driver.

One thing was nagging at Noah, though, and he shouldn't be hopping up on the *Anvil.*

"Knight, get up on her and, you know, sort of look inside."

Lewis looked at Noah with a confused expression on his face for a moment, then he blanched. It took a moment, but he nodded, then walked over to the *Anvil* and pulled himself up. Pure Dick gave him a dirty look that the corporal ignored. He hesitated, then leaned over the MGS connector ring and into the tank. He leaned back, and Noah could see him let out a big breath of air. The corporal turned, then jumped off the tank and came up to him.

"Clean. Nothing there."

The last time Noah had seen the inside of the tank, it had been covered in firefighting foam and the smell of burnt flesh. He'd been taken back before they'd extracted Ski, and he didn't know when Staff Sergeant Cremineli's remains had been removed. But he was pretty sure that no one had cleaned the *Anvil* in the field, and as far as he knew, there wouldn't have been a reason for any Marine to have worked on her. That meant that Pure Dick, along with Gretch Frieslander and Pop Maud, had cleaned out the mess inside. The team had arrived with Alpha Company, so this was the sixth tank that had needed this type of cleaning.

Suddenly, Noah wasn't as fed up with the head tech. That had to be pretty rough.

"So, Knight, tell me something about yourself," Noah said, wanting to move on.

"Me? Not much to say, Sergeant."

"There's always something to say. You're from Thomaston, right?"

"No, Tomas, not Thomaston."

"Oh, Tomas? Like in—"

"No, not like that at all. That's pure Hollybolly. It's not so bad, believe me."

"OK, so tell me, what's it really like? I mean, we're going to be getting pretty close, so you might as well spill."

Lewis seemed to be mulling things over, then he shrugged, and with a smile, said, "Well, parts of *Live or Die* were sort of true, but all that shit about the Ghost Oath, that's pure pig-piss. Never happens like that. I mean, when I was a sprout . . ."

Noah leaned back as Corporal Lewis began to tell his story.

****

"But I don't understand. I thought you said that was illegal," Noah said, almost an hour later.

"Yeah, it is, but not really. I mean, no one does anything about it. We just, I mean, it's fun, you know."

"Doesn't sound like fun to me," Noah muttered.

Noah had asked Lewis about himself because he wanted to know more about him, and he thought the corporal needed to focus on something else rather than on the loss of his two crewmates. But Lewis had turned out to be a good storyteller, and Noah had become interested in the story itself.

Maybe I need to focus on something else, too.

And it had worked. He felt better, watching Pure Dick bitch and moan over the *Anvil* and listening to the adventures of a young Knight Lewis on Tomas. If half of what Lewis was telling was true, then the real Tomas was much more interesting than what was portrayed in the movie.

"It's stupid, I know. But you have to consider it a rite of passage. Like humping Mount Motherfucker at Charles."

"Ah . . . I guess you have a point at that. I hated doing it—"

"Everyone hates doing it."

"But I was glad to have done it. Past tense."

"You were glad to have done what, Sergeant Lysander?" a high-pitched voice asked from behind him.

Noah turned around to see a short gunnery sergeant standing there. It took him a second before he tried to jump up, saying, "Drill Instructor Chimond . . . uh, Sergeant Chimond."

The gunny frowned, then looked down at the insignia on her collar and asked, "Have I been demoted, Sergeant."

"Oh, shit, no. I mean, sorry. Gunnery Sergeant Chimond. I just didn't expect to see you here. Did you just arrive with the mech company?"

"Yes, I came in with them. And you must be Corporal Lewis?" she asked.

"Yes, Gunny. Corporal Knight Lewis."

"In case you couldn't guess, I was Sergeant Lysander's DI at Charles, what, five years ago, was it?"

"Yes, Dri . . . Gunny. Six years. I'm just . . . I'm just surprised to see you here. And thanks for looking me up."

"Well, we'll be seeing a lot more of each other, Sergeant."

"Oh, yes. And we're glad you guys are here. Tanks with no infantry is bad news. But with you here, now, that's going to change things. And if you don't mind, I'd like to sit and chat if we have time, to find out what you've been doing since Charles."

"Oh, we're going to have time, Sergeant," she said, smiling as if she was enjoying an inside joke. "Starting now. What's the status of Charlie-One-Four?"

"The *Anvil*? Oh, she's taken a beating, but Pure Dick, I mean, Mr. Purile, the head tech, he thinks he can get her combat ready in six days."

"Come show me," she said, walking up to the *Anvil*.

Noah looked to Lewis, raising his eyebrows and shrugging his shoulders, then hobbled after the gunny.

Pure Dick was inside the open turret, back towards them as the three Marines reached the tank.

"Hey, Casper, you going to get this baby running, or is that more of your braggadocio?" the gunny asked.

Pure Dick turned around, disdain stamped on his face—until he saw who had spoken.

"Ivy, as I live and breathe, what brings you to this festering armpit of a planet?" he asked, a huge smile on his face as he pulled himself out of the tank and jumped down to hug the diminutive gunny.

"Orders, of course. Took me awhile to implement them, what with the company deployed. I had to hitch a ride with the Aardvarks to get out here."

What? She "hitched a ride" with them?

Noah had assumed she was with the rifle company, but that would mean she wouldn't have to hitch anything to get here. So, if she wasn't with the Aardvark platoon, and she wasn't with the rifle company, then she had to be assigned to Charlie. Noah had always assumed the gunny was infantry. She'd served with 2/3 during the Evolution and had fought on First Step, where his brother Ben had been killed. The gunny had even said that Ben and Yale Haerter had saved her platoon when they'd taken out the Armadillo that had been rigged as a mobile bomb. Then, there was the Silver Star she'd worn as a corporal, and it was usually the grunts who earned that. She'd also gone through a long regen, and as Noah had learned the hard way, when tankers were killed, it usually was permanent with no hope of resurrection.

And there was only one gunny in Charlie who was waiting a replacement—or had been waiting a replacement until the *Ba-Boom* had been destroyed.

"Uh, Gunny," he asked, interrupting a reunion that would normally have had his undivided attention, "are you, I mean, are you our new platoon sergeant?"

The gunny turned around, and her eyes clouded over.

"Yes. I should have arrived before you deployed, but the board was extended, so Gunny Hattori volunteered to stay on until I could arrive."

Shit. And that cost him his life.

"He was a damned good man and a friend," she said, her voice somber.

"Semper fi," Noah, Lewis . . . and Mr. Purile said.

"But we march on, right? And as I don't have a tank now, and you don't have a commander, Lieutenant Moore's assigned me to Charlie-One-Three. So, you two are my crew."

Chapter 23

Chili made a weird squeaking sound by using his hand up against his cheek, as Gunny Chimond left the E-5's tent where she'd just told Noah to meet her at the ramp at 1400.

"Cut it out, Chili," Noah said. "That's not copacetic."

"Well, you shouldn't have told me you guys called her 'Chipmonk' at Charles."

"I never did. Only some people did," Noah protested.

Chili was right, though. He should have kept his mouth shut, and he felt he'd betrayed the gunny. She'd been one of the few DI's who'd taken an interest in him at boot camp. The other DI's were all over Esther, who had been kicking ass there. They considered him the black sheep of the Lysander family, riding him hard. Chimond, who seemed to notice everything, had helped Noah get through the training.

And this is how I pay her back?

Short, somewhat squat, and with a high-pitched, almost cartoonish voice, she didn't look much like a Marine at first glance. But she missed nothing and was extremely competent. The fact that she'd just served on the staff sergeant's promotion board back at HQMC was a testament to her reputation.

Still, Noah was a little torn about her arrival. He respected her, and while he knew she could be demanding, he welcomed having her as their platoon sergeant. He wasn't as thrilled to have her as his TC. A Davis normally had a three-man crew, but they were still considered fully-manned with only two Marines. Noah wasn't a senior sergeant, but he'd hoped to remain as the *Anvil's* tank commander. Now, with the gunny taking over, that opportunity was gone.

It could be worse, Noah thought. *She's got to be better than Cremineli.*

And he immediately felt guilty for the thought. He'd never had much respect for the staff sergeant, but the man had paid the ultimate sacrifice.

No matter what he felt about the gunny taking over the *Anvil*, though, she was his TC, and he owed her his loyalty above and beyond for what she'd done for him at boot camp. He needed to bump up her street cred.

"I told you she earned a Silver Star, right?"

"Probably because she's so short the bad guys couldn't draw a bead on her," Cliff said to the laughter of the rest of the sergeants.

Noah rolled his eyes, then said, "What I didn't tell you was that at Charles, she was a corporal."

"So, there are other corporal DI's. Not many, but still . . . " Chili said.

"A corporal?" Barb McDavitt asked. "When the fuck did you graduate, Lysander?"

"I was with 9055. We graduated six years ago," he said, knowing that Barb had caught his point.

"Corporal to Gunny in six years? Bullshit."

"She's wearing the rockers, Barb."

"Holy fuck! Six years? What is she, a water-walker?" Chili asked.

Noah just shrugged.

"And she was with 2/3 on First Step during the Evolution."

"No shit? When was that? Ten years ago?" Cliff asked.

"Wait a minute," Barb said. "So, let's say she enlists during the Evolution. In five or six years, she only makes it to corporal? Then she not only goes to the drill field, but becomes a tanker and somehow makes it up three more ranks in six years? I'm calling bullshit."

Noah shrugged.

"Like I said. She's got two rockers, last I looked. Not only that, but the reason she was late reporting? Because she was sitting on the staff sergeant promotion board."

Barb leaned back in her chair, looking thoughtful. She was a big, burly Marine, almost as tall as Noah and so one of the tallest Marines in the company. A gym rat, she bulged with muscles upon muscles, which were very evident when she lounged around with her overalls top pulled down to her waist exposing her tight tanktop undershirt as she was doing now. Barb, a gunner in Second Platoon, tended to look down on those who didn't meet her standards of what a Marine should be, and she was harder on female Marines than males, as if any weakness a female Marine exhibited somehow reflected on her. She hadn't held back on her impressions of the gunny, but it seemed that Noah's comments had given her pause. If Chimond had made sergeant to gunny so quickly, if she'd been selected to sit on a selection board (probably the only E-7 on the board), then looks could be deceiving, and the gunny had to be good to go.

"OK, so she's hot shit. She still sounds like a chipmunk when she talks," Chili said. "So, are you going to call or not, Noah? Shit or get off the pot."

Noah looked down at his hand. He was sitting on a blockade, and if he could draw Barb or Chili to be more aggressive, that could give him the pot.

"I'll see you and raise you ten," he said, trying to show no emotion.

"Fuck, you've got nothing," Barb said. "Starting with having no balls. I'll see you."

The hand went around several more times before they presented, and Noah pulled in the pot. Cliff's spies would have won him the pot if he'd stuck with it, but he'd been right in egging on the other two Marines.

"So, you were just trying to distract us with all that crap about the gunny? That's how you're going to be playing it?" Chili asked.

"We do what we have to do. And with that, my fellow sergeants, I'd better go round up my driver and see what the good gunny wants," he said, standing up.

"Fuck that shit. You've got time for another hand," Chili said. "Sit."

"As much as I'd love to do that, I must be off, duty and all that, doncha know," he answered with a dramatic flourish.

He stepped back from the ammo container that had been serving as a card table, barely noticing the twinge in his leg. He'd been taken off the brace since the day before, and it frankly amazed him that only a week ago, he'd had a hole punched right through his leg, and now, he could go on a ten-klick forced march if he had to.

Battle was a four-hand game, no more, so as soon as he stood up, Myra-Jean Sassoon jumped off her cot and took his place. Chili was already dealing the next hand before Noah was out of the tent.

The E-4 tent was two steps away, and Noah stuck his head in the portal.

"You get the word?" he asked Knight.

"You heading out already?" Knight asked, checking the time.

"No reason to delay. She's probably going to tell us the *Anvil's* new name, so we might as well get it over with."

Lewis shrugged and pulled up his overalls. He'd been in the *Ba-Boom*, not the *Anvil*, so that name meant nothing to him. He joined Noah as they started towards the ramp, which had been expanded to hold not only the twenty-two tanks, but now six Aardvarks and the retriever. Two Aardvarks and a Davis were on sentry duty, but still, twenty-seven armored vehicles took up a lot of space.

The two crewmates headed for Bay 1, the expeditionary maintenance bay where the *Anvil* was being repaired. Noah could see the gunny on top, deep in conversation with Pure Dick.

"Gunny, you wanted to see us?"

She looked around, then checked the time.

"You're a little early, but that's OK. I think we're about there. Charlie-One-Three is combat ready, right, Casper?"

"As ready as she's ever going to be out here. Which is a freaking miracle, if you ask me, that we got as much done as we did. Not every team would have bothered, you know."

And she did look pretty good, Noah acknowledged. Maybe a little rough, but she looked ready for war. His eyes strayed to the front of the tank where the name was normally painted, and it was blank, covered over during the repairs.

In older versions of armor, a tank or APC's name was painted onto the main gun, but with a Davis and its interchangeable MGS, the name had been shifted to the prow of the tank, just where the frontal armor started sloping to the back.

He felt a degree of loss, which was stupid, he knew. A name was just a name, nothing more. A tank was her crew, not a label. And "Anvil" wasn't even his choice. Staff Sergeant Cremineli had named her, and he'd never even told the others his reasoning behind the name. But Noah had never known another tank other than his training platform, and it hurt a little to let that go.

"Tomorrow, we'll put her through her paces in a mini-shake-down, but there's one more thing we have to do," she said as Pop walked up, a small can of gold paint in his hand.

"I can't keep calling her Charlie-One-Three," the gunny said.

Right on that point, he agreed.

It had simply sounded wrong for her to be using the platoon designation. Crews didn't do that for their own tanks.

"So, we come to the name. My first tank as a commander was the *Boudicca*."

Noah kept his face neutral. "Boudicca" was not a name that inspired anyone, he thought. It wasn't bad, but an ancient warrior queen didn't convey the power of a tank. The first sergeant's *Night Witch*, which Chili had told him was in honor of a squadron of female pilots back in WWII on Earth, was better if going the historical route, in his opinion. But he guessed it wasn't that bad of a name. He whispered it as if trying it out.

"And I intend to keep that, with *Boudicca II*. But not yet."

Not yet?

"I'm only with you two until we get back to Archuleta. You'll get a new TC, and I'll be in the platoon sergeant's position with a new Davis. So, I don't think it's right for me to impose. This is your tank, and you'll be serving in her. So, what do you think?"

Noah was surprised at the lift that simple statement gave him.

"I think it's up to the sergeant, Gunny," Lewis said.

The gunny looked at Noah and asked, "Well, Sergeant?"

Noah hadn't been prepared for this. Like any tanker, he'd poured over names to have just the right one for when he'd become a commander, but this was too quick. Not that there really was a choice. Only one name would do.

"*Anvil*, Gunny. I think we should keep her as the *Anvil*."

Chapter 24

"Hug the left," the gunny told Lewis. "That scree on the right can make the tracks slip."

Noah hadn't even considered that, but the gunny was right. There wasn't much in the way of scree from the hillside, but even the small patch ahead could affect the *Anvil* if Corporal Lewis had to apply the power while they were on it. And if the Peters were going to ambush them, the spot would be perfect for that very reason.

Riding with the gunny was a 180 from riding with Staff Sergeant Cremineli. Where the staff sergeant was aloof and uncommunicative, the gunny kept up a constant dialogue, giving directions and offering observations. It might have been annoying to have a commander getting into the weeds like that, but her tone was neither critical nor condescending; it had more of a teacher-student feel. Already, Noah thought he'd learned more over the last four weeks with her than he had in almost two years now as a tanker. If he'd slightly resented her for taking over the *Anvil* before, that had long-since vanished. Every thing she taught Lewis and him was going to make him a better commander once he got his own tank.

It had helped that things had been fairly quiet since the fight. When Pure Dick had declared the *Anvil* battle ready, that hadn't been quite the case, as they'd found out during the initial shake-down. There had been some issues with the weapons turret. They'd gone back to the ramp where the gunny had taken Pure Dick aside, and Noah and Lewis had wagered how long it would be before the head tech erupted. To their surprise, he seemed to take it in stride, and when he jumped inside while Noah demonstrated the traversing problems, he'd simply nodded and told him his team would get right on it.

Even that was a lesson for Noah. There tended to be a bit of mutual disdain between the Marines and the civilian tech teams, but they were all in this together, and it didn't make sense to be at odds with the very people who kept their tanks up and running. He still thought Pure Dick could be an arrogant asshole, but that didn't mean they had to be antagonists with each other.

And now the *Anvil* purred. She could have been right out of the factory on Trappist 115. Noah wasn't sure how the gunny managed to be on a first-name basis with Pure Dick, but he was pretty sure that relationship had been good for the *Anvil*.

That was pretty important right at the moment. A slipped track, a problem with the motor now, and they could be in deep shit.

The *Anvil* was the lead in a two-tank patrol, and Noah felt the eyes of a thousand Peters on them. The day before, the *Kiss of Death* and the *Ball Shot* had gone out on a similar patrol. Today, it was the *Anvil* and the *Evangeline* from Second Platoon. The lieutenant hadn't encountered anything, but to Noah, all that meant was that the Peters had been alerted to the patrols.

Most of the Marines thought that the Pytor Velikiy forces had been spanked pretty badly and that they would lick their wounds and let the negotiations progress as they willed, but Intel was picking up signs that they were angling for another confrontation, one of which they could take advantage. No one thought they'd assault the combined task force, but they couldn't hit the Novyy Ural militia without going through the Marines. But a quick strike against a target of opportunity might be in the cards.

And what was two tanks off on a patrol but a target of opportunity?

"Hold up, Knight," the gunny ordered. "Noah, keep your attention here."

Noah looked at his display at the swash of color she'd splashed over a cut in the hills to the right. He wiped the color off, then focused 40% of his scans to the area.

The tanker in him didn't like sitting still. Tanks were made to move—they were not simply pill boxes that could be transported from position to position.

His scanners picked up some noise, but it could be anything. There was certainly no confirmation that the Peters were up there ready to pounce. But this had been a war of cloaking and spoofing on both sides. Their patrol was running cloaked, although not to the full employment of their capabilities. They'd be invisible to low-tech surveillance, but not to visuals nor to some of the more advanced scanners known to be in the Pytor Velikiy T/E.[5]

Noah's display flashed amber, and he grimaced. Gunny had just gone active, pinging the shallow valley in front of them. That ping could be picked up by almost anything. If there were Peters searching for them, that had probably given their position away. Instinctively, Noah hunched down in order to look into the sky, as if he could see the Pytor Velikiy version of the Marines' hummingbird and dragonfly drones.

"OK, I think that's long enough. Let's move on," the gunny told the corporal.

Lewis drove the *Anvil* down the slight decline, keeping off the trail itself and onto the grass on the shoulder. The *Evangeline* followed in trace. If the *Anvil* didn't hit a mine, neither would she.

Unless it's command detonated, and they want to block our retreat, Noah thought, then mentally kicked himself for bringing up yet one more thing that could go wrong.

He'd been less stressed during the last battle, if that made sense. There, he'd known what faced them. Now, he didn't know, and his imagination was running rampant. For all any of them knew, the entire Pytor Velikiy force was waiting in ambush for them, eager to take out two lone tanks.

As if she could sense his stress, the gunny said, "Nice and easy. We're just on a routine patrol between camp and the Peters, right?"

Noah focused on the area the gunny had highlighted, trying to occupy his mind. If they were hit, he was determined to strike back, and strike back hard.

But nothing happened as the two tanks slowly traversed the valley. In another time and place, he'd be happy with the hatches open, just taking in the sunny day. This area had been untouched since being revegetated with Earth trees and plants, and the wilderness was beautiful. It was hard to believe that the platoon had been in combat only 40 or so klicks to the east just four weeks ago.

---

[5] T/E: Table of Equipment

"Looks like this is coming up dry," Lewis said as they reached the edge of the valley—which was also the limit of their patrol.

"I wouldn't be so sure of that," the gunny said. "Let's turn her around and start back, but I want to see if we can make our way a little closer to the west, along the base of the hills."

"Off the trail?" Lewis asked.

"Affirmative. If it gets too congested, we can bring it back."

"Roger that."

Drivers generally loved to go cross-country. Noah certainly had while he was a driver. As a gunner, however, he was more concerned with his fields of fire. And if the gunny had been right about the high ground, then by driving the *Anvil* along the base of the hills, he'd be far more limited as to what he could engage if the need arose. There was also another problem—even if he was able to engage, a tank bucking up and down over rough terrain made keeping his gun on target all the more difficult.

"Yee-haw!" Lewis shouted as he smashed through the low foliage as if he were back on Quintero Crag and not in a potential combat situation.

Noah struggled to keep his butt in the seat as he was bounced around. He was getting beat up despite jamming his feet against the console frame in an attempt to lock his body into place.

At least we're not going to hit a mine, he thought. *They can't have enough to mine the entire wilderness.*

"Heads up," Gunny passed to both tank crews. "Be ready to bug out."

Noah looked at his display, wondering why her caution. He was still receiving some of the same noise, but nothing reached the level of an alert. He wasn't against caution—sometimes it was the best course of action. But he wasn't sure why she'd said it now.

He pulled up an overhead view, trying to figure it out when an energy bloom appeared, right at the cleft in the hills.

"Incoming!" he shouted.

"Hard right to the trail," Gunny said in a calm voice.

Lewis almost slung the *Anvil* around, dashing to the trail some 300 meters now to the east. Alongside them, 50 meters away, the *Evangeline* followed.

Noah rotated the turret until it was pointing to the rear. He ran a back trace on the missile just as the *Evangeline's* IA fired, knocking the missile out of the air. Noah ignored that, firing two of his 90mm HE rounds. His display started flashing with data points. Mortars were firing from beyond the cleft on the reverse slope, protected from retaliatory fire from either of the Davises, but Noah didn't think they had a round that would be too much of a threat to either one of them.

Noah didn't like riding facing the rear of the *Anvil*—it made him queasy—but he was part and parcel of the turret, and the known enemy was up on the high ground. But his display was beginning to show more forces, and as he expected, others were closing in on them, trying to cut off their retreat. He looked to his left and caught a glimpse of the *Evangeline* as she bounced along, her turret to the rear as well, so Noah rotated to his right to be able to react quicker as soon as he had a target. He wouldn't have been able to do that with the railgun. The barrel was long enough to protrude well past the side of the tank, and with them plowing through the vegetation, it could get caught on something sturdy and become damaged. The 90mm, however, was much shorter, and not nearly so vulnerable.

Explosions started to land around them as they reached the trail and Lewis started accelerating up the incline. The same tiny rockets that had knocked out the Federation tanks' Hashers in the first battle flew at the two tanks in waves, but with them at close to 70 KPH, none of the rockets hit their mark, instead flying past or impacting on the polycero armor without effect.

The *Anvil's* IA deployed twice, but Noah barely noticed as he started putting out rounds, simply aiming them as area weapons.

"Back off ten KPH," the gunny told Lewis.

Shit! Noah thought as he fired off another shot, his instincts screaming to speed up, not slow down.

He'd used 12 rounds without a confirmed kill, so he switched to the M104 and sprayed the hillside. A tank was not the best weapon of war against disbursed troops, so he thought his 104 might be a little more effective.

"Start the smoke," she passed to Staff Sergeant Patel, the *Evangeline's* TC.

Noah couldn't help but to glance back where a cloud of smoke started streaming from the back end of the tank.

Something hit the *Anvil* with a clang, but she never faltered. Along their entire left flank, the forest was swarming with what had to be at least a hundred soldiers, all converging on the two tanks to cut off their route of escape.

And two M249s opened up, raking the hills with 20mm rounds. Lewis spun the *Anvil* to a stop, facing the hillside as two PICS Marines rushed past them and on into the trees. Noah could see the smaller figures of straight-leg infantry as they advanced to meet the Peters.

Noah finally let out a huge breath of air. Their job was done. They'd suckered the Peters into an ambush. Tanks were not the best choice against a disbursed infantry force, but nothing was better against a foreign infantry than a company of infantry Marines. Or at least a company minus. One platoon of Kilo was over the line of hills and would now be converging on the weapons systems at the cleft. Here, in the valley, a platoon of PICS infantry, the remaining straight-leg rifle platoon, and the weapons platoon were taking it to the numerically larger, but far less capable Pytor Velikiy unit.

"You can turn off your smoke now," the gunny passed as the little generator on the back of the *Evangeline* kept spewing out the smoke that Pure Dick had rigged up to simulate a damaged tank, one that the Peters could kill if they just pushed a little harder.

The smoke was now settling around them, blocking visibility. Their role as bait was over, but they were supposed to be in support of Kilo now.

Not that it mattered, in the end. Noah never fired again. The Peters, intent on catching the fleeing Davises, must have been shocked by the sudden appearance of the infantry. Noah would have been, too. Who would have thought that the infantry would have infiltrated in three days prior to take positions, dug into spider holes and covered with tarnkappes? Who would have thought that a platoon of PICS Marines could get their combat suits into position, and then lay flat, for three days, not moving?

Well, the Marines would have thought it, but evidently not the Peters.

The plan was that the ambush would have been sprung the day before, but the Peters hadn't cooperated. They had today, though.

Noah almost felt sorry for the Peters. If he'd had to sit in a spiderhole for three days, if he'd had to lay down inside a PICS for three days, he'd have been ready to unleash holy hell on the reason for that.

Noah had popped open his hatch when the first of the prisoners, nine of them, were escorted back to the trail. Several glared up at him as if this was all his fault, which he easily shrugged off. He kept his 90mm pointed at them, but that was mostly for show. They'd surrendered, and the Peters had kept to the Harbin Accords so far, so the Marines owed them the same.

All told, 31 prisoners were taken, eight of them wounded and being treated by the corpsmen. Another 40 or so Peters had been killed, while the rest had managed to escape into the hills. Another 12 had been captured up in the cleft with 3 KIA. All at a cost of three Marine WIA.

Those numbers were astounding, to Noah. They'd had three KIA alone from the platoon in the first fight while only achieving about the same kill numbers against the Peters. Noah was proud of being a tanker, and he was a firm believer in a Davis' capabilities, but this only cemented his deep-set belief that the right weapon had to be used against a specific enemy. A tank might have problems against a well-trained, disbursed infantry, but it could take out a fighting position with ease that might hold up an infantry platoon for a day.

The Marine Corps was not considered a combined arms unit for nothing, after all. Now if they could only get the politicians to understand that.

Chapter 25

Noah tried to pull himself forward, but with his legs doubled up, it was hard to get leverage. He took a deep breath, readied his left hand, then pushed, jamming his body under the MGS' undercarriage to the point where he could just reach the access port. He touched his handheld to the port's interface, and a small beep acknowledged the transfer of data.

Now to get out of here.

He'd pushed himself in, but he couldn't push out. Squirming like a beached fish, he slowly edged back until he could grab the PSC-44's vertical handle and use it to extract his body. That wasn't what the handle was designed for, but he had to use what was available to him.

"Gunny, why the heck do they put these ports and readouts in so many grubbing hard-to-reach places?"

"For the same reason I told you three days ago. Simply because."

Noah shook his head. It made no sense. All of the displays and ports should be in easy-to-access places. It took a frigate's captain less time to get his ship's readouts that it took the three of them to get the *Anvil's.*

He glanced at his handheld's display.

"Right at 120. Perfect, just like every check for the last five months."

"As it will be for the next five months," the gunny said.

Noah's heart fell.

"Five more months? You heard something, Gunny? We've got another five months?"

"No, I haven't heard anything, Noah. But we were supposed to be relieved three months ago, and that didn't happen."

"Do you think it'll be that long, though? I mean, aren't the negotiations about over?"

"You must be mistaking me for some First Ministry hack. I'm just a lowly gunnery sergeant, keeping my head down and trying to do my job."

Noah didn't feel mollified. The idea of sitting on the planet for another five months was frightening, and he didn't think she should be joking about that.

The last five months had been a long, boring, exercise in wasting time. After the counter-ambush in the hills, the Pytor Velikiy command had agreed to a cease-fire. The task force had thought they would be recalled, and they'd even received a tentative date when an FCDC battalion was to relieve them. But the battalion didn't come, and they were extended on planet. So, for five months, they went out on patrol every three days, then sat back at camp for two. There weren't enough makeshift gyms they could build, enough books and flicks they could watch, that could fill up the time and keep their minds off home. Marines were dedicated hard-chargers, but they fared best when actively taking it to the bad guys. They were not a good police force.

More than a few fights had broken out, and the task force commander, a major from the regimental staff, had been busy with non-judicial punishment on close to a daily basis. Time-filling classes were now the norm for the grunts, and for the tankers, it was maintenance, maintenance, maintenance.

Noah's PA buzzed for attention, and he pulled it out.

"The first sergeant wants to see me," he told the other two.

"Well, then, I guess you'd better go see her. She's not been in a mood, you know."

"Oh, I know, Gunny. We all know."

It was true. As the time slowly fragged on, she was becoming more and more of a, well, asshole would be an appropriate term. Nothing she did was wrong, per se, and all was according to regs, but she kept demanding stricter compliance with the skipper's orders, letting nothing slide.

Noah wiped his hands on his overalls, then looked down at the grime that left behind. He momentarily considered changing into his other set, newly cleaned, but then shrugged that off. He was a tanker, and they were on the ramp. Being dirty was part of the job description.

The company office was only 40 or 50 meters from the ramp, and it took him only a minute to reach the igloo. There was no knocking on the hatch as when back in civilization, so he simply walked in.

The new igloos were impressive, he had to admit. Shipped folded up and fitting on a single pallet, when inflated, the outer skin foamed up, becoming hard within a few minutes. Air was filtered in by some sort of osmatic process, but noise was effectively blocked. After clanging around the ramp, inside the igloo was quiet and cool. If they could only get more of them for berthing, life on Novyy Ural would be much more comfortable.

"Sergeant Lysander, the first sergeant's waiting for you," Corporal Wythe, a driver from Third who had the company duty for the day said.

"I can see him, Wythe," the first sergeant said from her open office, which consisted of a partitioned-off section of the rear of the igloo. "Come on in, Sergeant."

"Yes, First Sergeant? You wanted to see me?" he said as he entered her office.

"We just received word from the Naval Hospital at Tainio—"

"About Miriam? Is she OK? What happened?"

The first sergeant held up a hand to stop him, saying, "She's fine, she's fine. And Chance is fine, too."

"Chance? Who's Chance?' he asked, confused.

"You son? That Chance?"

"My son?"

Noah sank onto one of the two chairs in front of the first sergeant's desk.

I'm a father? he asked himself. *I am a father!*

Noah had been expecting this, but not for another week-and-a-half, and it hit him hard. It was difficult to fathom.

And Chance? he wondered as the name sunk in. *What happened to Ryck?*

"He's your first, right?"

"Uh, yeah, First Sergeant. I thought we'd be back by now, and I'd be there."

"Doesn't always work out. I wasn't there for my first two," she said.

"Really? How did you handle it?"

The first sergeant looked at him as if he was an idiot, then said, "Uh, Sergeant Lysander, in case you haven't noticed, I'm a woman? You know, as in I'd have had to be there?"

Noah looked at her, trying to make sense of what she said before it sunk in.

"Oh, yeah. Of course, you were there. Sorry."

"I was just trying to lighten the mood, but you new fathers can get so discombobulated when you get the news. I was there, but Fierdor wasn't. He was deployed."

It took a moment for him to realize that Fierdor must be the first sergeant's husband's name.

"Uh . . . how did he take it?"

"Don't know. I wasn't there with him. But first, congratulations. Second, the skipper's getting a line back. Go to the comms shack, and you'll be able to talk to your wife."

"But's it's just after zero-two-hundred there," Noah said.

The first sergeant just let out a single laugh, then shook her head before saying, "She just gave birth, Sergeant. She'll be up, believe me."

"Oh, yeah. I guess so," he said, then as it all started to sink in, he started feeling excited, and he said, "I'm going over there now. Thanks, First Sergeant!"

He ran out of the company office and over the last of the six igloos.

The skipper was coming out as he rushed up, and he said, "Congratulations, Sergeant Lysander. I've cleared a line back for you. Mr. Drury said he'll have it in about five."

"Thank you, sir!" Noah said, barely waiting for the skipper to clear the door before he entered.

Mr. Drury was a retired Navy communications specialist, now working for the Corps. He and Staff Sergeant Oscar Lenz were the entire communications detachment for the task force. Noah barely gave a glance to the stretched-out figure of the staff sergeant, snores emanating from under a blanket, as he ran in.

"Congrats, Sergeant. Just hold on a second while we're routing."

Interstellar comms had been an issue since mankind started exploring the stars. The solution was hadron communications, where twinned receptors created by split-manufacturing allowed for instantaneous comms. The expense and requirements for military-only secured lines meant that a small task force such as this one had only two lines back to division. They could hook into the planet's commercial communications nodes, and for a call about a new child, that should be good enough, but their orders had been to limit all comms to the official military lines.

Noah waited impatiently until the routing was done, and Mr. Drury pointed to the small desk. Noah jumped up and sprinted to it.

"Miriam! How are you?" he asked her.

She smiled and said, "Tired, but happy. I'm glad I did it this way."

"This way," he knew, meant without drugs, a practice that had been becoming more popular over the last decade or so. She looked tired, though, her hair a mess, her face still a bit flushed, but she was smiling and seemed at peace with herself.

"Uh, where's, uh, Chance?" he asked, stumbling over the name.

She let the pickup pan down, and a small, very red body was at her breast.

"Say hello to Daddy, Chance," she said.

Noah didn't know what to say. That little guy was his son, and a feeling of protectiveness flowed through his body. It killed him that he was on some far-off planet, doing nothing, while his son—and wife, of course—were so far away.

"I'm so sorry I wasn't there, Miriam. I wanted to be, you, know."

"I understand, honey. It is what it is. Mann and Val were here, so it was OK," she said, panning the pick up to where her friend Mann and his wife, a staff sergeant with 1/11, were sitting.

Both waved and said "Hi, Noah," in unison.

Noah felt a small pang of jealousy. Mann and Val lived in the same complex as they did, but Noah hadn't really gotten to know either one of them well, yet both of them had been at the birth of his son.

"Thanks for being there with Miriam," he said, pushing his jealousy back.

"No problem. We love her," Mann said. "And she'd do the same for us."

Miriam panned the pickup back to her chest where Chance was suckling.

It was probably his first meal, he realized. *I wonder how many other firsts I'm going to miss?*

"What do you think? Isn't he beautiful?" she asked him.

"He sure is. Chance. I didn't know we'd considered that," he added, wondering if should even mention it.

"Oh, you know how it goes," she answered, seemingly unconcerned. "I know we mentioned 'Ryck' and a few others, but we never really decided on anything. And when they asked me here, I had to give them something, so I just told them Chance. Chance David Lysander, my little man."

Noah didn't know what to say, but he was a little hurt, and that dampened his joy at becoming a father. As he remembered it, they'd pretty much decided on Ryck. He'd told Miriam it was up to her, but that was him trying to be the understanding husband. He hadn't expected her to pick something entirely new.

I'm not going to let that spoil the moment, he admonished himself. *And Chance isn't a bad name. Kind of a strong name, in fact.*

"Chance is fine, and I can't wait to see him."

"When are you getting back?" she asked.

"Who knows? Soon, I hope."

Even if this was a secure line, deployment dates were never discussed in a call like this. But Noah hoped "soon" was OK to say.

"Oh, he's asleep," Miriam said, pulling Chance back and turning him around. "Here, look at his face."

If he'd felt the tug of fatherhood before, the minute he saw Chance's face, that tug became a tsunami. He wanted to reach into the screen and take his son into his arms.

He knew they weren't going home today. They weren't going home tomorrow. But they'd better go home soon or he was going to go UA and get back somehow to see his son, Marines be damned.

QUINTERO CRAG

Chapter 26

Noah stood on his seat, half of his body out of the hatch as Llanzo turned the corner in trace of the Gunny. The *Boudicca II* was barely a month old, and she still smelled of the factory, but Noah wasn't jealous. He was happy to be with the *Anvil*.

"Keep it tight. We've got eyes on us," he told his new driver.

"Roger that. I've got it."

Knight Lewis had gone with the gunny as the driver of the new Charlie-One-Four, which had been his original position on the *Ba-Boom*. Sergeant Llanzo Shearer had been with Third Platoon, but with the personnel shortage, he'd been pulled to bring the *Anvil* to a combat-ready status. Technically, Noah was still the gunner, but he was also the acting tank commander.

Noah was tail-end charlie for the platoon, but the platoon had the position of honor, leading the rest of the company after the skipper. As the company commander, in his *Eruption* and the first tank in the column, turned through onto camp Tainio's parade deck in view of the stands, the crowd erupted into cheers. The grunts were already in formation, five of the division's nine battalions, but even with the PICS Marines, they didn't offer the same visuals as the Davises did. Noah felt a surge of pride, and he tried to keep a stern visage, regardless of the fact that in the back of the division formation, he'd be a good 300 meters from the stands.

The skipper stopped the *Eruption* at his position, a lone Marine ground-guide leading him in. One after the other, the *Kiss of Death*, *Ball Shot*, *Boudicca II*, and the *Anvil* pulled in behind her. The remaining platoons fell in behind them, and then Alpha and Bravo Companies to their right.

And then it was time to wait for the rest of the division units to form up. Standing on his seat and looking forward, Noah pitied the grunts. The first company to form up had probably been standing there at attention for 20 minutes so far.

A loud, resonating fart sounded from below him.

"Grubbing hell, Llanz. Even here?"

"As I keep telling you, *unum saltum, et siffletum, et unum bumbulum.*"

"I'll freaking '*bumbulum*' you," Noah said, keeping his face locked to the front.

Llanzo was a senior sergeant with two years as a driver, and his quals were high, but he had digestive issues. Worse than that, he was pretty complacent about passing the resultant gas. Noah had the hatch open, so it wasn't bad, but in a closed tank, the filters were designed to keep bad things from getting into the tank, not releasing gas that originated from inside. Noah had a sneaking suspicion that Llanzo was sent by Third because of his flatulence.

Noah had to look up the Latin LLanzo kept spouting: it meant, "One jump, one whistle, one fart." Evidently, back on Old Earth, there were "flatulists," sort of court jesters, or later, comedians, who were paid quite well to entertain jokes and well-times farts.

The universe is a crazy place.

It took another fifteen minutes before the entire division, at least those units which weren't deployed, to form up. Finally, the last of the arty was in place behind everyone else, and in unison, every tube opened up, sending a shock wave over the division and up into the stands. The crowd erupted into cheers and applause.

"Ladies and Gentlemen," the narrator announced over the sound system. "Welcome to the Fourth Marine Division's Birthday Pageant. Today, the United Federation Marine Corps celebrates 317 years of service to our great Federation.

"The Fourth Marine Division has a long and glorious history, and the battle streamers on the division colors represent 67 different operations. Standing before you is Major Stanley H. Carrigan, the commanding general. Joining him in the staff is Sergeant Major Filipe L. J. J. Lopez-Sivla, the division sergeant major.

"If I can turn your attention to the reviewing stand, our guest of honor is Vice-Minister Patricia Q. Howland, accompanied by Lieutenant General Kristof K. Kravitz, the United Federation Marine Corps Chief of Research and Development.

"Please stand, as we present the colors. The color guard, composed of six Marines and one Navy corpsman representing each regiment and separate combat arms battalion, is led by Sergeant Gustavio Miller."

The crowd rose to its feet as the drummer commenced with a beat. Noah was standing at attention the best he could considering he was on top of his seat, and he could only peripherally see the color guard do its thing. Then it was 45 minutes of speeches, and Noah quickly zoned out. The grunts were at parade rest, but he couldn't do that standing on his seat, so he simply leaned back a bit, his butt on the edge of the hatch. LLanzo was sitting, his head out of his hatch, but that didn't stop him from "bumbulumming," if that was even a word.

Finally, those giving speeches must have been tired, and the adjutant yelled out, "Pass . . . in . . . REVIEW!"

There was almost a palpable sigh of relief as the drum picked up the beat, and the color guard marched to the far right-hand side of the formation before doubling back to cross in front of the bleachers and spectators. Both the guest of honor and Lieutenant General Kaufmann saluted as the Federation colors passed them. Behind them, a line of Marines, all in historical costumes going back to the formation of the Marines marched past, the narrator explaining each uniform. And then, at last, the first of the grunts stepped off.

Noah had never actually stood as a grunt in a division-sized formation, but he could imagine the feeling as blood started flowing back into legs pushed into motion. He was in the *Anvil*, but he shook out his legs, too. Eventually, it was their turn. With the skipper leading, First Platoon followed four tanks abreast, and in turn were followed 50 meters back by the four tanks from Second Platoon.

"Eyes . . . right!" the skipper passed over the net, saluting as he reached the reviewing officer. LLanzo kept his eyes straight ahead, but Noah snapped his head to the right at a 45-degree angle. Once the Third Platoon passed the vice-minister, they were essentially done. A ground-guide was waiting for them at the end of the parade deck, and First Platoon turned into the parking lot while Second and Third proceeded to the lowboy for transport back to Camp Archuleta.

The four tanks were parked ready to be a static display for the crowds and newsies.

"You've got it, Llanz," Noah said, jumping out the hatch. He'd relieve his fellow sergeant later, but at the moment, he needed to track down his family.

Family. It still sounded odd to him.

There were at least 6,000 spectators, but Noah had told Miriam where to wait, and sure enough, as he reached the reviewing stand, there she was, Chance on her hip.

He gave her a kiss—yes, he was in uniform, but he didn't think that constituted PDA.[6]

"And how's my man?' he asked, taking Chance's hand and giving it a gentle shake.

"Your man is asleep, but he woke when you came rumbling past," Miriam said.

"That's 'cause he's a tanker, just like his daddy."

Miriam merely snorted.

"Well, what did you think?" he asked her.

"Much bigger than on Wayfarer Station," she said. "But I kind of liked it better there. We were so much closer to the Marines. This was impressive, but not as personal. Anyway, that's just my opinion."

On the station, with much more constrained space, both the Patron Day and Marine Corps Birthday parade and pageant took place in the Alpha Corridor, and the spectators could reach out and touch some of them while they marched. There was a lot to be said for that. But seeing almost a whole division on the parade deck had been pretty impressive, he thought.

"Any word on a sitter for tomorrow night?"

---

[6] PDA" Public Display of Affection.

Miriam hugged Chance a little tighter as a frown just creased the edges of her mouth.

"Not yet. I'm not sure we're going to be able to go. I mean, me. I don't think I can go. You can still enjoy it."

Miriam was still rather possessive of Chance, and while Noah knew for a fact that there were arrangements at the ball for children, he was also sure that Miriam simply was not willing to let go, even for an evening. She'd enjoyed the four other balls she'd attended, but that was before she'd become a mother.

In another two months, she'd be off maternity leave, and she'd have to let go then, so he really didn't understand her reluctance now.

For a moment, he was tempted to say he'd go on his own. If she didn't want to go, that was her choice. But there would probably be a cost to pay if he went alone.

"Nah, it's OK. We've been to them before, and we'll be to others in the future. Chance is only going to be a baby for a short time, so we need to enjoy him like this."

Miriam nodded, but her smile let Noah know he'd made the right choice.

Chapter 27

Noah tasted the mashed peas from the blender.

Too bland, he thought to himself.

It took an effort of will not to reach for the sherry vinegar to give the peas a little kick. But Miriam had been on his case about making Chance's food too spicy. She thought it was bad enough that he made baby food from scratch instead of relying on "doctor approved" food from the fabricator, but he held firm, insisting that Chance at least experience "real" food.

He realized that fab food was nutritionally sound, and with the infant add-on pack, it was probably better from a medical standpoint than what he was making. Miriam said he just wanted Chance to be a little Noah, and she might be right. But Noah wanted him to at least be introduced to food made from natural ingredients, to "pre-load" his taste buds, so-to-speak.

"You like it, though, right?" he asked Chance, who gurgled back something from his highchair.

He looked up at the clock: 1922. Miriam was running late again. With the day care on base, Noah could pick up Chance easily enough when he wasn't in the field or on duty, but he thought Miriam would have been home by now. Not that he was really concerned about it. He welcomed the opportunity to be alone with his son like this.

He fed Chance, changed his diapers, then sat with him on the rocker until the little guy fell asleep. He considered putting him in the crib, but he just sat there, holding Chance against his chest. Times like this were all too few.

Noah nodded off himself before the door opened and Miriam came in. She dropped her bag on the couch and picked Chance off his chest, holding him close as he squirmed in her arms.

"Everything OK at work? It's . . ." he paused, looking at the clock. ". . . 2115."

"We were shorthanded and I had to take two stations," she answered, looking Chance over as if making sure Noah hadn't screwed up with him. "Let me put him down."

Noah stood up, stretched, and went to the cooler, pulling out some pork cutlets.

"Do you want these? I can make them piccata."

"No, I'm beat. This is good enough," she said, spooning out some of the remaining peas from the blender.

Noah shrugged and put the cutlets back into the cooler. Miriam wasn't a fussy eater. If it was calories, then it was fine. She ate to live, not lived to eat. He went to the couch and sat down, and a few minutes later, she joined him.

"We need to talk," she said.

"About what?"

"This," she said, pointing at her waitress uniform.

"You don't like to wear it?" Noah asked, confused.

"No, not that. Well, yeah, I don't like it. But the work. The hours. I take Chance to day-care at 1100 each morning, then go to work. I don't see him again until late when he's already asleep, at least until he wakes up in the middle of the night and I've got to tend to him."

"I pick him up—" he started before she interrupted him.

"You pick him up when you can, but what about last week during your field ops? That was three days when I had to, and never earlier than 2000. It's not good for him to be at Day Care for so long."

"Maybe," Noah said, although not convinced there was a problem. "But what are we going to do? I mean, you can ask for fewer hours, but is that going to make a big difference?"

"No, and that's my point."

"So, what do you want to do?"

"I think I need to quit. I need to stay home."

Noah looked at her in surprise.

Stay at home? How can we afford that?

"But, you've never mentioned anything about that before."

"I am now. I thought it would work out, but it isn't."

Noah paused, trying to marshal his wording, before he asked, "But what about your pay? Can we survive without it?"

She let out a big breath, then said, "Not really. I mean, of course, we can, but it'll be tough. We'd have to really watch our spending. But you'll be a staff sergeant sometime, and if not that soon, your enlistment will be up and we can look at something else."

That was a gut-shot to Noah. They'd never discussed yet what they'd do after his enlistment expired, but he'd half-assumed he'd just re-up again. Now it seemed as if Miriam wasn't sold on that idea.

"I . . . we need to look at this. We're barely scraping by with what we make between us. Can we really make it on my salary alone?"

"Not just your salary. I can try some home-based work. Lots of people do it, you know."

"What kind of work?"

"I don't know. But I can figure out something."

Noah leaned back, letting it all sink in. The silence between them was getting uncomfortable.

Finally, he said, "Maybe we should think about it. Let's see if we can come up with some work before you quit your job."

"Too late, Noah. I already gave notice. Next Saturday will be my last day."

"What?" Noah said, unable to articulate the rush of thoughts that smacked his brain.

"I gave them notice."

"You didn't think to tell me?" he managed to get out.

"I'm telling you now."

Noah was shocked. He thought they worked things out between them, and to hear that she'd just acted out like that unilaterally took him by surprise.

"Oh, and one more thing. I gave them the notice today because I just found out."

"Found out what?" he asked, feeling numb.

"I'm pregnant again. We're having another child."

Chapter 28

"Staff Sergeant Cain? I'm Sergeant Lysander."

The broad-shouldered staff sergeant stood up from the chair in Gunny Chimond's office, hand out to shake. He had the typical physique of a heavy-worlder, but all Noah knew about the man was that he was to be the *Anvil's* new commander. He'd just gotten the word from the gunny, and trying to stifle his disappointment, had come from the ramp to pick him up.

"If there's anything you need, my door's always open," the gunny said. "But you've got one of the best in Sergeant Lysander."

"Thanks," the staff sergeant said, squeezing Noah's hand hard.

Noah didn't squeeze back but simply tensed his hand so it wouldn't be crushed. He wasn't into pissing contests, but he wasn't about to back down.

"Everyone says you're hot shit, Lysander. That true?"

The staff sergeant was smiling a kilometer wide, and his voice was friendly—Noah wasn't sure if the man was joking or not, but he chose to play it like that, responding, "That'll be up to you to decide, Staff Sergeant."

"Well, I guess I will at that. Why don't you take me down to the ramp so I can meet . . . LLanzo, is that his name?" he asked, then before Noah could answer, ". . . and see the bucket of bolts that'll be my home for the next three years."

"OK, then. Just follow me and I'll take you to the *Anvil*."

Noah looked over his shoulder as he left the gunny's office, and to his surprise, the neutral expression on the gunny's face changed to something, well, not so neutral as they left. He didn't think the gunny noticed him looking at her, and he wondered what the change in attitude meant.

Maybe there's just something else on her mind.

He led the new TC past the battalion CP and down Meunster Avenue to the ramp. Llanzo was waiting beside the *Anvil*, anxious to meet the new commander.

Over the last two months, the two had formed a pretty tight team, both relying on and trusting the other. It couldn't last forever, though. A Davis crew was three Marines, not two. Noah had just hoped to get a new driver instead of a new commander, but he guessed that had never been in the cards.

"Sergeant Llanzo, good to meet you," the staff sergeant said, reaching out to bump fists. "I gotta tell you, I was stoked when I found out you were my crew. We're a bro crew."

Noah wasn't sure he heard the staff sergeant correctly.

"A bro crew?"

"Yeah, you know, bros," the staff sergeant said, looking around to see if anyone was listening, then saying quieter, "Guys. Bros. All male."

"Yeah, I guess all three of us are guys," Llanzo said.

"I mean, the gunny? Give me a break. She sounds like Meerkat Momma," he said, referring to a popular children's figure in the toons. "You make sure you pick up your toys, kiddos," he added mimicking her.

"Gunny Chimond's OK, Staff Sergeant. She was my commander on Novyy Ural after Staff Sergeant Cremineli was killed," Noah said.

"Hey, no offense. I know you've got to be loyal and all that, and I'm sure she a nice gal. But a Marine? Give me a break. And the platoon commander and first sergeant are bitches, too?"

"I'm not sure your point, Staff Sergeant. There are lots of women in the company. We're a tank company, after all," Noah said, still confused by the staff sergeant's attitude.

"Oh, don't get your panties in a twist, Lysander. We don't have to be PC here. I'm just saying, it's good to be an all-guy crew. We can relax with each other and not get turned in for sexual harassment if we say someone's got a great ass or something. You know what I mean. Am I right?"

When neither Marine said anything, he added, "Look, I know there are some good broad-ass Marines, some real hard chargers. But person for person, they're just not our equals, and they get special treatment, you know, coming right from MacCailín's office. She made Chairman, and look at the social experiments going on since then. But you, Lysander, you have to see it. Your twin, she's an officer now, right? But where are you? Did some magic hand reach down and pull you up, too? No. You're a guy, and you have to do it all yourself.

"I'll serve with them, so don't think I'm some misogynist cretin. Hell, I love me my ladies," he said, punching Llanzo in the shoulder. "Am I right? Anyway, all I'm saying is that I'm glad I've got two bros as my crew. It just makes it easier, that's all."

Noah knew he should say something else, to stick up for the gunny, for the lieutenant. To tell the staff sergeant that Esther earned her commission, and that he'd never even wanted one. But he didn't, and he wasn't sure why.

"So, is this our girl?" he asked.

"Yes, this is the *Anvil*," Llanzo said, patting the side of the tank.

"*Anvil*? Weak-ass name. Well, first things first. Let's get that shit off of her. From now on, she's the *Hombre*."

Hombre, Noah thought, his heart falling.

He hadn't really thought of losing the Anvil name, but Staff Sergeant Cain was the new TC, and the tank was his to rename, even considering the irony of his referring to a tank named "Hombre" as a "she."

"One thing about me, boys, is that I always win, and I'm going to make you into winners, too," he said as he clambered up onto the tank. "We're going to be the best fucking tank in the battalion, mark my words."

Llanzo looked at Noah behind the staff sergeant's back, eyebrows raised in a question. Noah shrugged, then motioned for Llanzo to follow their TC.

He wasn't sure what to make of the staff sergeant. He was a 180 from the quiet, detached Staff Sergeant Cremineli, it was pretty evident, and Noah would have thought that would be a good thing. Now, he wasn't quite as sure about that.

Chapter 29

"Congratulations, Lieutenant Moore," Major General Carrigan said as he pinned the Silver Star on her pocket flap.

Noah stood at attention beside her, eyes focused on the bleachers in front of him where Miriam and Chance were sitting.

"You've made the division proud, and you are going to be a fine addition to Armor School."

Lieutenant Moore, now a captain-select, had receive her orders to Armor School as part of the staff. Noah thought the general was right—the lieutenant would excel in training new tankers and APC crewmen.

Because of his background where he'd grown up mingling with colonels and generals, a lieutenant just didn't impress him based on the bars on his or her collars. It had taken him awhile to get a feel for his platoon commander, but slowly and surely, he'd come to realize that she was an officer well-worthy of his respect. Sometimes a little unorthodox, she nevertheless was fearless in combat, and she put the welfare of her Marines above that of her own. A Marine couldn't ask much more in a commander.

The general shook the lieutenant's hand, then came to attention and conducted a right face, marched two steps, then snapped a left face until he was looking straight into Noah's eyes.

The narrator, Gunny O'Fell from Third Platoon, read the citation:

The Chairman of the United Federation of Planets takes pleasure in presenting the Silver Star medal to:

Sergeant Noah Lysander
United Federation Marine Corps,

for service as set forth in the following

CITATION:

for conspicuous gallantry and intrepidity in action against the enemy as a member of First Platoon, Charlie Company, First Tank Battalion, Fourth Marine Division in support of Task Force 54-03 on Novyy Ural on 4 May 319. During the operation, First Platoon was tasked to cut off an infantry advance. Outnumbered by the Pytor Velikiy aggressors, Sergeant Lysander engaged the enemy with tremendous success, destroying several crew-served weapons positions. Shortly after the battle commenced, Sergeant Lysander's tank commander was killed by enemy action, and he assumed command of the vehicle, continuing to press the battle. One of the platoon's tanks was destroyed and another was damaged, rendering it unable to maneuver. With the situation becoming dire, his platoon commander ordered an aggressive assault of the main enemy line with two of the remaining tanks, and Sergeant Lysander, acting as both gunner and commander, destroyed numerous enemy positions until his tank was damaged by entrenched infantry and rendered combat ineffective. Sergeant Lysander immediately exited his tank and boarded his platoon commander's tanks. Standing on the outside of the vehicle, fully exposed to enemy fire, he used his personal sidearm to engage and kill enemy who were closing in on and attacking the tank. Sergeant Lysander, at great personal risk, protected the platoon commander's tank from almost certain destruction. After an intense fight, the enemy attack was broken, and the surviving enemy were forced to retreat. Sergeant Lysander's zealous initiative, dogged actions, and fearless performance of his duties reflected great credit upon himself and upheld the highest traditions of the Marine Corps and the United Federation Naval Service.

For the Chairman,
Picolli J. Emerson-Ito

First Minister, United Federation of Planets

Noah stood still as the general took the medal from the sergeant major and slowly pinned it on his pocket flap.

"This is special to me, son. I served with your father three times, and there was never a better Marine. What happened to him is a travesty, a travesty. But you and your sister, you're making him proud, and I'm sure he's watching over you."

He stepped back, and Noah brought his hand up into a salute.

"Thank you, General. I appreciate that."

The general returned the salute and said, "And I appreciate your service. I've talked with Lieutenant Moore here and looked at the recordings. I agree with her. If you hadn't decided to ride shotgun on the *Kiss of Death*—that's the right name, isn't it, Lieutenant?" he asked before turning back to Noah, ". . . the *Kiss of Death*. If you hadn't jumped on top, the battle would have turned out differently, and the Pytor Velikiy forces would have reached the Novyy Ural AO, causing all sorts of problems. Sometimes, the actions of a single Marine can change the course of a battle, and this was one of those times.

"I told you your father would be proud, and I mean it."

The general stepped back, the signal for Lessa, the far right Marine to say, "Hand . . . SALUTE," then "Ready . . . TWO" after the general returned it.

Every Marine who'd been at the battle had received some sort of medal, from a BC3 on up. Staff Sergeant Mauser-Lopez had been presented with a Bronze Star, and then Noah and the lieutenant had received the Silver Star.

"Left . . . FACE!" Lessa ordered, then "Forward . . . MARCH."

Noah, as the far-left Marine stepped off, knowing the rest would match his cadence. He tried to keep it steady, but the tears in his eyes were making it hard to see.

The general had told him that his father would be proud of him. Noah knew in his heart that Ben had been his father's favorite. Heck, Ben had been everyone's favorite. And Esther was now an officer, one with a Navy Cross no less. His father would probably have been shocked to see Noah follow him into the Corps in the first place. But Noah hoped that the general was right, and somewhere, somehow, his father was looking down at him and finally proud of the man, of the Marine, he'd become.

Chapter 30

"Hey, Noah. You've got a fucking asshole for a TC," Lessa said, her eyes looking like they could shoot out sparks at any moment. "You can tell him to keep his fucking dick to himself or I'll cut the tiny little thing off and feed it to him."

What the hell? Noah wondered as he looked up from the readouts.

"What are you talking about?"

"Your TC, Staff Sergeant Cain, that's who," she said, standing in front of him in gym shorts and tank top, the anger emanating from her.

"I guess he can be an asshole, Lessa, but what's this about his dick?"

The staff sergeant was full of himself, Noah had discovered, and he was free with his opinion on civilians, the Navy, the FCDC (who he seemed to hate with a passion), and yes, women in "his" Marine Corps, but his opinions seemed to be just bullshitting with Llanzo and him. Noah wasn't particularly comfortable with the bitching and pontificating, but the guy knew tanks, and he was a wizard at maintenance. Noah had already learned more about keeping the *Hombre* (the name still stuck in his throat) up and running than he'd managed to learn over the previous three-plus years.

"Oh, the little fact that he likes to stick it in my face? How about that?"

"What are you talking about, Lessa?"

"What I'm talking about is at the gym. I'm on the bench, and he comes up, saying something like "That's a lot of weight for a little lady like you. I think you need a spot,'" she said, lowering her voice in a mocking imitation.

"So, he comes up, and I think what the fuck, if he wants to spot, no skin off my nose, right? I start lifting, and since he's spotting, I'm going for failure. And I get up to 17 reps, right? And

181

he keeps yelling 'You got it,' only I don't. But when he moves to help me rack it, he sticks his dick in my face."

"What? He took out his dick?"

"No, not out. In his shorts, but he tea-bagged me."

"I . . . what did you do?"

"I was so fucking pissed that I got out of there before I unloaded on him."

Noah didn't know what to think. Sure, the staff sergeant had his opinions, but that seemed a little much, even for him.

"Are you sure he did it? Could it have been an accident?"

"Accident? I could feel him, half hard and shit. No, he fucking meant to do it."

"What are you going to do about it?"

"I'm telling you, that's what I'm going to do. I should just turn his ass in to the new lieutenant, but you pass the word to him that if he does some shit like that again, I'll come down on him in a fucking world of hurt."

She leaned forward and poked Noah in the chest with her forefinger, saying, "You tell him that."

She spun around and stalked off.

Noah sat back. In his mind, he tried to put together what she'd said. It did seem odd, as he pictured the staff sergeant in back of her spotting. If he'd had to take the weight, he should have bent back at the waist, taking his crotch away from Lessa, not towards her. Something didn't make sense, and with a sinking heart, he knew he had to confront the staff sergeant.

He closed the assessment, calling out to Pure Dick that he'd be back and have it finished before chow.

"Make sure you do, Sergeant. I don't want to have to chase you down."

Noah checked in the gym first, but the staff sergeant wasn't there, so he headed to the SNCO barracks. Cain wasn't married, so he lived on base.

"Staff Sergeant, it's Sergeant Lysander. I need to talk to you," he said, speaking into the interface.

"What do you want, Lysander. I'm in the shower."

"It's important, and I don't want to say it out here."

"Shit, Lysander. It can't wait? OK, give me a moment."

Noah stood there, nervous as he waited. After about a minute, the door opened and the staff sergeant, naked except for a towel around his waist, stood there.

"What's so fucking important that you've got to pull me out of the shower?"

"Uh . . . it's about Sergeant Franklin."

"Franklin? What does she want?"

If Noah was expecting some sort of guilty reaction, the staff sergeant didn't produce. He just stood there, looking annoyed.

"She just came and told me that you spotted her at the gym . . ."

"Yeah. What of it?"

"She says you stuck your dick in her face while you spotted her."

The staff sergeant looked at him in amazement, then a huge smile took over his face as he broke out into laughter.

"Is that what the little bitch is saying? For reals?" he asked.

"Well, yeah. That's what she's saying."

"In her dreams I did that."

"What do you mean?"

"I mean, she wishes she could see my cock," he said, grabbing it with one hand through the towel. "Look, she comes in the gym with shorts five sizes too small and a tanktop that flashes her titties. What do you think she's trying to do? What do you think she wants?"

"Uh, Staff Sergeant. I think you might have the wrong impression of things. Lessa's got a wife. She's not into guys."

"She's a lez? No shit? But she's kinda hot. But no matter. If she's a lez, that's because she's never had some guy give it to her good. Am I right or am I right?"

"Staff Sergeant, what she is doesn't matter. She said if you do it again, she's not going to hold back."

"What, little bitty Franklin's going to jump me? Me?" he asked, flexing his pecs.

He had a point, Noah had to admit. Lessa was a small Marine, maybe tipping the scales at 50 kg. Staff Sergeant Cain was short like many heavy worlders, but also like other heavy worlders, he was a big, muscular man, probably 120 kg. Lessa could be full of bluster, but there wasn't a way she could take the staff sergeant in a fight.

"Maybe, maybe not. But she said she'd take it to the new lieutenant if it happened again. She was going to do it this time, but she came to me instead."

The smirk on his face disappeared, and he said, "Look, Lysander. I don't fucking know what she thought happened. I spotted her. When her spindly arms failed, I grabbed the bar, you know, to protect her. Maybe the front of my shorts got close to her, maybe they didn't. I wasn't paying attention, you know, 'cause I was trying to keep the bar from slamming back down on her. I can't help it if she's got it into her head that I was trying to get my nut off that way."

Noah stared into the staff sergeant's eyes, trying to read what was behind them. Maybe Lessa had misconstrued what had happened. Maybe the staff sergeant hadn't intentionally done anything. And it wasn't like it was that much of an event. Noah had probably done worse during MCMA[7] training when fighting female Marines. He'd sure had more than a few dicks in his face while rolling around the ground, after all.

I've done my duty. I've passed along Lessa's message.

He was about to tell the staff sergeant that and leave, when the mental image that he'd constructed came back to him. Physics was physics, and there wasn't a way that the staff sergeant could have accidently brushed her like that. Unless Lessa was lying—and Noah was pretty sure that she wasn't, given her anger—he'd meant to do it. Whether he was joking or meant something more serious, he'd done it, and now he was lying. Standing in front of Noah, he had a look of disdain on his face, but there was something else there, something he was trying to hide.

He was scared.

---

[7] MCMA: Marine Corps Martial Arts

And Noah knew for certainty that Cain had done it. Whether it was a joke, disdain for women in the Corps, or some perversion, Noah couldn't tell, but he was sure it had been a purposeful action.

"Bullshit, Staff Sergeant. You did it and you know it. If you pull that kind of thing again, Lessa, or whomever else it is, won't have to report you because I will."

Anger flowed across the staff sergeant's face replacing any fear he might have had.

"Fuck you, Lysander. I thought you were a man, not a fem. Oh, yeah, I spoke with Leto Smith, from your recruit platoon. He told me you were a pussy, but I thought how could General Lysander's son be one? I wanted to give you a chance, but here you are, siding with the bitches. You're what's wrong with the Corps, let me tell you. And let me tell you one more thing. Your sister? She's got more balls than you. Your father would be sick to his stomach if he could see you now."

He shoved Noah in the chest, pushing him back out of the quarters, and slammed the door in Noah's face.

Chapter 31

Things had rapidly gone downhill since his confrontation with the staff sergeant. The *Hombre* was an arctic landscape, cold and bitter. Staff Sergeant Cain didn't speak a word to him unless it was related to the tank. He kept Noah busy with every imaginable scutwork, but he never went over the line, he never raised his voice, even to the level of removing all profanity while addressing him.

He'd tried to broach the matter with Llanzo, but his fellow sergeant refused to be drawn in, saying he wasn't going to get between his two crewmates. Noah resented that. He'd done nothing wrong. But it had become painfully obvious that Llanzo was not going to stick his neck out.

It wasn't just within the *Hombre's* crew, either. Several other male Marines, including Cliff, had turned a cold shoulder to him. Lanny Hirokyu had gone as far as to call him a "snitch" to his face, which made no sense. Noah had tried to tell Lanny that he'd snitched on no one, but Lanny wasn't having any of it. He accused Noah of trying to get rid of Staff Sergeant Cain so he could become tank commander, which shocked Noah into silence.

Nobody—not one person—came up to Noah with support. To be fair, most Marines didn't seem to either know or care what had transpired. They treated Noah as usual. But no one told him he'd done the right thing, not even Lessa, who acted as if she'd never brought Noah into the confrontation in the first place.

Noah had been lonely as a recruit, without much in the way of friends. Over the course of his two tours, he'd started to feel the joy of being part of something bigger than just himself. He'd felt as if he belonged in the Corps. Now, he was feeling isolated, like an outsider, once again.

And it wasn't as if he was getting support at home. Now well into her pregnancy and taking care of Chance, Miriam had seemed to pull back from him. He'd tried to talk to her about his situation, but she seemed to think that everything would pass, and when he'd tried to bring it up a second time, she curtly told him to "be a man" and to take care of things himself.

Noah tried to bury himself in his work, and the staff sergeant was helping him in that, at least. Noah had just spent the last eight hours testing every one of the *Hombre's* tracks, which was both a mind-numbing and back-breaking task. He'd called Miriam earlier to tell her he'd be late, and now, he was doing something he'd never done before. Instead of going home immediately, he'd walked into one of the many bars on Gasperson Street. He'd been in a few before, but never alone, and not when he should be going home.

He stared at the glass of arak sitting in front of him. The milky color did not look as appealing as any of the whiskey family, the "uisce beatha" water of life, but Noah had been curious as to the resurgence in popularity of the ancient grape and anise liquor. He'd stepped inside the bar on a whim, and on a whim, he'd ordered a glass of it.

Neither of his parents had been heavy drinkers, and his mother had always told him never to drink when he was depressed, advice he'd always tried to follow. And now, it looked like he'd ignore that advice.

His tour would be up in less than a year, and he'd have almost another year before his enlistment was up. Miriam expected him to get out, but he'd been leaning towards re-enlistment. Until now. With all the crap he was taking, he was beginning to wonder if it was worth it. Maybe it would be better out in the civilian world.

"You gonna stare at that all night, or you gonna drink it," the bartender asked, stopping in front of him.

Noah looked up at the bartender, but he couldn't detect any animosity in the man's question.

"Drink it," he said, reaching down to pick up the glass and send the sweet liquor cascading down his throat.

Chapter 32

"One more push," the nurse-midwife said from between Miriam's legs.

Noah watched as Miriam first grunted, then shouted as Hannah Belle Lysander made her entry into the universe. He felt an ache in his heart as his daughter opened her mouth and screamed her displeasure.

With deft hands, the nurse-midwife cut the umbilical, gooped it shut, and placed the baby girl on Miriam's chest. Noah crowded close, putting his hand on Hannah's back, marveling at the pulse he felt. What had before been to him merely a concept, an idea, was now a living, breathing person.

"She's beautiful," he said, his voice in awe.

There'd been no way he was going to miss her birth. No deployment, no duty, and thanks to the first sergeant running interference for him, he'd made it, catching an Albatross ride in from the Winston Training Ranges when Miriam started labor. Six hours later, Hannah Belle had made her appearance.

Unlike with Chance, this time, Noah was going to be part of the naming. "Hannah" was from his mother's first name. Miriam had chosen "Belle" simple because she liked the sound, and Noah was OK with that. Right now, they could have named her "Hombre" and he'd love her no less.

Hannah's squawls quieted, and she fell asleep on Miriam. Noah leaned over and kissed his wife's head.

"You did great, honey."

"Yes, I did, didn't I? Look at her."

"I can't keep my eyes off her."

While things could always change, it looked like Noah would finish up his enlistment with Third Tanks. He hadn't re-enlisted, so the Corps was not about to PCS[8] him with a year left in service. Gunny had even asked him if he wanted to transfer up to the

---

[8] Permanent Change of Station

battalion staff for the remainder of his time, and Noah was seriously considering it.

Things had gotten better with the company. Staff Sergeant Cain still kept him at a cold arm's length, but when nothing happened to the staff sergeant, the other Marines who'd rallied to him seemed to forget about Noah. They weren't as welcoming, but neither were they antagonistic. From comments they'd made when things were tense, Noah was pretty sure Cain had misrepresented what had happened, but Noah's pride was such that he never tried to set the record straight.

Still, Gunny had sensed the tension, even pulling Noah aside to find out what was wrong. Noah denied that there were problems, but he knew the gunny didn't believe him. He was pretty sure, though, that was the reason she'd asked him about moving up to battalion.

Looking at his daughter, he'd just about made up his mind to accept the offer. He'd miss the *Hombre*, but this way, unless the battalion deployed as a unit, he'd be there every night for Hannah and Chance. It seemed like a good trade-off.

"Hannah Belle, don't you worry about a thing. Your daddy's here to take care of you."

Chapter 33

"Chance, leave Tabitha alone!" Miriam said.

"Come here, little man," Noah said, lowering himself to one knee, and when his son slowly wandered over, continued, "You have to remember not to bother other children. Tabitha wants to talk to her mommy now, so don't interrupt."

Chance lifted a hand to the back of his head and said, "I'm not bothering her. She wanted me to."

"Don't fib to Daddy," Miriam said, pushing the stroller with a sleeping Hannah in it back and forth.

"I'm not fibbing!"

"Look, Chance. I told you I've got to go away for awhile. You have to be a good boy and do what mommy says, OK?"

"Why do you have to go?" he asked.

That tugged on Noah's heartstrings, but he kept his voice calm and said, "It's my job, Chance. But I'll be home soon, I promise."

He didn't have to be going at all, he knew and as Miriam kept reminding him. He'd delayed accepting the battalion job, wanting just one more exercise, one more chance to play. And it wasn't as if it would be forever. Rampant Force was only scheduled for twelve days. In three weeks, he'd be back, and then it would be up to battalion to work on the training schedule until his release from active duty.

"So, you'll be a good boy? You'll take care of Hannah?"

"Yes. I love Belle."

Noah didn't hold back his smile. He called his daughter "Hannah." Miriam called her "Hannah Belle." Somehow, Chance chose to call his sister simply "Belle." It was probably going to screw up the little girl once she got a bit older, but for now, he liked that Chance was making his own relationship with her.

"OK, come give me a hug."

Chance leaned into Noah, content to accept the embrace.

"Come on, people, load 'em up!" the Gunny Speck shouted.

"That's us," First Sergeant St. Cloud said, kissing each of her kids, then Fierdor.

Noah squeezed Chance a little tighter, then stepped to the stroller and kissed the sleeping Hannah on the forehead.

"I'll see you soon," he told Miriam, kissing her cheek, his hand straying to her belly where child number three was incubating. It seemed that they'd barely settled into their new routine with Hannah when she became pregnant again.

"Remember to get your resume out," she reminded him. "You promised."

"I will, I will."

"Let's go, Sergeant," the first sergeant said. "We're last again."

He followed her to the bus where Gunny Speck scanned them in. One step up, he turned to wave, but Miriam was in deep conversation with Fierdor, and she didn't see him.

No one had saved him a seat, so he slid into the empty one beside Barb McDavitt who was already head back and fast asleep.

He looked again as the bus pulled out, but he couldn't spot Miriam. He'd liked to have gotten in one more wave, if for nothing else, to help assuage the feeling of guilt he had. Miriam hadn't wanted him to go on this last exercise, and he hadn't been 100% truthful in telling her he had to go. The bottom line was that he wanted to go—and with little Hannah waking up throughout the night, as much as he loved and would do anything for her, he was a little relieved to be getting a break. And that relief he felt was eating him up inside.

A good father would never feel that, right?

Still, he felt a little thrill as the buses left the battalion area and headed for the main gate.

ITZUKO-2

Chapter 34

"Tank, four o'clock," the staff sergeant said. "Priority 1."

Noah immediately swung his turret around, abandoning the line of APCs advancing at about four klicks out. The tank was solo, emerging from depression, and it was cock-eyed to the main battle. He instinctively knew that the driver would over-correct, and that would cause the gunner to fall short in trying to acquire the *Hombre*.

"Goose it, Llanz!"

Using the combat assist instead of full auto, he smoothly brought his 75mm to bear and thumbed the trigger. From the staff sergeant's shout until round downrange had been just over four seconds.

The railgun round was fast, but somehow the opposing tank managed to snap off a shot. Llanzo's sudden acceleration, however, coupled with the opposing gunner's mistake that Noah had foreseen, rendered a clean miss. Not so with the *Hombre's* shot. It was a clean hit, knocking the other tank out of action.

"Now back to the APC's," the staff sergeant said.

But it was too late. The other three tanks had already engaged and destroyed the opposing Aardvarks.

"Shit, get back to school, zeroes," Llanzo said. "You expect to be tankers with that weak shit?"

Noah looked down at the opposing forces list, then said, "I think that's it. There's no one left."

"No shit? In one day? I bet there's going to be some heavy ass-chewing tonight. So, what now?" Staff Sergeant Cain asked.

Less than two minutes later, he had his answer. They were to return to the ramp.

Rampant Force was a two-pronged exercise. During the first phase, the participating units acted as the OpFor for Armor School. The next phase would be a force-on-force against each other. In this case, due to scheduling, the OpFor mission came first. It was fun to beat up on the students, and it was always embarrassing for a tank or Aardvark to get taken out by them, but the real thrill was the force-on-force. This was just a warm-up.

Beating up Armor School wasn't that difficult, but to wipe them out in one day was almost unheard of. Normally, it took two to three days. During the third reset during Noah's own Armor War, three student Mambas had managed to evade destruction for almost the entire four days, falling within an hour of endex.

The net was alive with chatter as they returned to the ramp. Marines were feeling their oats. Noah had to admit it had been fun, but he felt a little sorry for the students. Their confidence had to be crushed. Still, it had probably been a good lesson. With the first set ending so quickly, there would probably be time for three more sets before the war's endex, and he was pretty sure they'd do much better the next go-round. They'd be going next against Bravo and a platoon of Aardvarks, though, while Charlie sat it out.

After that, though, would be four days of intense combat, with Bravo and Charlie, along with Alpha Company, Third Tracs, against Fourth Tank's Alpha, Bravo, and Charlie Companies (Fourth Tanks' Charlie Company was a Mamba company). It should prove to be interesting. This would be Noah's last hurrah, and he was bound and determined to kill lots of bad guys without getting the *Hombre* killed.

It was a three-hour drive to the ramp, and they arrived shortly before chow.

Noah hopped out, his stomach growling, when the staff sergeant said, "Start clean-up, Sergeant Lysander. I'll send someone to relieve you after we eat."

Which meant once chow was over, and Noah would be left with field rats. This wasn't the first time this had happened.

"Roger that," Noah answered.

No one else was left behind from the other tanks, and he could see only one tracker over with the Aardvarks. He idly wondered what she'd done to piss someone off. Sitting on his turret, he wasn't in a hurry to get going, and he knew the staff sergeant wasn't expecting him to do much. There were a few things that really should be done before stopping for the night, but they had at least a full day and probably even longer, if the students could make a better showing of themselves, before the vehicles would be taken out again. He was half-tempted to just take a nap until he was relieved, but finally, his sense of duty got the better of him, and he climbed down off the *Hombre*, grabbed a mud pick, and started levering off slabs of mud from the tracks and road wheels. That had to be done long before the power washers were brought out.

He'd cleared most of the major chunks of mud when Llanzo came back to relieve him.

"Sorry about that," Llanzo said, which was as close to saying this was bullshit as he was going to get, Noah knew.

"What was for chow?"

"Some sort of breaded patty, spaghetti, or ansome rolls. And the typical sides. Mostly shit, you know."

"'Shit' I can't get now that the chowhall's closed up for the night."

Llanzo just shrugged.

He'd been right, though. That would have been mostly shit. The spaghetti was universally detested, and the ansome rolls were almost inedible, some new "full-nutritional" meat roll with a red sauce that couldn't quite figure out what it was supposed to be. Even the word "ansome" made no sense to anyone.

"Well, I've got most of the mud off. You can probably start with the power washer. The turret's gone through analytics, but I haven't connected yours or the TC's interfaces."

"You know, he said I can leave after you go. We're supposed to meet back here at zero-seven-hundred."

"Yeah, I know you'll be bugging off, but our SOP is to pass on what's happened, so consider yourself informed."

Noah turned and stalked out of the ramp. He could be angry, but that would only be a waste of energy. A few more days of this, and he'd be heading back to a desk job until his EAS.[9]

He stopped by the chowhall to see if there was anything left at all. The old lady cleaning dishes gave him half a key lime pie, so he took it and walked to the overlook, a bluff that gave way to the Area 4 Training Range. There was nothing much to see—the Itch's minor moon was low in the sky, so illumination was minimal. But it was peaceful. Behind him, he could hear laughter. He knew the mood was high, and with Fourth Tanks arriving in three days, Marines were getting excited.

He swiveled to look beyond the camp, across the creek, to the lights of Alpha Camp. It wouldn't be such a happy place there, he knew. The students were not at boot camp, but the instructors couldn't be happy about their dismal showing today. He wondered if Mr. Duval was with these students, if the B103 was. Heck, maybe the B103 was one of the two tanks he'd taken out during the too-brief battle. The thought made him smile.

He looked down at the pie, realizing he hadn't thought to bring a spoon. With a shrug, he reached in with his hand, ignoring the crud from washing the *Hombre*, and grabbed a handful, stuffing it into his mouth. To his surprise, it wasn't bad. If he didn't know it was fab, he wasn't sure he could tell. He wondered if the dining chief would give him the programming.

Or maybe it's the mud and grime, he thought to himself, smiling widely.

He finished the pie, licking the plate, wishing he had more. He wasn't in the mood to draw some field rats. He stood up, looking down the bluff, when the thought hit him. Slowly turning back, he tried to pierce the darkness between him and the camp to see if anyone was there.

Turning back around, he cocked his right hand back, holding the pie tin.

I can't believe I'm about to do this!

---

[9] EAS: End of Active Service

With a one-step assist, he flung out his arm, sending the pie tin spinning out into the darkness. He followed it down the best he could, but it went far enough out and then down into the shadows that he lost sight of it.

Flying a pie tin wasn't the most egregious sin a Marine could do, but it was so unlike Noah. And he felt great. Somewhere down there in the darkness, was a piece of trash, trash that he, Noah Lysander, had tossed there.

Yeah, I'm such a grubbing outlaw!

He turned back, feeling surprisingly better. Life was too short to go through it angry, he knew.

Both Alpha and Bravo camps were semi-permanent, which meant they had hot showers, and Noah sure needed one. He walked down the trail to the large warehouse-like building that served as billeting, dumped his overalls, put on gym shorts, a shirt, and flip flops, and grabbed his kit before heading back out to the showers. There was a plasticrete sidewalk leading to the showers, but Noah didn't like the way it grabbed at his flip flops, so he padded alongside it on the well-packed dirt.

The showers were off from the rest of the buildings, set on top of a huge French sump. The wastewater went through an initial filtration unit, then out onto the gravel of the sumps before eventually making its way into the aquifer. Marines or anyone using the camp were restricted to approved soap. It was supposedly a green system. The heads, however, flushed human waste into holding tanks that were regularly sucked empty with the waste going to a processing plant. With the two different systems, they were not supposed to piss in the showers, something that was taken as a standing joke.

Noah was wondering if he should have made a stop at the heads first. He'd already flown trash off the bluff, and could he live with himself being such a criminal?

Yeah, I think I can.

He was chuckling at himself when he heard a muffled curse off the trail, then mumbling. Someone was upset. He stopped, trying to see through the foliage, but the darkness defeated him. He was about turn back and continue when he was sure he recognized Lessa's voice, and he knew something was wrong.

Off the sidewalk to the left was mostly scrub and low trees. Small trails led into the brush, and Marines had been known to use them for illicit and licit activities that required privacy. Noah couldn't imagine that Lessa would have need for either. To the best of his knowledge, she wasn't a stim-freak, and with her devotion to Tammy, he didn't think she'd be there with someone else for a little extra-marital fun.

Noah searched the brush line until he found a trail, then half-ran down it, barely getting ten meters before it opened up, and he could see Lessa sitting on the ground, knees bent with her head between them. Another Marine was kneeling, hand on her back. One of her flip flops was missing, and the acrid smell of vomit reached up to him.

The Marine, who Noah didn't recognize, looked up at him and said, "I was going to the showers when I heard her throwing up in here. I want to get a corpsman, but she says no."

"No corpsman," Lessa said, sounding dazed.

"What happened?" Noah asked, kneeling on the other side of her.

The light of the minor moon barely penetrated the small opening, and it wasn't until Noah leaned in close that he saw the dirt smeared on her face, the blood coming out of her nose. He pulled her arms from around her knees, pushing her upright, and he saw that the front of her shirt had been ripped open. His heart fell.

"What happened, Lessa? Who did this to you?"

"I . . . I don't know. I don't remember!"

"Were you . . . you know . . ." he asked, not voicing his fear.

"I . . . I . . . maybe. I can't . . ."

Noah was sick to his stomach. The torn shirt, the face that had been held against the dirt, the dirt on her chest: he was afraid what they indicated. At the least, she'd been jumped. At the most . . .

Whether she wanted it or not, Noah knew she had to see a corpsman. He didn't have his PA, which he'd left back in his locker, so it was up to the other Marine and him.

"Here, help me get her up," he said, taking her right arm.

Lessa cried out as they lifted her to her feet, and she barely helped move her feet as they brought her down the tiny trail to the sidewalk.

"You!" Noah shouted to two Marines heading to the shower. "Get a corpsman, now!"

The two took off for sickbay, and Noah and the other Marine laid Lessa down on the sidewalk. She was moaning, barely conscious, but she had a death grip on his hand. It looked like one of her eyes was swelling shut, but other than that and the blood dripping from her nose, she didn't look like she had any major injuries. But given the torn shirt, given the dirt where she'd been obviously held down, that wasn't Noah's only concern.

He knew he should leave it to the MP's, but he asked again, "Who did this? You can tell me."

"He . . ." was all she said.

And then the duty corpsman ran up, his stretcher trailing. He scanned Lessa first, then physically examined her while more Marines who'd seen the commotion gathered around before placing her on the stretcher.

"You're going to be OK, Lessa," Noah said, letting go of her hand as the corpsman trundled her down towards sickbay.

A lieutenant showed up, taking charge, and ordering any witnesses to wait until the MP's arrived.

Noah disobeyed the order, slipping off and back down to billeting, sticking his head inside the SNCO cubicle. It was empty, so he headed for the Swamp, the all-ranks recreation center. He stepped in, still in his flip flops and gym clothes, and peered around until he saw him.

He marched up to him, then demanded, "You. Right now. Outside."

Staff Sergeant Cain looked up from the table where he was sitting with Gunny Speck and Staff Sergeant Muser-Lopez.

"You done cleaning the *Hombre*?" he asked, smiling.

"Outside. Now!"

The staff sergeant looked at the other two, shrugged, and said, "Give me a moment to see what my junior Marine's crying about."

Noah waited until the staff sergeant was moving before following. He looked at him closely, trying to see any evidence that he'd been involved. He didn't know what he expected, but he hoped he'd recognize it when he saw it.

They passed through the door and turned to the smoking table to the right, and the staff sergeant said, "OK, we're outside. What the fuck do you want?"

"I know you did it," Noah said, watching to see him flinch.

"Did what?"

"Up there, on the way to the showers."

Noah thought he might have seen the slightest tic in the staff sergeant's eyes, but he couldn't be sure. He knew if he accused the man, and if he were wrong, his final days in the Marines would be a living hell. But he was sure he was right.

"What the fuck are you talking about?"

"Lessa."

"Lessa who?"

"You know damn well who that is. Sergeant Lessa Franklin."

"Oh, your little girlfriend?" the staff sergeant said. "What about her?"

Noah felt the first tendrils of misgivings. The staff sergeant wasn't looking guilty. What if he was wrong? But Lessa didn't get hurt stumbling off the sidewalk. Someone did that to her. But what if it was someone else?

"She was assaulted, maybe half an hour ago."

"And?"

"And I know it was you."

The staff sergeant stood silent for a moment, just staring at Noah, before saying loudly—too loudly—Noah thought, "Wasn't me," and looking around as if to see if any of the half-dozen Marines standing outside the rec center were listening.

Noah grabbed the staff sergeant's shirt, pulled him in close, then quietly, almost in a whisper, said, "Oh, there might not be proof, Staff Sergeant, and maybe you'll get away with it, but between you and me, I know you did it, and you know you did it."

It looked like the man was going to deny it again, but his expression changed, and in his own whisper, he said, "You were wrong, Lysander. Your little hottie isn't a lez. She just hadn't met a real man yet. But when she saw me leaving the shower, she just had to have me, so she dragged me off into the woods, begging for it."

He took Noah's wrist in his hand and pulled it down, tearing it off his blouse.

"And let me tell you, Lysander, she was a tiger, a fucking tiger."

Staff Sergeant Cain was big even for a heavy worlder, and sane people rarely messed with them. But as the staff sergeant brought up a massive bicep and flexed it, Noah reared back and put every ounce of his strength into the blow that smashed into the man's smiling face, dropping him to his knees. Noah immediately kicked the staff sergeant in the head, knocking him onto his back.

It took five Marines to pull him away from where he was stomping on his tank commander's head.

Chapter 35

Noah sat outside the skipper's office, staring at the splints on his fingers. He'd broken two of them when he'd hit the staff sergeant, and the pain he'd be feeling as the nanos went to work over the next couple of days would remind him of what he'd done and how he'd destroyed what little was left of his career.

Still, he'd do it again.

No one would tell him anything about what had happened. After being pulled off the staff sergeant, he'd been taken to the makeshift holding cell at Alpha Camp only to be pulled back to the Bravo Camp sickbay some four or five hours later to get his hand treated. He'd asked about both Lessa and Staff Sergeant Cain but received no answer. The clear plastic disposal bag in the treatment room, with the bloody swabs inside visible, however, was a pretty good indication that he'd done a number on the staff sergeant.

A civilian inspector had arrived, looking like he'd been pulled out of bed, and had asked Noah what had happened. He said very little other than whispering comments into his recorder as he took in certain points of Noah's testimony.

And it was a testimony, Noah knew. But he was willing to accept the consequences of assaulting another Marine, and he'd refused the offer of an attorney. After another hour, the first sergeant had come and got him from sickbay and escorted him to the company office, never saying a word. Noah didn't bother to ask her anything, and he felt guilty for letting her down. He'd come to greatly respect the first sergeant, and if he had a regret, it was that she'd think less of him.

The hatch to the office opened, and the first sergeant stuck her head out and motioned him to enter.

Noah marched in, centered himself on the small field desk, and said, "Sergeant Lysander, reporting as ordered, sir!"

"At ease, Sergeant," the skipper said. "Well, you rather went overboard, don't you think?"

"Yes, sir!"

"You do know that you can't just assault other Marines, right? That there are ways that are accepted to handle situations like this?"

Noah wanted to blurt out that Lessa was assaulted, and while that might be true, it didn't excuse his actions, but he said "Yes, sir," instead.

"So why, for all that is holy, did you decide to take it upon yourself to fall on Staff Sergeant Cain like an avenging angel?"

"Sir, Lessa . . . Sergeant Franklin . . . is my friend. When I found out what he did to her, I just lost it."

"So, do you have a habit of losing your temper? Your platoon sergeant and commander don't think so," he said, tilting his head to where the gunny and lieutenant were sitting on folding chairs.

"No, sir, I don't."

"So why did you this time? Just because Sergeant Franklin is your friend?"

"No, sir. Not just because it was her. I've been thinking about it. It's not just because it was her. It could have been anyone. But sometimes, you have to protect others, Marines, civilians, or whomever. That's what we do, right sir? I mean when we become Marines. To protect people. I know I screwed up, sir. I should have just let the MP's and MCIS handle it. But when he admitted it . . ."

Suddenly he paused. He'd told the MCIS guy that Cain had admitted assaulting Lessa, but he wasn't sure anyone in the office knew that.

When none of them commented, he continued, "When he admitted it, I just had to act."

He'd considered telling some cock-and-bull story that Cain had thrown the first punch, but he couldn't bring himself around to lying. He figured he'd just stick with the truth and hope he'd not get court martialed. He didn't want to lose his Honorable Discharge, but "honor" was right there in the word, and he'd thrown honor out the window when he made himself judge, jury, and executioner.

"Are you, well, are you back to normal now? Do we need to send you for a psych eval?"

"No, sir. I'm fine. But if I can ask, how is Sergeant Franklin? No one will tell me anything."

"She'll be fine. She had a slight concussion, a broken nose, and bruising, but she'll stay here and return with the company."

"And . . . I mean, was she . . ."

"Staff Sergeant Cain is being charged with Class B aggravated assault and Class C sexual assault."

Noah tried to digest that, thinking back to classes on the UCMJ. A Class B aggravated assault was a step down from trying to kill someone, but it was still serious. A Class C sexual assault was the least serious type of sexual assault, something a Marine might be charged with for exposing him or herself where it was not welcomed. Then it became clear.

The grubbing fucker bragged about something he hadn't even done! This was just a beat down on Lessa for revenge, and he'd said the rest of that shit to mess with me.

It didn't make Noah any more sorry he'd taken down the staff sergeant. The bastard was more than twice the size of her.

"Thank you, sir, for letting me know."

"Is there anything else?"

"What about the staff sergeant? I mean, was he hurt bad?"

There was snort from behind him, and in front, the captain smiled and said, "Multiple facial fractures and a broken rib. As I said, you went rather overboard on him."

"Yes, sir. I realize that, and I'm ready to accept the consequences of my actions."

"You are, are you?" the captain asked. "OK, then I guess you better get going, then. You're back to being the temporary commander of the *Hombre*, and you've got to be ready to go if we get a third reset."

"What?" Noah asked, stunned.

"Lieutenant Durand, I thought you told me Sergeant Lysander was a bright young man. He doesn't understand Standard?"

"Sergeant Lysander, you do speak Standard, right? The skipper told you to get back to the *Hombre*, and that sounded like an order to me," the lieutenant said.

"Yes, sir, and thank you sir. Thank you!" Noah said, wheeling about and rushing out of the office as if he thought the skipper would change his mind. He ran outside, where the morning sun was just rising over the horizon.

He'd never expected this outcome. It shouldn't have played out this way, not that he was complaining. The gunny, the first sergeant, and the lieutenant really must have gone to bat for him.

With the huge weight off his shoulders, he ran back to billeting, changed into overalls without bothering to shower, and rushed to the ramp.

"Oh, Noah!" Llanzo said as he reached the *Hombre*. "You're back."

"Yeah, surprised the hell out of me, too."

"So, I mean, you're really back? Here on the *Hombre*?"

"No, Llanzo, I'm not."

"No? Oh, yeah, I guess not. It's just when I saw you here . . ." he trailed off as Noah started rummaging around in the parts box.

Noah found what he was looking for, a can of Ferroshield. A small number of parts on a Davis were made from ferrous metals, and even when treated, they could be subject to rust. He took the can to the front of the Hombre and shook it, then wielding it like a handgun, sprayed over the word "Hombre," covering it with a dark yellow patch.

He shook the can one more time, then underneath the patch and in large, clumsy letters, sprayed A-N-V-I-L.

He stepped back, admiring it for a moment. He'd get Pop to tidy it up later.

"I'm back with the *Anvil*, Llanz, not the *Hombre*. It's you and me again."

Chapter 36

"Where you at, Llanz?" Noah asked as he tightened the lock-down.

"Just starting on the D series now."

"Push it. Load-out's in less than two hours."

"Roger that."

Noah looked at the manual, swiping to the next page. Each and every lock-down had to be done in order, and now that he'd finished the MGS mount, he needed to make sure of what was next.

Rampant Force, with a day left in the Armor War, had been cancelled. A contingency, in-system, had arisen, and the three Marine companies, along with the battalion of FCDC stationed on Lowe's Retreat, were being ordered to Saint Gallen. Half of the Aardvarks had already been lifted off the Itch aboard shuttles that would take them across the system.

Trappist 1 was an ultra-cool dwarf sun with three planets in the Goldilocks zone. Lowe's Retreat already had a habitable atmosphere and its own fairly advanced life forms. St. Gallen was a Class 2 world, requiring minimal terraforming, while the Itch had required more aggressive terraforming. There was even talk of terraforming Lowe's Retreat's moon, a mineral-rich planetoid, and with four habitable planetary bodies in the system, that would break the current record.

All three planets were members of the Federation, with St. Gallen maintaining a degree of autonomy. One of the oldest systems settled since the Age of Expansion and fairly close to the homeworld, Noah would never have imagined a contingency on any of the planets, much less on St. Gallen. But the bad guys rare cared for such logic and niceties.

St. Gallen was one of the few refugee worlds for the Capys, who'd been driven from their planets by the Klethos. Noah's father had fought the Capys until their situation had become clear. Now, only a few million of them survived, with about 300,000 of them, according to the brief they'd received the day before, on St. Gallen in seven different enclaves.

Enter the bad guys, in this case, a group affiliated with the Human First movement, a loose political party that stretched across humanity and that advocated total human withdrawal from the current agreement with the Klethos. Based out of Brotherhood space, one of their basic tenets was that the Klethos had attacked only because humanity had sided with the Capys against them.

This was just as ridiculous as the Children of the Dragons, who worshiped the Klethos as gods. The Klethos' history was one of expansion, and whether humans sheltered the few remaining Capys or not had zero effect with regards to the Klethos and their gladiatorial combat.

A group of armed fighters had taken over the old walled city of Wallenstadt. Most of the 40,000 Capys in the adjoining refuge had been killed, and about 15,000 humans within the walls were being held hostage. The terrorists threatened to kill them all unless the remaining Capys on the planet were put to death.

The FCDC battalion would be the point of main effort in the hostage negotiation and/or rescue, but being so close to the home system, it was a light battalion, organized for normal policing but with little in the way of heavy equipment. The Marines were going to provide that heavy punch, either to simply help cow the terrorists, or if it came to it, to support the FCDC troopers in a hostage rescue.

Noah wouldn't lie and say he wasn't excited. He'd accepted that Rampant Force was to be his last hurrah, and he'd told Miriam that. But this was beyond his control. He knew Miriam would be royally pissed if the mission lasted longer than a week or so, but he didn't feel guilty about the mission itself, only that he welcomed it.

"Sergeant Lysander, you in there?" a voice called from outside the *Anvil*.

He twisted his body around and stood, sticking his head out of the gunner's hatch. Vikky Wallace, the company supply sergeant, stood there with an unfamiliar corporal standing beside her.

"Yeah, what do you want?"

"You're short a body, and the skipper wants to know if you want him," she answered, hooking a thumb at the corporal.

"What? Who the heck is he?"

"'He' is Corporal Diego White Bear. Just about to graduate from Armor School. The first sergeant found out who out of the class was coming to the company, and it was either him or another guy. The skipper said grab him now if you wanted him."

"He's not even graduated," Noah said, ignoring the corporal like he wasn't even there.

"I will be in four more days, Sergeant," the corporal said.

"Hell, there's no time to get locked in, and in a combat zone, that's not so good."

"The skipper says it's your call," Vikky told him.

Noah was about to dismiss the idea, but something in the eager, almost pleading look in the corporal's eyes stopped him.

"You, Corporal. You can drive a Davis?"

"Yes, Sergeant, I can," he answered.

"What was your qual score?"

"Ninety-six," he said, pride evident in his voice.

Grubbing hell, that's better than my score was.

Llanzo had stuck his head out of the driver's hatch when he heard the talking. He wasn't saying anything, but Noah knew his decision would affect him as well.

"What do you think?" he asked his driver. "You ready to move up to the gunner's turret?"

"I'm ready, but it's up to you."

Noah looked back to the corporal, who was waiting anxiously for his decision. He wanted to go, that much was evident.

Hoping he wasn't making a mistake, he said, "OK, get your butt over here. We've got load-out in less than two hours."

Noah thought the corporal was going to start jumping up and down in excitement.

"This is only temporary, Corporal, so don't piss yourself. I'm only the temporary tank commander, so when we get a new one, I'm back to gunner, Sergeant Shearer's back to driver, and that means you're out on your ass, understand?"

"Yes, Sergeant," the corporal shouted, throwing his pack on the ground and jumping on the *Anvil*. "What do you want me to do now?"

Noah swiped the next checklist to the corporal's PA and said, "Get working on that. Like I said, we've got less than two hours to be ready."

SAINT GALLEN

Chapter 37

"Please, folks. Keep behind the yellow tape," Noah said for the hundredth time today.

"When are you going to do something," someone yelled from the crowd.

What do you want me to do? Fire on the city? Jeesh!

Noah had been pretty excited to get a last, actual mission. Now he almost regretted it. This was far from what he'd expected or in what he and his crew were trained. They'd been on the ground for ten days now, simply sitting and watching while throngs of family, gawkers, and newsies had invaded the city proper. The gawkers were there to witness, the newsies to record, but the families ate at Noah, and there was nothing he could do to help them.

The terrorists held the old walled city. Noah still didn't quite understand why the walls had even been built. They might have been a tourist draw over the last few centuries, but at the moment, they provided pretty good protection for the terrorists and a pretty good jail cell for the hostages.

With a population of 250,000, Wallenstadt was much larger than just the walled city and sprawled along the Rhein where it flowed into the Lake Bodensee. The city, the lake, and the river, framed by snow-capped mountains, was truly beautiful, but it had lost its allure earlier on as the platoon essentially parked and watched, 200 meters from the walls. Noah had felt a little exposed at first, but the terrorists hadn't shown any anti-tank capability so far—in fact, they had shown no aggression so far. Their demands were simple: kill the Capys on the planet, and they would release the hostages and surrender.

Judging from the placards and augmented chants from the crowd, it sounded like most of the people thought that was a reasonable price. Just this morning, effigies of Capys appeared, hanging from handmade gallows.

"Hey, Marine! You in the tank. I want you to talk to my sister," a middle-aged man shouted, stepping under the yellow tape and holding out his PA.

"Please, sir, you need to step back," Noah answered as one of the FCDC troopers came over to manage the situation.

"My sister! She's in there!" the man shouted.

Somewhat to Noah's surprise, the Homo Primes, as the terrorists referred to themselves, allowed for full communications with the outside. No PA's had been confiscated. That's how he knew that just over that wall, not 30 meters in, over 2,000 of them were being held in a church. He knew that there were fewer than 30 guards on them. If it weren't for the walls, the 30 guards couldn't hold back their captives should they make a break for it. But the damned wall, 19 meters of unbroken plasticrete, stamped to look like stone, was as good as a jail cell's bars.

There were two ships in geosynchronous orbit over the city, scanners peeling back the inner city, layer by layer. Thousands, probably millions of nanodrones had been sent over the walls. The FCDC commander, a full two-star general who'd arrived to take over the operation, had an excellent picture of what was going on inside the city. What he didn't have was a way to rescue the hostages without thousands of them being killed. So, the negotiators negotiated, but for show, not with the expectation of a breakthrough. This was turning into a major clusterfuck and huge public relations disaster—not to mention the 15,000 lives at stake.

"I'm coming in," Gunny Chimond passed on the net.

With the mass of people, it took them more than a few minutes to move to the sides and let the *Boudicca II* through. A trooper cut the tape, then waved the gunny forward. Corporal Giscard-Suez, the driver, neatly brought the *Boudicca II* alongside the *Anvil*.

The crowd was chanting again, so Noah passed on the net, "Nothing much new, except for the Capy effigies."

"Saw them coming in. Tension is rising. No aggression towards us, though?"

"Nothing. Just the usual, I mean. They want us to do something."

"I want us to do something, Noah. I understand them. But if that's all, consider yourself relieved."

"Roger that, and see you in twelve," he passed, then to WB, "Let's take her back—and we're going through Whoville."

"Shit," Llanzo muttered.

Noah let it slide. They weren't physically doing much, but the mental stress was taking its toll. He knew Llanzo just wanted to get back and out of the *Anvil*, and the direct route to the stadium was Victory Boulevard. "Whoville" was the name the Marines had anointed on the area to the north of Victory, a warren of small, winding streets and alleys. Noah would never want to enter a maze like that under combat conditions, but this wasn't exactly combat, and WB, as he and Llanzo had taken to calling Corporal White Bear, was still an untested variable, and while he'd performed fine so far, Noah wanted to fit in all the driving time he could for the corporal.

"Got it, Sergeant," the driver said, his voice full of eagerness.

Noah had to smile. It wasn't so long ago that he couldn't wait to drive the *Anvil*. Now it was WB's turn.

"OK, here's your route, Corporal," he said, sending over a convoluted route with more than a few tight turns and a switchback. "Don't touch a single building."

"No problem, TC. I've got it."

Lessa gave Noah an unobtrusive wave from the *Boudicca II's* gunner's turret as they drove past the trooper, who was still holding the tape for them. It took several minutes for WB to creep the *Anvil* through the press of people, but finally, they left the people and the foreboding height of the wall behind.

Chapter 38

Noah tuned out the crowd as he dug his spoon into what was left of his Canadian Cobbler, scraping out the last tiny bits clinging to the bottom of the packet. It hadn't been that long ago that he was making the dessert for Miriam, trying to lessen the blow of having to postpone their wedding. Now, he was a married man with two kids and another on the way. He'd changed a lot since then, and not just as a family man.

Like with this cobbler, for starters.

Noah, as a dedicated foodie, tended to sneer at fab food, but here he was, rummaging like a rat in trash to dig out every last morsel. He'd been surprised to see the dessert on the rotating menu, and he'd tasted it with more than a little trepidation, but it was actually delicious, and Noah tried to trade with his crew when either of them received it and he didn't. Llanzo always told him to get bent, but WB usually traded, probably to try and get on his good side more than he wanted whatever dessert Noah had received in his meal packet. Noah felt a little guilty about using his rank for that—but not too much.

He'd never have even been eating in the *Anvil* back when he first joined the crew. Staff Sergeant Cremineli wouldn't allow it. But he was the commander now, even if temporarily, so he made the rules now. He wouldn't let Llanzo or WB toss their packets out of the tank, especially given all the eyes on them every moment that they were on station, but the *Anvil* was their home, and it seemed ridiculous to implement rules that had no effect on their combat readiness.

His food habits were minor, though, not too important in the grand scheme of things. He'd changed much more as a Marine. He'd originally enlisted more out of a sense of duty to his father's memory, in part, he knew, because he'd always wanted his father's approval. Over the course of his first tour, however, he'd started to love the Corps, to relish being part of the brotherhood. Going to tanks had been an exciting continuation of the journey. Now, as he was approaching the end of his enlistment, things had changed. The luster of being a Marine had faded.

That's not really it, he corrected himself. *Be honest with yourself.*

His situation had changed, not the Corps. The deployments, while he actually enjoyed them, were hell on family life. Miriam had long gone past resigned acceptance and now actively resented the time he spent away. And Noah hated it, too, in that regard. Growing up, he'd sworn that he'd never be like his father, an absentee figure to be revered, but who wasn't there for birthdays and school plays, for football games and holidays. Noah looked at the pictures of Chance and Hannah, downloaded and printed out only a week ago, that he'd affixed alongside his TC display. What was he missing as they grew?

The bottom line was that he still loved being a Marine—he just feared what kind of father that made him.

He burped, then folded up the cobbler packet and put it in the trash bag that he'd hung from the hatch release lever before he checked the time.

Five more hours, he thought, disappointed that more time hadn't passed.

This mission was becoming excruciating to bear. They did nothing but sit, staring up at the wall. Just over it, Federation citizens were in dire straits, but they couldn't do anything about it. The gouge was that the FCDC general, now assisted by a Marine full bird, had several plans ready to conduct a rescue, but he couldn't get the OK. Meanwhile, the hostages, having been held for almost four weeks now, kept up communications with the outside.

He swiveled around to look at the crowd. The numbers of looky-loos had dwindled, but the hardcore observers, the family members, were there day in and day out. Noah had gotten to know many of them.

Sasson de Vries was one of the more vocal of them. Early on in the mission, he'd offered his PA and challenged Noah to speak with his sister, who was being held right in the church just over the wall. Sometimes, the terrorist guards would escort a hostage or two up the steeple in full sight of the crowd, like dangling bait, and just three days ago, his sister had been one of them.

While Sasson demanded action, he understood the situation. Noah had spoken with him on a few occasions, and he understood the man's position. If Esther were being held, he'd be going crazy as well. The Marines were supposed to defend people like Sasson, like his sister Julia, yet they were doing nothing for the 15,000 of them inside the walls.

Noah didn't have an answer, though. If they just assaulted, hostages would be slaughtered. But they couldn't just sit like this forever. Something had to break out, one way or the other. Until then, though, he and his crew would just have to wait.

Chapter 39

The crowd was in an uproar, with more people streaming to the area. The FCDC troopers were having a difficult time holding them back. The Spec 5 in charge had asked Noah to swing a gun around to simply point at the crowd, but he'd refused. The crowd wasn't the enemy, and he was not going to treat them as such.

He understood their anger. Half-an-hour before, the terrorists had lined up five hostages on the city wall and executed them with the warning that more would be killed unless their demands were met. That had been outside the main gate into the walled city, on the opposite side from where they were, but the holos had immediately hit the undernet.

Already, people were marching on the Capy refuge, and FCDC troops were scrambling to intercept them. Here, at their section of the wall, the troopers were nervous. A block to the north, the lieutenant was conferring with the FCDC sergeant first class. He'd already recalled the *Boudicca II* and the *Ball Shot*, but for the moment, the *Anvil* and six troopers were all that separated a hundred or more angry and scared civilians from the city walls.

The holos had made Noah sick—sick and angry. The end game was approaching, and he'd be damned if he'd just sit and watch it unfold. He wasn't sure what the Federation forces could do, but they had to do something.

Whatever the general had planned, though, in such a contingency, did not involve either tank company. They were there only for show, which pissed Noah off. If it came to a rescue attempt, two Mamba platoons, which had arrived two weeks ago, and a mechanized company aboard Aardvarks would support the FCDC troops who were to be lifted over the walls with their own aircraft as well as Navy and Marine Albatrosses. The intent would be to swarm the terrorists and rescue as many of the hostages as they could before they were executed. Estimates that up to two-thirds of them would die had kept the Federation from launching an assault, but now with hostages being executed, that could change the command's mind.

From what little had been passed to the Marines, Noah thought the plan, despite the huge number of projected casualties, was about as good as could be developed. When he looked at the overhead images, though, he could see that there was no way to land an Albatross or one of the FCDC V-33's anywhere near the church over the wall. Just over two thousand hostages were being held inside, and with nowhere for aircraft to land, and with no gate in the wall, those 2,000 wouldn't have much of a chance should a massacre commence. FCDC BlackOps or Marine Recon could jump in, but not with the numbers to protect that many people until they could be escorted to safety.

With 15,000 hostages, 2,000 might not seem as important, but to the people behind him, they were. And to Noah, after staring at the church steeple for five weeks, after seeing 20 or 30 being paraded around the steeple, these were "his" hostages. He felt attached to them.

"Charlie-One-Four, Charlie-One-Two, divert to London," the lieutenant passed on the platoon circuit.

"London" was the Capy refuge. If the lieutenant was ordering the *Boudicca II* and the *Ball-Shot* there, things must be getting hotter.

"It's just us now, guys," he told his crewmates. "Keep your heads up."

For what? I sure don't know.

He found out less than 20 minutes later when the simple words "Pink Dragon" were passed over the general net.

"We've got an alert!" Noah said as he triggered the activation.

Noah didn't know what "Pink Dragon meant, and neither would anyone else hearing it. The *Anvil's* AI compared it to an ever-shifting quantum cipher, and the actual command was displayed. The rescue was on.

A quick glance revealed that Plan B was being put into action. Noah scanned first to the subordinate units, but nothing had changed for them. First Platoon, now minus two tanks, were to protect the civilian crowd and to take action as needed to protect hostages who managed to reach their position as well as apprehend or kill and terrorists trying to escape.

"It's on," he told Llanzo and WB.

"About fucking time," Llanzo said.

"Nothing's changed for us. Keep the friendlies out of the way, rescue any hostages who make it over the wall, and if any of the terrorists make a break for it—"

"Drop their asses," Llanzo said. "With fucking pleasure."

According to the operations order, it would take 15 minutes before Federation Forces were crossing the city walls. That was a lot of time should the terrorists get wind of it and start their killing spree. Noah looked behind him at the crowd, and part of him wanted to tell them the rescue was one, but the risk was too great. A spy in the crowd, or even an overeager relative giving hope to those inside could result in a bloodbath.

He swung back, hiding his face so that no one watching could pick anything up from him. As usual, his vision focused on the steeple. It was so close, but still, with the wall, it might as well have been a hundred klicks away. If it wasn't there, the hostages could make a break for it once things went south. Noah had asked the lieutenant why combat engineers couldn't just blow the wall if it came to that, and the answer was first that the plasticrete was designed to withstand standard explosives, diverting the force of the explosions to the sides. A slowly detonating explosive as was used in mines could work if it had enough power at the point of attack, almost pushing a hole in the wall, but Intel was pretty sure the church had been wired with sympathetic explosives that would detonate when another charge, even a slow, earth-moving-type charge, detonated within range, and the wall would be within that range. The lieutenant said that if they had a medieval-type siege catapult, they could batter the wall in with huge rocks, but that was just wishful thinking.

The irony was not lost on Noah. Here they were, essentially laying siege to the modern version of a medieval walled city, and they needed a medieval weapon to break the siege.

"Ten minutes, guys," he said.

He considered ordering the crew to button up, but that could alert the crowd that something was up. His nerves were getting tighter and tighter, but he tried to act calm, at least. It was hard, though, when he realized that in a few short minutes, thousands of hostages could die.

"Check your load," he told Llanzo.

"HE, Sergeant, same as always."

"I can see the readout, same as you. I want a visual."

He heard a grunt, then the thunk of the autoloader being opened.

"HE, visually checked."

"Roger that."

Noah understood why the 75 mm railgun round and the Mad Mike would be useless against the wall, but the 90mm HE was a slower-acting round, even if "slower" was relative. He didn't want to initiate a sympathetic detonation of charges placed inside the church, but if all other hope was lost, it might be better than nothing. Besides, the *Anvil's* main gun, along with the coax, were locked onto the church's steeple. He could imagine a terrorist climbing it to fire on the crowd, and if that happened, he'd blast the sucker into his component atoms.

Noah kept looking down at the clock on his display. The timer under the GMT LED was slowly ticking down. For the last 30 seconds, he didn't lift his head. As it hit zero, changing from red to green, Noah half-expected to hear something, anything, but H-hour indicated the aircraft crossing the LOD, which was almost 20 klicks away. The ground forces wouldn't move until the aircraft passed PL Brown.

Five hundred FCDC troops and almost 200 Marines were about to enter the inner city, but behind him, a few of the relatives were barely chanting with most of them taking a break. The newsies were mostly lounging under their tents as well, editing their human interest stories, which were about all they'd had since the start of the emergency. He wanted to shout out, to get them on their feet, but he held his tongue.

It didn't matter. A few moments later, four FCDC V-33's flew overhead, trailing flares like Tenth of August fireworks.

Relatives jumped up, and newsies scrambled for their holocorders as the V-33's banked around the church and flew out of sight.

Deep explosions sounded from the direction of the two main gates into the city, and Noah's display lit up. As a tank commander, he couldn't delve too deeply into the details, but he needed to know where friendly forces were, and blue avatars pushed through the gates while others appeared as their aircraft landed where they could.

Sasson's voice pierced the general commotion as he screamed, "They're killing our people in the church!"

Noah could hear the sounds of firing and muted screams from over the wall, and he stood on top of his commander's seat as if that would help him see better. Less than 200 meters away, Federation citizens were being murdered.

"Get back, get back!" one of the FCDC troopers was yelling, something that barely registered as his mind faded out, trying to put together the pieces of all his thoughts over the last few days.

And it suddenly gelled. He realized all along that he knew what had to be done.

"Get out of the tank!" he yelled at his two crewmates, then turning, "Sasson! Sasson! Tell your sister to make a break for it to the wall!"

The man paused from where he'd pushed through the barrier, one of the troopers trying to hold him back.

"The wall. Tell them to head to the wall, but hold back!"

Understanding seemed to take over him, and he waved and nodded. He grabbed his throat mic and started talking.

"Get out? Why?" Llanzo asked.

"I'm taking over, now. There's no time!"

As if to emphasize his point, the firing at the church rose to a crescendo. Both Marines looked from Noah to the wall and back to Noah again.

"You're right, no time," WB said. "Let's go."

Noah hesitated only a split second. He didn't want to put them at risk, but by the time he'd have gotten into the drivers' seat, how many more would have died?

"Petal to the metal, Diego!"

Jonathan P. Brazee

The *Anvil* jumped forward like a Jaguar X-20, pushing Noah back into his seat.

"Button up!" he shouted.

Corporal White Bear smashed a line of bushes, crushed a statue, and bounced over a walkway as he accelerated 40 tons of polycero armor, fusion generator, and gun turret forward. Noah watched the wall getting bigger and bigger through his vision blocks.

"Miriam!" he shouted as he hit the fire control foam.

White embraced him an instant before the *Anvil* hit, 40 tons of tank at a single, concentrated point. The shock knocked him senseless. A second, a minute, he didn't know, but he suddenly realized he couldn't move, but was amazed to be alive, as the *Anvil* shook and jerked him around him with some sort of impacts.

He tried to yell out, to see how Llanzo, how WB were, but as he opened his mouth, it filled with something heavy, something he pulled down into his lungs. He instinctively reached for the emergency release, his arm barely obeying his commands, but the hatch would budge.

He needed air, his body screamed for aid, but with each gulp, his lungs took in something heavy. He coughed, but if anything came up, it was immediately replaced with more. He was suffocating.

Noah fought—he'd expected to die, but now that he'd somehow survived the impact, he wanted to live. Chance and Hannah needed him. His future child needed him. But no matter how hard he struggled, it was a losing battle. Within moments, darkness replaced the white foam that had him entrapped.

220

QUINTERO CRAG

Chapter 40

"Why don't you just come home, now?" Miriam said. "No one expects to see you now."

"Yeah, daddy. Come home," Chance chimed in.

"I'm only going to be a few minutes, honey. You can wait here if you want."

"A few minutes? More like a few hours."

"Come on. I'll be home soon, and I've got a week off, with only a final check on Wednesday. Give me this, OK? Please?"

Miriam frowned, then said, "I can't have you moping about all week. OK, do what you have to do, but be back for dinner. Fierdor and Eve are bringing something over."

"With their kids?" Noah asked.

He was feeling better, but he wasn't sure he could handle seven kids at the moment.

"No, just them. I told them they can stay half an hour, no more."

"Oh, good, and that's why I love you," he said, leaning over to give her a kiss. "I promise, I'll be there."

He got out of the car, feeling only a twinge of guilt as he waved at Chance. He'd just been released from the Naval Hospital, and the first thing he was doing was going to the platoon. It might be screwed up, but he needed it.

His stay in the hospital had been short, only four days. And since he'd been in stasis ever since they'd dragged him out of the *Anvil*, for him, the fight on St. Gallen had only been four days ago. He'd seen his family every day in the hospital, and most of his fellow Marines had stopped by to see him, but he still didn't have a firm grasp of all that had happened, only hearing some of the basics. The rescue had gone about as well as could be hoped, he knew. Over 5,000 hostages had been killed, but that meant that 10,000 had been saved. And when Noah had ordered the *Anvil* to breach the wall, 1,314 of the hostages had managed to escape through the opening they'd made. One-thousand, three-hundred, and fourteen. That number, at least, had been cemented into his brain.

Crashing the *Anvil* into the wall hadn't been a sure thing. The *Anvil*, which had been written off as a total loss and had been left on St. Gallen at their request, had hit with enough force to penetrate the wall, but not bring it down, at least not immediately. The mass of wall had stood for close to a minute before tumbling down, burying the *Anvil* and her crew, but leaving a large gap over which the hostages could scramble out. The terrorists had pursued, shooting some hostages even after they had reached the other side before the FCDC troopers engaged the terrorists in a fierce firefight.

He hadn't yet seen a recording of the crash, but Lessa had told him it was pretty spectacular. The commonly held opinion was that without the foam, none of the three would have survived. The foam had acted as a cushion.

Technically, none of them had survived. Diego, who as the driver was located at the furthest point forward in the tank, had been killed upon impact. Noah and Llanzo had survived the impact, but suffocated after; however, the fire foam had been designed to take into account that a tanker might not be able to exit a tank after the foam had been activated. While a human could not breath the foam (oxygenated foam wouldn't put out fires, after all), it was treated to help prevent cell trauma to the lungs as well as lower the activity of brain cells. It had taken almost six hours to dig out the *Anvil* and retrieve the three Marines. Six hours was longer than what was recommended for a body before it could be put into stasis, but for Llanzo and Noah, the foam mitigated the delay. Even with Diego, the foam had lessened the trauma to his body. He was still in regen, but the docs expected a full recovery.

And that's about all Noah knew. But he needed to find out more before his enforced week-long vacation at home.

"Look who the cat dragged in," Lessa said as Noah entered the office.

She stood and came to him, kissing him on the cheek.

"Is that Sergeant Lysander I hear out there?" the lieutenant shouted from his office.

"Yes, sir, it's me."

"Well, get your ass in here!"

The lieutenant met him halfway around his desk, hand out to shake, saying, "Good to see you're back, but I didn't expect to see you for another week."

"Just stopping by, sir, to get up to speed."

"Good on you. Do you want to make your report now?"

"Well, sir, I'm supposed to be on light duty, and I just came in to check in—"

"Of course," the lieutenant said, holding up a hand to stop him. "We've got plenty of time to get to it when you're back on full duty.

"The CO, that's the battalion CO, wants to see you 'as soon as that young man gets back,' as he said, but I think that can be next week, too.

"Actually, I'd love to talk to you, too, but I've got a maintenance meeting with the Four[10] in a few minutes that I can't miss."

The lieutenant had seen him every day while he was at the hospital, but they'd almost assuredly been told to steer away from "serious" conversations while he recovered.

"Gunny Chimond," he told his PA, then as she picked up on her side, "Gunny, we've got our prodigal son here. Why don't you stop by and pick him up?"

"Roger that, sir," she replied.

"Look, sorry to run, but I'm going to be late. Stop by again before you go, OK?"

"Aye-aye, sir."

---

[10] Four: Short for S-4, the logistics officer of a battalion or regiment.

As the lieutenant left, Lessa came strolling in, her hand in a fist and rubbing her nose in the space between her folded forefinger and thumb, coughing out "Brown-noser, brown-noser."

Noah gave her the finger.

"So, now you're a zombie," she said, sitting on the corner of the platoon commander's desk.

"Yeah, I guess you're right," he said, realizing it for the first time.

Being resurrected was an exclusive, if not desired club. To Noah, a zombie better referred to someone like WB, or his father, for that matter. He and Llanzo had merely suffocated, and with foam that was designed to act as it did. Since coming to in the hospital, he hadn't really considered the fact that he'd "died."

"So, how did it feel? I mean, what was it like?" she asked, her eyes bright.

"I don't know. Like I went to sleep on St. Gallen and woke back up here."

She seemed a little disappointed he hadn't anything more profound to say, but he hadn't really considered it much until she'd mentioned it.

They chatted about their respective families while waiting for the gunny. One thing that wasn't mentioned was Staff Sergeant Cain. Aside from a single thanks hurriedly given on St. Gallen, it wasn't mentioned between the two of them. And that was more than fine with Noah.

"Sergeant Lysander, coming back to the scene of the crime?" Gunny Chimond asked, stepping into the office.

Somehow, she and Noah hugged, something that had never happened before. It was short, quickly broken off, but it was a hug, nonetheless.

"How's your family?" she asked as if trying to change the subject. "I'm surprised your wife let you come in."

"It was touch and go with her, Gunny. But I promised to be a good boy until next week if I could just stop by."

Both Lessa and Gunny laughed at that, and if the gunny hadn't been there, Noah was pretty sure Lessa would have had a dismissive, if profane, comment about him being "whipped."

The gunny pulled out her PA, touched the screen, then held it out to Noah, saying, "We weren't supposed to show you this while you were in the hospital, but you're out now, so here it is."

Noah took a look and saw a frozen image of a tank, an open area, the city walls, and the church. He immediately reached forward and hit the play command.

It seemed weird to watch, the image, a tank that was the *Anvil*, but didn't feel like it to him, race across the parkland, picking up speed, then slamming into the wall with a cloud of dust. The *Anvil* slowly appeared as the dust cleared, three-quarters of the way through the wall. People started running out of the church, most headed for the wall, which still stood. They slowed, and some started to change directions when slowly, ever so slowly, the wall started to lean before collapsing in a shower of rubble, burying the *Anvil* from sight. Within moments, the people started scrambling over the rubble and emerged on the outside of the wall, running to meet the other people who were rushing forward.

Noah turned off the recording. He knew that the terrorists would appear and start killing the people before the FCDC troopers took them down, and he didn't need to see that.

"Pretty fucking awesome, huh?" Lessa said.

Noah shrugged, not knowing what to say.

"At least this time, we've got proof of someone destroying Marine Corps property," the gunny said, lightening things up.

"Oh, yeah, Gunny. My man Noah's going to have his pay docked for a hundred years. What's a Davis worth these days?"

"Heck, I wasn't driving. It was WB!"

"You were the tank commander, Sergeant."

"Temporary, Gunny. Don't forget that."

"OK, OK, you win!" the gunny said, accepting defeat.

All three laughed, and it felt damned good. It brought a sense of normalcy to him, a reset. He'd been feeling a little off, as if the universe had been skewed by a few degrees, and now it suddenly clicked back into place.

"If you're up to it, how about coming with me to the ramp?" the gunny asked.

"Sure, but I'd like to know more about what happened. I know the big stuff, but what about the other Marines? Even the troopers we had with us."

Lessa was a font of knowledge, which she spewed out like a mini-volcano as they walked to the ramp. From the Marine point of view, there had only been eight WIA's and five KIA's, the *Anvil's* crew being three of them, and the other two were also in regen. That wasn't too surprising. Marines were professionals, after all, and terrorists generally weren't.

The FCDC had suffered more, with over 50 WIA and 35 KIA—ten of the KIA were too far gone for resurrection, to include Spec 5 Nelson, who'd been killed protecting the hostages fleeing from the church.

That piece of news sobered Noah. He hadn't been too impressed with the specialist, but evidently, the soldier had stepped up, and stepped up big.

She was still relating all the facts she could dredge up when they reached the ramp, and almost all of the Marines there gathered around and welcome him back. The hug-fest continued with most of them grabbing and enveloping him. Noah wasn't anti-hug, but this was something new to him.

He kind of liked it.

Then as if they were the Red Sea parting, the gathered Marines stepped aside to where Pure Dick, Pop, and Gretchen were standing up against a brand new Davis, so new he could still smell the polyurethane coating that was sprayed on every tank before it left the factory.

Despite the gunny's affection for the maintenance chief, Noah was still not overly fond of the man, but he could greet the man. He stepped forward, hand out to shake.

"Try not to break this one, Sergeant," Pure Dick said.

Noah faltered, his hand half-lowering.

"What?"

"I said, try not to break this one. We can't just keep going back and getting new ones every time you decide to smash one into a wall or something."

Noah turned around to the gunny, confused.

"He's right. She's yours, so yeah, try not to break her."

"But—"

"Unless you don't want her. I'll have to tell Sergeant Shearer that he'll have to find a new TC. He's already claimed the gunner's spot."

Noah had less than a year on station, and he was supposed to spend that behind a desk in the Three shop. He certainly hadn't expected to be back in a tank. And with the *Anvil* gone, there weren't any openings, either. Until now, he realized, looking at the tank with covetous eyes.

He knew he should say no. He knew Miriam expected him to say no. But he looked around at the rest of the Marines, almost the entire company, and there was only one thing for him to say.

"Oh, I want her."

"I thought so," the gunny said. "And one more thing. The skipper said you're the tank commander. No more temporary, so if you break this one, you really will have to pay for her."

Epilogue

"You hanging in there, WB?" Noah asked.

"I keep telling you, I'm fine," the corporal said as he shut down the tank's motor.

"Yeah, I know you did, but it still took me a few days to get my rhythm back. Same with Llanzo."

Noah had been surprised when Corporal White Bear had returned after less than three months. In Noah's experience, most people who underwent regen took nine months or longer to return to duty. Knight Lewis was still in rehab, for example. Doc Anders told him that WB was back because while he'd suffered skull fractures when the *Anvil* had hit the wall, his cause of death had been a severed carotid. He'd bled out. The regen techs had regrown his blood vessels, which evidently was not a lengthy process. It has taken longer for his brain to knit and then for him to undergo cerebral rehab. The bottom line, though, was that his driver was back. He had to let Corporal Lin go, which hadn't been fun to do, but she'd known her position had been temporary until White Bear returned.

Noah looked at his driver for a moment, trying to see if the corporal seemed at all woozy. He looked fine, and if his driving over the last four hours was any indication, he was fine.

"OK, let's get her cleaned up," Noah said as he hopped out. "I think we can go right to the power-washer," he added after checking the tracks, which were mud-free.

That's one benefit of all this dry weather we've had lately, he thought.

"I've got it," Llanzo said, walking into the gear shed.

Noah conducted a simple walk-around, inspecting his tank. As usual, he stopped as he got to the front, and then reached out, touching the gold *Anvil II* painted there. He wasn't sure why he did that, but it had become a habit.

"So, what do you think of the power?" he asked WB as the corporal started uploading the data from the morning.

"Me likey. Very much."

The *Anvil II* was the first tank in the battalion with the new Springer 405 motor. The fusion generator was still the same and so put out the same amount of power, but the new motor was supposedly 18% more efficient, could create more torque, and was supposed to last up to 30% longer than the older motors. But like any new innovation, factory numbers were not always replicated in the field, so the *Anvil II*, along with eight other tanks throughout the Corps, were the final field trial for the new Springer. And that was why uploading the data back to the Marine Corps rep at the Springer plant was so important.

The data was holding true so far, and Noah was pretty sure that when the trial was over in another month, the switch-out with the rest of the Corps' Davises would commence.

Llanzo rolled up with the power-washer, handed Noah a nozzle, and the two of them began spraying the *Anvil II* clean. With both of them on the two spray nozzles, WB grabbed the hand vac and jumped back in the crew compartment.

Twenty-five minutes later, in almost record time, with the *Anvil II* clean and the analytics completed, they were done.

"Early chow's about to start. You going?" Llanzo asked.

"No, you two go ahead. I've got to go up to company. We've got class at 1330, don't forget."

"Hell, wills and powers of attorney, how can I forget that fun-filled afternoon," Llanzo said as he started up the ramp to return the power-washer.

Noah left the ramp, walking toward the company offices. He took his time, going over everything yet one more time. Even now, he was wavering back and forth, and he wished he had longer. But with his EAS at exactly 90 days, he had to make his decision before COB or have it made for him.

This morning hadn't been fun. Miriam was at seven months, and as with Hannah, she was pretty cranky—and from what he'd been told, she'd been even worse with Chance with Noah gone. Noah's job search had not been going well. He'd had offers, but to both his and Miriam's surprise, when benefits were added to his Marine Corps salary, none of the jobs except for one paid as much as what he was now pulling in. Of course, some of those jobs had nice upsides, but with a baby on her way, expenses were going to increase, and a raise in two years after probation was not going to do them much good.

The one job that paid better—much better, in fact—was on Prophesy, working for his Uncle Barrett. Noah knew nothing about water management, but his Uncle assured him that he could learn. Uncle Caleb had offered a job to his father as well, probably the same one, which financially would have paid him more than when he was a general, but he'd told Noah more than a few times that he knew nothing about a working in a civilian business, and, more than that, he would never have been able to live on his brother-in-law's largess. Noah thought that his father was being a little harsh on himself; if he could become the Chairman of the Federation, he could learn water management. As for Noah, when it came to his family, what mattered is that he provided for them, not if a job was "fun" or not.

Miriam went back-and-forth on the job offer. She professed to love his extended family, and she thought it would be good for the kids, but then she chaffed sometimes at the idea, telling Noah she didn't want to be controlled.

Finally, as he left early this morning, she'd told him to do what he thought he should do. Noah tried to read into that, to know what she wanted, but he was lost. It really was up to him. He had a gut feeling that no matter what, Miriam would find reason to complain, but he also resented the fact that she was laying everything on him. They were a family, and some decisions should be made by the family, not just one person.

He hesitated outside the company offices, checking the time. It was 2237 GMT, so technically, he had almost an hour-and-a-half. He almost turned around to go to the chow hall, hoping that with a full belly, things might be clearer, but he knew that was just an excuse to delay. He took a deep breath and opened the front hatch.

An unknown corporal had the duty, but during normal working hours, she was there more as a runner than to check who was entering the building. Noah walked past her and down the passage to the Charlie Company office. He didn't hesitate, pushing the door and stepping inside. There wasn't anyone at the desk, but the first sergeant's door was open, and she looked up as he entered.

"Sergeant Lysander, cutting it close, aren't we?"

"Still time, First Sergeant."

Noah's relationship with First Sergeant St. Cloud was strange, to say the least. Miriam and Fierdor had become quite close, and Chance's best friend was Hans, the first sergeant's youngest, so the two families socialized quite often. Miriam called the first sergeant Eve, and Noah called Fierdor by his first name, but between them, it was always "Sergeant" and "First Sergeant."

"Well, are you ready?" she asked.

"Yes, I think I am."

"You think? You'd better know. Once you leave, there's the reserves, but coming back into the active forces will be pretty tough."

"I know, First Sergeant."

He'd had more than a few talks with her, the last only two days prior at his house. She'd been pushing for him to reenlist, he knew, even if she'd tried to simply be a sounding board. He was also pretty sure that Miriam had told Fierdor everything, and he would have told his wife, so she undoubtedly knew to the credit what he'd get paid working for his uncle.

"Let me see if the skipper's free," she said, sending him a message.

Her PA bonged, and she told him, "Two minutes."

"Your CPM1 has gotten through the board, and it's just waiting for the commandant's signature."

His command thought Noah's action on St. Gallen deserved an award, but evidently, there had been much debate as to just what to give the *Anvil's* crew. A Silver Star, or possibly a Navy Cross, had been discussed, at least that was the scuttlebutt, but some of the Old Corps types thought that as the *Anvil* wasn't facing an enemy, exactly, a combat award wasn't appropriate. In the end, the three of them had been put in for the Civilian Protection Medal First Class, which was given for saving lives at the risk of their own. The award was pretty rare, and now Noah would have both the First Class and Second Class CPM's, possibly the only such Marine so honored.

Noah would be happy with that, and he was pretty sure Llanzo and WB would be, too, and he asked, "That's official? I'd like to tell the other two."

"Sergeant Major Çağlar himself called me with the news."

"The Sergeant Major? How is he?"

"How is he? I sure don't know, but I imagine he'd take your call to find out," the first sergeant said, one of the very few times she'd referred to Noah's place as a Lysander.

Sergeant Major Çağlar had been his father's friend, Man Friday, and confidant. He was the last person to see Noah's father and mother before they'd taken off on their final flight. He'd just been assigned as the Sergeant Major of the Marine Corps a few months prior. Noah could call him up, he knew, but ever since he'd enlisted, he'd tried to avoid his father's posse.

"Sergeant Lysander, come on in," the skipper called out.

Noah stood up, followed by the first sergeant, and as the Second Platoon commander left the skipper's office, he entered.

"So, Sergeant Lysander. It's decision time. I know we spoke last week about your options, and First Sergeant St. Cloud has briefed me that she's spoken to you at length. I know you've got your tracks greased for a pretty sweet job, but all I can say is that a salary isn't the most important thing in life. Duty, I'd say, is more important, right First Sergeant?"

"Yes, sir."

"I think you can have a great future in the Corps, Sergeant. You're a shoe-in for Staff Sergeant next year, and who knows after that?"

Noah wasn't sure if the captain was asking him a question or not, so he said nothing.

"Well, uh, of course, you know that. I'm sure you've considered everything, and so let me just say, I only wish you the best in your future. I've been honored, Sergeant, honored," he said, holding out his hand.

"Thank you, sir," Noah answered. "And I've been honored as well, and I'm so grateful that you made me the TC for the *Anvil II*."

"You earned it, Sergeant.

"Well, if that's all over, let's get this done," the skipper continued, picking up the Unit Diary. "Lysander, Noah," he muttered, swiping the face. "OK, here we are. This is your Form 308. I need to inform you that this is a legal document," he began, reading from a script. "Once your intent has been entered and you've been scanned, it is binding, subject to the provisions of the UCMJ. The subject Marine has 24 hours to rescind his or her decision . . . well, you don't, Sergeant, given how late you've delayed . . . after which time this form will become part of the official United Federation Marine Corps records.

"So, any questions?" he asked.

"No, sir."

"OK, then let's get it done," he said, handing the diary to Noah.

Noah looked at the form. It was pretty straight-forward. His service information was listed at the top, and there was some military legalese at the bottom, but the bulk of the form simply had two boxes. The first was to be checked if he wished to reenlist, and it was annotated that his reenlistment had already been approved by HQMC. The second box indicated that he wished to decline his reenlistment and wished to be released from active duty on his EAS.

Noah had seen holo service contracts that were more complicated. It seemed odd to him that a Form 308 was such a simplistic document, but one with such heavy implications.

He stared at it for a moment, then thought, *I hope I'm making the right decision.* He reached forward and affixed his thumb, indicating his choice.

A yellow light in the image of an eye flashed, and Noah held the unit up and looked right at it. There was a chime, and the eye turned to green. It was done.

"Well, thank you for your service," the skipper said, taking the diary.

"Don't forget the reserves, Sergeant," the first sergeant added. "You've still got 90 days to decide on that."

Noah didn't say a word. A feeling of calm had swept over him, taking away the stress of the last month. He'd made his decision, and for good or bad, it was done.

"So, if there is anything . . . wait. It says here you reenlisted, Sergeant," the skipper said, sounding confused.

"Yes, sir."

"But, I was led to believe that you were going to get out to take that cush job with your uncle," he said, looking at the first sergeant.

"I'd considered that, sir, and it was tempting. But what you said about duty was right, and when it comes down to it, I can't imagine leading a life as anything other than a United Federation Marine."

Thank you for reading *Noah's Story*. I hope you enjoyed it, and I welcome a review on Amazon, Goodreads, or any other outlet. The series will continue with Esther's missions in her new APOC billet.

If you would like updates on new books releases, news, or special offers, please consider signing up for my mailing list. Your email will not be sold, rented, or in any other way disseminated. If you are interested, please sign up at the link below:

http://eepurl.com/bnFSHH

Other Books by Jonathan Brazee

The United Federation Marine Corps' Lysander Twins

Legacy Marines
Esther's Story
Noah's Story (Coming)

The United Federation Marine Corps

Recruit
Sergeant
Lieutenant
Captain
Major
Lieutenant Colonel
Colonel
Commandant

Rebel (Set in the UFMC universe.

Women of the United Federation Marines

Gladiator
Sniper
Corpsman

Jonathan P. Brazee

High Value Target (A Gracie Medicine Crow Short Story)
BOLO Mission (A Gracie Medicine Crow Short Story

The Return of the Marines Trilogy
The Few
The Proud
The Marines

The Al Anbar Chronicles: First Marine Expeditionary Force--Iraq
Prisoner of Fallujah
Combat Corpsman
Sniper

<u>Werewolf of Marines</u>
Werewolf of Marines: Semper Lycanus
Werewolf of Marines: Patria Lycanus
Werewolf of Marines: Pax Lycanus

To the Shores of Tripoli

Wererat

Darwin's Quest: The Search for the Ultimate Survivor

Venus: A Paleolithic Short Story

Secession

Duty

<u>Non-Fiction</u>
Exercise for a Longer Life

<u>Author Website</u>
http://www.jonathanbrazee.com

Made in the USA
Monee, IL
28 January 2021